Waterloo Sunset

*To Jan + Roy
Best wishes from
Richard*

RICHARD AYRES

authorHOUSE®

AuthorHouse™
1663 Liberty Drive
Bloomington, IN 47403
www.authorhouse.com
Phone: 1-800-839-8640

First published by AuthorHouse 6/3/2009

ISBN: 978-1-4389-8254-0 (sc)

Printed in the United States of America
Bloomington, Indiana

This book is printed on acid-free paper.

To my wife, Sally, for her forbearance,

and

*to Dave, Iain, Martin, Geoff and Barry in whose company
in London the idea for the story had its inception,*

and

to Roy, Pat and Ian, whose company we missed.

Thanks are due to Phil Emery and Paul Forrester-O'Neill for their critical advice on the creative writing process, and to my fellow-writers at Keele University and those meeting fortnightly in my living room for their encouragement and friendship.

Thanks also to Dexter Petley and to Hilary Rich for their invaluable advice.

Chapter 1

THE PILLARS OF HERCULES, GREEK STREET, SOHO

Alan sank back in the seat in the snug, too exhausted even to raise his pint to his lips. Why was this of all days the first real scorcher of what had so far been a lousy summer? Sheila had told him, often and at length, that it was a crazy idea for him to tramp round London; that he'd be knackered after only a few hours. She was right. He was already totally buggered. Clapped out. It was the tube journey from the hotel to Tottenham Court Road that had done for him; sweltering, overcrowded, the carriages packed with ill-temper and incipient aggression. Too much for anyone, he told himself, let alone an old geezer in his sixties.

No, that was bollocks. Who was he trying to kid? He was panting, feeling faint. The average sexagenarian should be able to undertake a short journey on the underground without feeling that he'd run the marathon. But then he wasn't an average sexagenarian, was he?

His mobile phone chirruped. He groped for it in the top pocket of his shirt. He hated the bloody thing and only carried it in case of emergencies. Today it was needed to ensure that Eric and Vivienne, if they came, would know where to rendezvous with them. In any case Sheila had insisted that he switched it on as soon as he left the house. She thought central London was akin to the wild west since the attempted bombings in Haymarket several weeks before.

It was, in fact, she who was ringing.

'Hello, Sheil,' he said.

'Just ringing to see if you got there ok,' she said, her south London accent accentuated by the medium. 'Where are you?'

'The Pillars. The others haven't arrived yet.' He kept his voice low. He loathed those who evidently believed that the entire world would be enthralled by their half of a conversation.

'What? I can't hear you.'

'I'm in the Pillars.'

'Have any of the others arrived?'

'No.'

'Are you all right?'

'Of course I'm all right. Look, Sheil, I hope you're not going to keep ringing me every few minutes. It'll be embarrassing.'

'OK, darlin'. Just look after yourself, won't you.'

'Of course I will. I'm ok. No need to keep on.'

'How's the hotel?'

'All right, I think. I was too early to get into the room but they let me leave my case in the lobby office.'

'I don't know why you had to get there so early. It makes it a very long day for you.'

Alan sighed. He was ready with an impatient retort but knew that in the coming months he'd come to regret hasty words. 'I told you, I just wanted to be sure I was here before the others. It's me that's organising this gig, after all. Stop worrying, Sheil, I'll be ok.'

'OK, darlin'. Bye.'

He made to replace the phone in his pocket, but fumbled, dropped it. Cursing under his breath, he groped for it under the chair, checked that it was still functioning, and inserted it with the care that was beginning to characterise all his movements. He realised he'd stopped panting, and took a first swig of his beer. It was IPA, and was rather heavy. Secretly he would have preferred a lager, but didn't wish to be caught by the others in a heretical act, particularly by Jim. No doubt they'd all start this session pretending to be paid-up CAMRA members. He wondered which pub they'd reach before Tony started on his whisky chasers.

He found himself relaxing, and peered round the room. It had only just turned 11, and the place was almost empty. He was sitting in the small slightly elevated snug near the entrance: it provided a good view of the bar area which, devoid of other customers, revealed itself to be seedier than he remembered, the dark oak surrounds scuffed and the walls nicotine coloured. As usual when he had a pint in his hand he felt the old familiar craving even though, nagged by Sheila, he'd kicked the habit three years previously, much good it had done him. He was grateful for the absence of ashtrays and the prohibitary notices on the walls, and wondered if Jim and Tony still indulged; it was difficult to imagine the former without his bedraggled roll-ups (always held between thumb and forefinger) and the latter without his small cigars. No doubt he'd have to listen to them both ranting about the iniquity of the recent ban: Tony would inveigh against the nanny state while Jim would see it as a conspiracy against the working classes. One thing to be said for the hot weather, they could take their habit outside when their urges became overpowering.

3

His phone rang again. Nigel, no doubt. He was always the most punctual, and with his impeccable manners the most likely to call with an explanation for his delay. But it was Sheila again.

'What now, Sheil?'

'Sorry, darlin'. Just wanted to remind you to give me a call when you get back to the hotel tonight.'

'I said I would, didn't I? Please don't fuss.'

'OK darlin'. Sorry.'

Poor old Sheil, he thought. She was finding it more difficult than he to cope with the situation in which they'd recently found themselves. After 38 years of marriage he still blessed his good fortune in having her. She was his rock, his soul-mate, his ever-supportive companion through a life that many would have described as disappointing. He'd been reunited with her, his teenage sweetheart, when his mum's final illness had prompted him to return to Woolwich immediately after graduating. She'd been his bedrock during the year while he juggled nursing his mother (he was an only child who took his filial responsibilities seriously) with studying for his Cert Ed at London University. Things had then happened very quickly: his mother died, he obtained his Cert Ed, proposed to the only girl he'd ever loved and was accepted. They'd moved to Ealing where Alan had obtained his first teaching post and had remained there, unpromoted, ever since. His life had come to revolve round his family (Sheila had borne him three sons and a daughter, piling on weight with each confinement), his neighbourhood, Arsenal football club, the local pub, a Friday night curry and the occasional jazz or blues concert and, though it had never occurred to him to consider it until recently, he'd been a happy man.

Sometimes, he was accepting of his fate. Once past 60 you no longer believe you can continue for ever. You know you'll probably go sometime within the next 15 to 25 years. The issue was not so much when, as how. A massive heart attack was probably the best bet. He told himself that even cancer, given the availability of palliative care, was preferable to the slow and agonising deterioration of motor-neurone disease, or the destruction of the personality brought about by Alzheimer's. At least he, and Sheila, would be spared the deadliest aspect of a prolonged decline – the warping of the personality. Sheila was his only real sadness: he worried how she would cope. For himself, he wasn't really sad, but he was frightened, scared shitless in fact. He had never been a believer. But not for him the proselytising zeal of the evangelical atheist, just an acceptance that there was nothing afterwards. Now, it was that very nothing that he feared the most.

Reality was hard to bear, week in, week out. That was one reason why he had sought this reunion. It would provide a temporary escape, just for a day. He needed a break from his family and his London friends. He had lived in the metropolis all his life apart from the three years at University, had kept up with his boyhood mates from Woolwich, had made numerous friends in Ealing, his home for nigh on forty years. All of them knew his recent history, the onset of his pains, his loss of weight, his diagnosis, his subsequent immersion in the arcane bureaucracy of the NHS – visits to specialists, tests, scans, reassurances, more tests – and then the solemn prognosis followed by renewed reassurances, this time about pain relief and palliative care.

But his old Leeds University friends knew nothing of this. He'd last seen Nigel, Tony and Jim a decade ago. The other two, Eric and Vivienne, he'd had no contact with since graduating, apart from Christmas cards. He wanted to see them all for one last time, wanted to be with people who weren't embarrassed in his presence, people who'd be neither inarticulately over-solicitous nor determinedly but inappropriately cheerful, nor cross the road when they saw him approaching. Today was important. With these friends he would be the Alan he had always been. More than that, he wanted to observe how the men interacted with each other, and each with Vivienne, assuming she'd be present. He thanked the God in which he did not believe that he'd not been subjected to chemo, that his hair was still thick, the risible ginger faded to a more pleasing pepper-and-salt.

He shook himself and glanced at his watch. 11.25. He'd said elevenish, and was surprised that none of the others had yet appeared, especially Nigel, who'd always been a stickler for promptness. Jim's arrival time would of course depend on his state of mind: his lateness pointed to him being in one of his depressive phases. Alan hoped fervently that the Jacksons had decided to come, for those times when Jim had been on a downer it was only Vivienne who'd seemed able to reach him. As for Tony, well, he was probably on his phone closing some lucrative property deal before he chose to set out. On the other hand perhaps the three of them had met up at the hotel and were waiting for the slowest to emerge from his room before proceeding as a trio to the pub. Alan wouldn't mind betting that Tony and Jim had already exchanged words about the hotel: Jim would have railed at its expense, while Tony would have sneered at its three stars. Bugger them, thought Alan; it had taken weeks of protracted research on the internet before he'd decided on the Tavistock as being a reasonable compromise, and he'd then had to spend hours reassuring Sheila that its proximity to the site of the 7/7 bus bombing did not represent an ill-omen for his night away.

The idea for the reunion had come to him three months previously when he'd begun to sort through the lifetime of old photographs that were stuffed into old boxes kept under the stairs, and to insert them, carefully presented in date order, into a series of large, black hard-covered albums that he'd purchased from Boots at £15 a time. Such concern for order had only come after he'd received his sentence. Sheila didn't understand. She said it had become an obsession, and he found it hard to explain to her why he, once so careless and carefree, had become so anally-retentive, not that she would have understood the term. He felt the need to catalogue his past, to codify, classify, somehow to make sense of all that had gone before. It was the same with his record collection: he'd spent hours re-organising and storing his CDs according to the date he'd purchased the original vinyl releases, so that the soundtrack to his life had visual expression on the shelves of his study.

It had been a painful process handling the photographs of his early teenage years in which a slim, attractive, precociously sexy Sheila figured so prominently. Even as he'd inserted the small black-and-white photographs (contact prints taken with his Box-Brownie camera) he'd felt sorrow welling behind his eyes, remembering Sheila's distress at their parting when he'd left her to go to University. They both had known that home-town romances rarely survived across such a geographical and educational chasm. In those days before mobile phones, emails and student car-ownership, 200 miles might well have been 2000.

It was with relief that he had turned to the task of sorting the photographs dating from his time at Leeds. They'd been taken mostly in his final year after he'd joined the Union Entertainments Committee. Looking at them for the first time in decades, it was like seeing a still from a TV documentary on the Summer of Love – droopy moustaches abounded on the men, the girls' eyes were hidden by fringes, jeans were flared, miniskirts revealed a startling variety of legs. The youthful faces stared at him across the chasm of forty years, his friends just as they still appeared in his mind's eye – Nigel, tall and blond, conventionally attired; Jim, skinny, lank dark hair, eyes cast down; Tony, handsome, swarthy, jet black curls over his collar, denim jacket; Eric, boyish, slim, wearing a flowered shirt and a headband, his arm around the stunning Vivienne with her long auburn hair, willowy figure and those amazing legs. Suddenly, he needed to see them all again, to recapture the essence of that year. The meeting in Leeds with Nigel, Jim and Tony ten years before had not been a success, for Eric and Vivienne hadn't been there. They should have been, to have made it work – especially Vivienne.

So he'd phoned the others to suggest a second try. Jim and Tony had proposed they once again meet up in Leeds, both seemingly unconcerned about the terrible things that had already happened to the pubs along Headingley Lane at the time of their earlier nostalgia trip. Fortunately Nigel had agreed with him that London would be a better venue, and when Eric had emailed to say that there was no way that Vivienne would sanction a return to Leeds though she might be persuaded to join them in London, then Jim and Tony had fallen into line. He hadn't, however, mentioned to them that the attendance of the Jacksons was still in doubt: to have done so would probably have resulted in

Jim blaming Eric and Tony cursing Vivienne, just as they had before when the pair had cried off. On that occasion Nigel, ever the reasonable gentleman, had pointed out that as a married couple they might find the company of four males free of uxorious restraint somewhat discomforting, to which Tony had replied *he'd* be bringing along *his* new woman and that in any case four unrestrained males were just what that uptight bitch Vivienne needed.

He wondered how much Jim, Tony and Nigel had changed since their last meeting. Then, though in their early fifties, they had retained traces of the young men they had once been, and it had taken only a few pints before their youthful countenances seemed to emerge from behind the creases and bags of their middle age. That reunion had been blighted by Tony's young woman, a scantily dressed blonde whose mouth turned down every time they mentioned the 1960s. Tony, obviously eager to impress, had kept boasting about his talent for wheeling and dealing, and berating the Labour government even though Blair had been elected only four weeks previously.

Now, ten years on, he wondered if there was any trace of their former selves remaining. When you were fifty, still working, with younger children still at home, there still remained a connecting thread, albeit tenuous, with the passage of one's mature adulthood, and through that with the days that had gone before. But to be over 60 and retired, with grandchildren: now, a corner had been turned, gates had clanged shut on aspects of the past. He felt a surge of apprehension about the day to come. Could they still connect? And what of Eric and Vivienne? He'd had no contact with them since leaving Leeds until last February when Nigel had provided their phone number, and after their first stilted conversation Eric had only communicated on-line, his initial enthusiasm for the reunion seemingly dissipating with each successive email.

He finished his pint. The snug was filling up and he felt embarrassed to be sitting nursing an empty glass. To go to the bar however would risk the loss of his seat: predatory eyes were already being cast towards the empty chairs around him, and he knew it wouldn't be long before the question, 'Is anyone sitting there, mate?' would be asked of him, to which his answer would have to be in the negative. These days it wasn't wise to give the obvious facetious response. He glanced round at drinkers, an oddly assorted bunch of varying ages; the clientele of Soho taverns still retained a touch of the eclectic, unlike the tribal gatherings of youth in most of the pubs in Ealing. There, he'd begun to feel uncomfortable sitting alone in what had once been his local; there was about it a touch of the old man hanging around school playgrounds.

'How long do I have to bloody stand here before you recognise me, then?'

The question came from a short, balding man dressed in jeans, loose tee-shirt and trainers standing alongside his table.

'Bloody hell! Jim!' Alan got to his feet and made to give his friend a bear hug before substituting a hearty handshake, his free hand grasping the other's elbow. 'How long have you been in here?'

'Only a minute. Spotted you right away. You were miles away, or perhaps you're going ga-ga?' He gave one of his rare smiles, hastily raising his hand to his mouth as he did so.

'Good to see you, mate. How are you? What kept you? Have you seen any of the others?'

'I aren't answering any questions till you get me an ale in.'

Jim still retained his Potteries dialect. Alan betted that it wouldn't be long before he started calling everyone 'duck', loudly.

'Sorry, mate. What do you want?'

'I suppose it's all London piss. I'll leave it to you.' He sat down.

'Try and keep two seats free for the others,' said Alan, and began to fight his way towards the bar.

As he waited for a chance to be served he kept glancing back to the snug, managing to catch occasional snapshots of Jim behind the kaleidoscope of customers in constant movement between them. He'd been taken aback by his first sight of him, expecting that he, of all the others, would have shown the most evident signs of deterioration. In 1997 his thinness had verged on emaciation, his face scoured with deeply etched lines, his complexion muddy under the two day growth of beard, the thinning grey hair lank and covering his ears. Now, the face was still lined but less haggard, the eyes were clear, he was clean shaven, the hair fashionably cropped, and he'd put on some weight. In fact he looked younger than he had ten years ago. Alan felt a twinge of envy.

'IPA suit you, I hope,' he said, setting the pints down on the table.

'It'll do,' said Jim, 'Cheers.'

He took a deep draught. 'Not bad,' he conceded, high praise from him.

'Have you seen the others?' asked Alan. 'You're all bloody late.'

'Don't blame me, it's all the fault of Virgin Rail. Fuckin' train was 20 minutes late arriving at Stoke and it lost more time after that. Half an hour late into Euston. Bloody rail privatisation. Why didn't Blair re-nationalise them, Thatcherite wanker? Don't reckon Brown's gunna be any better, and – '

'But did you see the others at the hotel?'

'What? Oh, yeah, Nige was in the foyer when I arrived. Bastard still looks like an overgrown schoolboy; that blond hair's dyed, I reckon. We were gunna set out together, but just as we were leaving he had a phone call from his missus, what's'ername – '

'Melanie.'

'Right, Melanie. She was obviously giving him an earful, so he told me to get on, he'd catch me up. He looked a bit hassled, did our Nige.'

'I bet it was a problem with the kid.'

'The kid? Oh yeah, of course. Forgot about that. Poor bugger.' Jim looked slightly embarrassed and took refuge in another lengthy swig.

'Tragic,' said Alan, 'Remember how chuffed he was when we last met? Melanie was pregnant at the time. Terrible thing to happen.'

'Aye, well, it's always risky at their time of life. Melanie's not much younger than Nige, is she?'

'A bit. Think she was in her mid forties when they got married. Strange, old Nige getting spliced so late in life. Thought he was a confirmed bachelor. Anyway, Jim, what about *you*?'

'What d'you mean, what about me?' Alan noticed the defensive tone that Jim had always adopted when asked about his welfare.

'How you keeping? How's life treating you?'

Jim's response was to drain his pint in two swallows and ask if Alan was ready for another.

'Blimey, mate, just a half for me: we've got a long session ahead of us.'

As Jim headed towards the scrum at the bar Alan cursed himself for asking the sort of direct questions that had always made his friend clam up. Throughout their time at university Jim had been something of a man apart. He'd approached his membership of the Entertainments Committee with dour seriousness, seeing it as a vehicle for his mission to educate his peers about folk and blues, and had been scathing when the committee opted instead to invite flower-power oriented rock bands to play at the union hops. There'd been the occasion when he'd arrived at Eric's flat one evening to find the rest of them reverentially listening to *Sergeant Pepper* which Eric had purchased only that morning: he'd marched straight to the record player, lifted the stylus and made to hurl the disc across the room, only Vivienne's soothing intervention forestalling the act of sacrilege. He'd poured scorn on the shaggy hair, flared jeans and colourful shirts that Eric had begun to adopt, saying he was a dupe of the consumerist capitalist conspiracy to keep youth compliant. At that point Nigel, who still affected blazers, flannel trousers and a side parting, had expressed amused agreement, only to be rounded on and informed that he, Jim, didn't need the support of a fucking public-school toff.

But in those laid back times, thought Alan, such non-conformity was tolerated, so long as the nonconformist was under thirty, of course. Let it all hang out, man: do your own thing. Jim's distaste for youthful ephemera, his class consciousness, his political activism, his pessimistic taciturnity punctuated by drunken aggressiveness had all been accepted as a collectable eccentricity, and it was easy to forgive the peccadilloes anyone who could play the guitar as sweetly as he. What placed Jim apart, what they could not handle, had been those times when he withdrew to a place of his own, silent, dull-eyed, unreachable. 'Jim's really, really down again,' they used to say, but as he was unwilling or unable to express the reason for his sadness they could think of no way to help him, and only Vivienne had had the patience to try. In the Union bar one evening Tony had told him to pull himself together and stop being such a drag: they'd all stood aghast, waiting for an aggressive outburst, but to their horror he'd burst into tears and walked out.

It had not been until after the results of their Finals had been published that Jim, buoyed by his 2.1 in Sociology and mellowed by the cannabis that had recently made its appearance in their group, had confided to Alan that he'd suffered from severe bouts of depression since his adolescence. 'Well, we all get down now and again, man' Alan had said, at which Jim had shaken his head and replied sorrowfully that he didn't really expect anyone to understand who'd not experienced it.

Forty years on, Alan felt again the familiar shudder of shame at his uncomprehending response to Jim's admission, but then began to excuse himself: after all, back then, few in their age group had understood depression; it was something middle aged housewives suffered wasn't it? It was mothers who needed Little Helpers, hadn't the Stones said? Something to be ashamed of, not to be spoken about. These days, it seemed to be a common complaint – even some of his pupils had been thus diagnosed. He glanced over towards Jim, still waiting at the bar. Poor old sod, he thought: if only he'd known we might have been more supportive. But would they have made any difference? Jim's affliction had dogged him all his life, evidently ruining his career and resulting in a succession of failed relationships.

'These seats, they are free, yes?' The question, in heavily accented English, was posed by a burly young man standing behind Jim's vacant chair.

Alan looked up. 'Well, that one isn't, my mate's getting a drink in: I'm saving the other two for some friends who – '

'So, they are free. Come, Katya, sit.' He beckoned to a startlingly attractive girl standing near the entrance.

'Hang on a bit, mate.' Alan's mild-mannered tone belied the irritation he was feeling. 'My friends'll be here any minute. Can't you find some seats through at the back?'

He was ignored. The young man sat down, followed by the girl. They began to converse in a foreign tongue. Russian? Polish? Czech? Some eastern European lingo, thought Alan; London was full of them, Ealing Broadway at rush hour was like Warsaw. Sheila said they had no manners, any of them. Alan said she should give them time, they'd settle in, soon get used to our ways, just like the lot who came over in the war. This couple, however, evidently hadn't. You couldn't deny some of the women were real lookers, though: when was it that east European women suddenly stopped resembling Soviet shot-putters and became Anna Kournikova look-alikes? This Katya was a real stunner: despite his displeasure, Alan found it hard not to stare at her breasts, half revealed above the tight low-cut tee-shirt. Décolletage seemed to have become the fashion in recent years, he thought, and realised he probably found the phenomenon as disturbing as his father would have found the young Sheila's miniskirt had the poor old bugger lived long enough to meet her.

He was suddenly conscious that the girl was looking at him and she was obviously displeased. She muttered something to her companion, who treated Alan to an aggressive stare.

'You have problem?' he said, loudly.

'Pardon?'

'I ask, you have problem? Why you look at my woman, old man? Find yourself old lady.'

Alan was mortified. Notwithstanding his long years of faithful matrimony, he'd always had an eye for a pretty girl, and his admiring glances had occasionally been reciprocated until he started piling on weight in his late 30s. Since then he'd been resigned himself to sexual invisibility and had abandoned his discreet oglings – until the recent emergence of breasts, that is.

'Sorry, mate,' he muttered, 'I was miles away.'

His apology seemed further to agitate his accuser.

'What you mean? You not far away, you here, staring at Katya. You think me stupid?'

'No, no, you misunderstand me. I meant I was thinking of something else.'

The young man glowered at Alan from under beetle brows. He was drinking from a bottle of lager (why did young people eschew glasses?), which he began slowly to tap on the table top. Alan began to feel rather more than merely discomforted.

He was rescued by the sound of smashing glass and an affronted 'Fuckin' hell!' from the area by the bar, followed by silence. He looked across to see the other customers had backed away from Jim, who was standing in a pool of beer and shards of glass, his tee-shirt soaked, one hand holding a pint, the other ineffectually dabbing at his chest. A slightly-built middle-aged man, obviously the cause of the incident, was making apologetic noises, but his female companion, made of sterner stuff, announced loudly that anyone with any sense would ensure that no-one was standing behind them when turning from the bar. She had a clipped old-fashioned Home Counties accent of the sort rarely heard these days, an accent certain to provoke a tirade from Jim. Alan seized the chance to escape from European Union tensions and hurried across to the bar to bridge the English north-south divide.

'You can bloody well buy me another pint, you clumsy wanker,' Jim was saying.

'Hey, come on, Jim; it was an accident: no need to get heavy,' Alan interjected, wondering as he did so why he always reverted to the slang of his youth in times of stress.

'Of course I'll buy you another drink,' said the mild little man, 'What was it you were drinking? No, leave it be, dear,' he added as his wife (she had to be his wife) started a shrill response to Jim's insult.

Five minutes later, normal service was resumed at the bar and Alan and Jim had joined the drinkers standing on the pavement outside the door, their seats in the snug having been snapped up during the brief altercation, much to Alan's relief. On their way out he'd received a meaningful glower from the East European.

'You didn't tell me these pubs of yours were gunna be full of middle-class prats,' said Jim, 'Suppose I should have expected it in London.'

Alan was determined not to be provoked. 'How's life treating you, mate? How's work?' Jim, a social worker still on the basic grade, was the only member of the group yet to retire.

'Work's shit. No resources, deprivation getting worse, it is in Stoke, anyway. Got to carry on till I'm 65, of course, and even then I won't have enough years' service for a full pension. You don't know how lucky you are, comrade.'

'You're looking well enough on it, though. To be honest, Jim, you look younger now than you did ten years ago.' As he said it, Alan noticed that Jim's teeth, previously snaggled and discoloured, had obviously been capped.

Jim took a quaff from his glass. 'Aye, well.' He looked embarrassed. 'Might be summat to do with giving up smoking.'

'Christ! Yes, of course! I thought there was something missing. No roll-ups! Well done mate: what made you give up?'

Jim looked distinctly shifty and glanced up the street in the direction of Soho Square.

'Well, you may as well know. Me partner don't like me smoking in the house, but look, no need to tell the others – '

'Partner! That's great, Jim! I thought you were looking well cared for. Who is she? Why don't you want the others to know?'

'Nicky's a colleague. We've been shacked up now for a couple of years. I just don't fancy Tony taking the piss, that's all. Remember last time when he found out that women keep walking out on me? He was merciless. Dunna want him going on about how long this relationship will last. Dunna fancy the others doing their patronising, 'Oh we're so pleased for you, Jim', act either. At least you're from working class stock, even though you're a bloody southerner: you won't make a fuss.'

Alan recognised the coded warning not to pursue the matter further. He was in any case getting uncomfortably hot, the sun now shining directly down Greek Street with no shade on either side. He needed to sit down.

'Jim, I'm getting bloody toasted. Let's stand under the archway while we wait for Nige.'

They took up their new positions in the covered alley leading to Manette Street.

'How about you, then?' asked Jim. 'Keeping all right, are you?'

'Yup. Mustn't grumble, as me old mum used to say.'

'Lost a bit of weight, haven't you?'

'Well, I could afford to, couldn't I?' Alan peered out from under the arch, and to his relief saw Nigel's unmistakeable six-foot two inches, topped by a still-luxuriant blond quiff, approaching from Soho Square. Thank God for that. Now they could move on to the Coach and Horses, where seats might be available, and he wouldn't be subject to further observations from Jim about his weight loss.

Chapter 2

They walked slowly down Greek Street, Jim a few paces behind the other two. Nigel had greeted Alan effusively, but back at the hotel all Jim had received was a handshake and a 'Good to see you again, old boy'. Old feelings of inferiority had poked their snouts above the protective wall of his new-found security, and all the ambivalence of his feelings about Nigel Templeton had come flooding back. At Leeds he'd been the golden boy, tall, lean but muscular, with a mane of straw-coloured hair framing chiselled features, and he had all the easy charm of the public schoolboy. Buggers like that, Jim had thought, shouldn't be at a provincial university in a northern industrial town: why hadn't he gone to Oxford where his class belonged, or failing that to London, or Bristol? Nigel's accent had immediately grated on him, and his use of such terms as 'old boy' and 'old chap' Jim had taken to be condescending and insulting.

Jim had deliberately chosen Leeds as a means of reinforcing his northern credentials following the good-natured taunting of his Lancashire-born Geography master who insisted on referring to Stoke as a midlands town, but he'd been unpleasantly surprised to find that a sizeable minority of students came from south of the Trent.

Though he'd finally come to accept, grudgingly, that some Londoners might have as impoverished a background as those in the Potteries, he could not entertain the idea that anyone with a public school education could empathise with the underprivileged. When Nigel had revealed his membership of the Labour Party, he'd been suffused with rage at further evidence of condescension and had railed that the working classes didn't need the sympathy of toffs. But already Leeds had opened his eyes to a world beyond the Potteries, so when he discovered that Nigel was a Yorkshireman, Jim felt the crumbling of all his certainties. It was only much later that he discovered Nigel's parents' home to be a substantial house in the Yorkshire Dales, and that the Dales themselves contained pockets of affluence that would be the envy of many in the home counties. But by then he'd learned to suppress his preconceptions, and in any case there'd begun to be times when he felt alienated from all his peers, regardless of their origins. The vague feelings of sadness and malaise that had first afflicted him as an adolescent had, at university, deepened and darkened into interludes of desperate hopelessness when it felt as though an opaque curtain had fallen between him and those he'd begun to think of as friends. During his better periods however he'd begun to warm to Nigel, grudgingly admiring him for his resolute refusal to be seduced by the trappings of the swinging sixties. He still remembered the occasion of the first group obeisance to *Sergeant Pepper*: when the final crashing crescendo of 'A Day in the Life' had faded away to Eric's *Yeah Mans* and *Far Outs*, and Nigel had raised a sardonic eyebrow and said that yes, it was rather fun, wasn't it, but totally divorced from the blues.

'Come on Jim, what's keeping you?' Alan shouted back along the pavement: he and Nigel were standing outside a pub, the latter gazing appreciatively up at its façade.

'I always thought the Graeco-Roman exterior was rather fun,' Nigel observed, 'It must be twenty years since I was last here. How about you, Al?'

'Not as long as that, mate, but this wasn't here then.' Alan tapped a wooden structure, akin to a Western horse-hitching rail which ran the length of the pub wall. Between the wall and the rail and segregated from the pavement stood the lepers of the 21st century, smoking in the blistering sun.

'Aren't you glad you've given up?' he said, as Jim finally caught them up.

'Aye, in a way, but we ex-smokers live from day to day. I could murder a cig right now, couldn't you? And there's summut about the company of smokers I'll always like. Where does the working man go to have a pint and a fag? This bloody legislation's another nail in the coffin of working-class culture.'

Alan raised an eyebrow in Nigel's direction. Nigel appeared not to notice and said, 'It's certainly destroyed the ambience of many of the old pubs. I can't imagine what it'll be like inside here without the fug. I imagine Peter Cook would have had something to say – '

'Peter Cook?' said Jim, 'What's he got to do with it?'

'Oh, didn't you know? The *Private Eye* crowd used to drink in here. I remember when I first came to work in London – '

'Bugger that,' said Jim, 'Let's get inside. I've worked up a right sweat just walking down the street.'

He led the way inside. 'I'll get 'em in,' he said.

'No, I'll get them, old boy. What are you having?'

'I said I'll get 'em.' Jim was insistent. He didn't bother to ask what his friends wanted, but hurried off to join the crowd clustered round the bar.

Nigel and Alan secured seats at one of the heavy round-topped tables grouped close to the entrance. Each was adorned with ancient condiment sets, crusty sauce-bottles and cutlery wrapped in paper serviettes.

'I hope he doesn't start getting impatient,' said Nigel, glancing at Jim who was shuffling around behind the backs of those waiting to be served in an obvious effort to secure a place in the queue. 'He always gets testy when he's kept waiting for his pint. It was bad enough in Leeds, remember? I can't see him being very tolerant of being delayed by Londoners.'

'Just as long as he doesn't start exaggerating his Stoke accent. He'll confuse the barman.'

'If he tries that then it's a good job we weren't here last year,' said Nigel, 'old Norman would have refused to serve him; probably chucked him out, in fact.'

'Norman?'

'Yes, Norman Ballon, mine host here since the year dot; had the reputation of being London's rudest landlord. He retired last year. Didn't you ever come across him?'

'Blimey Nige, I was never a regular in these central pubs: I first came here yonks ago, just the once, until last February when I was planning this gig.

'I had some good evenings in here, in the old days,' Nigel said wistfully. He suddenly pulled back his shoulders. 'Anyway, I must say Jim looks very well. Last time we saw him I thought he was on his way to an early grave.'

'Well, he's given up smoking for a start.'

'Has he, by God? And what else?'

Alan glanced round at the bar where Jim was evidently attempting rudimentary sign language in an effort to be served.

'He's got a woman, but for God sake don't let on. For some reason he doesn't seem to want you all to know.'

'A woman? Jim? Are you sure?'

'That's what he said. Why, don't you believe it?'

'It just seems unlikely – after all the problems he's had with them, I mean. Anyway, best of luck to him. What about his mental state?'

'No more breakdowns, apparently.'

'That's good to hear. And what about you, Alan?'

'I'm ok. Mustn't grumble, as me old mum used to say. Bloody glad to be retired, as no doubt you are. I envy you the Cotswolds; Sheila and me used to go there for weekends before the kids came along.'

'How is Sheila? And your children?'

It was evident that they were about to exchange ritual enquiries about families neither of which were known to the other. Alan steeled himself for the necessity to ask about Melanie, and Nigel's son, and realised to his shame that he didn't even know the lad's name.

'She's ok, misses the kids now they're all married. Got six grandchildren now and another on the way. What about Melanie?'

'She's coping, Alan; that's about all I can say. Oscar's ten, now. It's getting to be very hard work.'

Alan wished he had a pint in which to take temporary refuge. 'It must be, mate,' he said eventually, 'I was so sorry to hear about it, Nige: why didn't you let us know sooner?'

'We just shut down after it was diagnosed; didn't want contact with anyone who couldn't share the problem. It's far worse for Mel, of course. You don't get much in the way of support networks in the Cotswolds. Sometimes I think it would have been better to have moved back to London. All Mel's friends are there of course. Look, Alan old boy, I appreciate your sympathy, but I don't really want to talk about it today, not with all the others around. Insofar as I can forget it, I've been looking forward to today as a break from horrendous reality.'

'*Tell* me about it.'

'No, Al, I said I don't want to talk about it.'

'I didn't mean – oh, never mind. Oh, Christ ...'

'What?'

'Nige, I've just realised. When I phoned everyone about this gig, I told Jim and Tony about….. about Oscar. They didn't know; didn't you want me to tell them?

'Oh, I'm glad you did: that sort of news is best revealed by a third party – leastways it's still something I find difficult to impart myself. I assume you told the Jacksons as well?'

'Well, no, I didn't, Nige. I only spoke to Eric once on the phone, after that it was all emails. I thought they knew – I mean, Eric was your flatmate, wasn't he? I assumed you'd have told him. In fact once you'd moved to Stow-on-the-Wold I thought you might have seen something of them; they're not that far from you, are they?'

Nigel hesitated for a moment before replying. 'I haven't seen either of them since about 1970. My news wasn't the sort you divulge on a Christmas card.'

Jim, still in the crush by the bar was glad to have fought off Nigel's insistence that he should buy the first round. He still wanted space to acclimatise to Nigel's presence and to overcome the lingering feeling of resentment that

Alan's attention had been diverted by the arrival of a third party. He'd wanted more time alone with Alan: of all the Leeds crowd he had been the nearest to an intimate, apart from Vivienne of course, but then she was a woman. He was disturbed by Alan's appearance: like most people of former ample proportions the weight-loss had not had the desired enhancing effect: his face had sagged, the once rounded cheeks were pouchy. And he was more subdued, less ebullient: at odd moments Jim had caught odd fleeting expressions of extreme sadness. He looked happy enough at the moment, though, chatting with Nigel at one of the tables near the door.

He began to resign himself to a long wait. The elderly Irishman behind the bar seemed a throwback to another age, hard of hearing and slow on his feet, though this was a comforting change from the glib chatter delivered by youthful bar staff confident in their possession of NVQs in Customer Services. In fact Jim felt comfortable in here. The absence of music had been the first thing he'd noted, then the faded, stained carpet. With its scuffed light-wood panelling and fly-blown mirrors the pub was the total opposite of anything he'd expected to find in the centre of London. Most reassuring, the clientele was almost exclusively middle-aged, or even older.

Jim had agreed to London being the venue for the reunion out of loyalty to Alan. He didn't like the capital; it felt like an alien land. His arrival at Euston and the journey to the hotel and then on to the pub had done nothing to re-assure him – everyone seemed expensively dressed, confident, cosmopolitan, attractive, and they walked so bloody fast, whether on the streets or on the escalators. And they all seemed to be in the first flush of young adulthood, not like the elderly shapeless women and their nobblyfaced anorak clad partners, so ubiquitous on the streets of Stoke, and the overweight teenagers in tracksuit bottoms and trainers, the boys with their shaven heads and the girls with their hair scraped back in what Nicky, in an un-pc moment, had called a council house facelift. All his mistrust of metropolitan culture had come flooding back, to be reinforced by that posh bitch in the Pillars of Hercules. He still retained a fierce defensive allegiance to the town of his birth, to which he'd returned to live and work immediately after graduating, despite the fact that his partner, a Brummie (almost a southerner, in Jim's eyes) was still inclined, albeit gently and humorously, to deride the locals. Nicky had joined Stoke Social Services Department nine years previously after a period working in Manchester. Initially Jim had felt intense dislike for the way the newcomer extolled the cosmopolitan Manchester with its modern architecture and vibrant night-life, and constantly disparaged the Potteries. Jim had let fly with a rant about how Stoke's deprivation was the result of the nation's wealth being unfairly distributed to other less deserving areas of the country. Nicky spiritedly responded that the area might attract more inward investment if the natives shook off their narrow-minded parochialism that bordered on xenophobia and stopped reading that bloody local rag with its daily diet of self-pitying mawkish sentimentality. Outraged, Jim had resorted to the personal, vilifying his new colleague's penchant for fashionable clothing ('You're a bloody social worker, not a fashion model') to which Nicky had retorted that Jim was the Potteries personified – shabby, impoverished and with little of architectural merit. There had followed a month when the two had exchanged not a word, except in the line of duty in case conferences.

He jerked out of his thoughts to realise he'd missed a chance to get to the bar, and reconciled himself to a further period of waiting. But at least this pub was acceptable, once one had acclimatised to the estuary English of the clientele, though some of the older men clung to the speech of the past, either cockney or BBC. Like the décor, they were all slightly shabby, and the absence of cigarette smoke allowed the occasional waft of body odour to compete with the smell of cooking fat seeping from somewhere in the recesses of the building. Occasionally strident Transatlantic or Oriental accents could be heard from couples hovering hesitantly at the open doors, only to cease abruptly when it became evident that this was no place for tourists.

At last he secured a place by the bar. The Irishman was engaged in the protracted delivery of an order placed by an elderly man dressed, despite the heat, in a dark suit, greasy with wear, the jacket liberally dusted with dandruff. There were at least two other customers ahead of Jim in the queue waiting to be served. Risking loss of eye contact with the Irishman he glanced over his shoulder to see if Alan and Nigel were showing signs of impatience, but they were engaged in animated conversation. He'd forgotten that Nigel's working life had been spent in London and that the two probably had much in common. At the gathering ten years before, Nigel had been very vague about the nature of his job beyond saying that it was in an obscure department of the Civil Service, and such was Tony's insistence in including his bimbo in all the conversations that it hadn't been possible to quiz Nigel further. He was certain to have been a high-flier, though: he'd achieved a First in history without any apparent effort, and had moved to London to take up a post immediately after graduation. Perhaps now he'd retired he might be a bit more forthcoming, though one of the problems about Nigel was that he was so bloody modest.

Jim had agonised about attending this reunion. He wasn't sure that he wanted to revisit a past for which he had few fond memories, especially after the disaster of the previous get-together in Leeds where that bastard Tony had been just as big a pain in the arse as he remembered. But Alan had been insistent, pleading almost, and had waved the carrot of the Jacksons' probable attendance. While Jim could take or leave Eric, he remembered Viv with great affection. London might be tolerable if she were present. When he told Nicky of his intention to go, his partner's first question had been 'You'll tell them all about us, of course?', a question which presumed the answer 'Yes' which Jim was unable to give. Trying to connect with others after years of separation would be fraught with enough angst without him being subject to a prurient reappraisal. Even in these enlightened times the reactions of those whose attitudes were formed in the years before Roy Jenkins' time at Home Office were hard to predict. Nigel would be relaxed about it, no doubt – after all, he'd been to public school, hadn't he? Al would be ok as well – old Al was tolerant of everything. Eric was an unknown quantity. Of all of them, Tony was the one most likely to condemn. And there was Viv, of course ....

'Yes, sorr?'

Behind the bar the Irishman had been joined by a faded blonde who rapidly dispatched two drinks orders, leaving Jim to struggle to communicate with one whose evident deafness seemed to be worsening with every pint he pulled.

'Fuckin' hell! That barman's geriatric!' Jim arrived with three pints on a battered metal tray which he placed on the table. Alan and Nigel grabbed their glasses and quaffed greedily, both thinking how unusual it was for Jim to be a welcome distraction. He further obliged by commenting that the place was a right dive, just his bag, and that it would be ok by him if they stayed here for the rest of the day.

As Alan began a rather weary defence of the other pubs that were on their itinerary, Nigel fell silent. He was relieved that the subject of Oscar had been introduced, relatively painlessly, early on in the day. Alan's reaction had been worrying him: his talkative, warm, open nature had always been of the sort that expected an exchange of confidences, and failure to reciprocate would have hurt him. However, there seemed to have been a change in Alan; he was less ebullient, less optimistic than he remembered. Perhaps it was the effect of the diet to which he'd obviously been subjecting himself? Jim would be less of a problem, he was always rather detached from the sorrows of others. As for Tony – well he'd never cared for Tony at university: their mutual dislike had been reinforced during the 97 reunion, and condolences were unlikely from that quarter. It was having to cope with Vivienne's sympathy that he dreaded.

'Do you think Eric and Viv'll turn up?' Alan said, echoing Nigel's thoughts.

'Your guess is as good as mine, old boy. You're the one who's had most recent contact with them.'

'If they didn't come last time I don't see why they should now,' said Jim, already half way through his pint. 'Dunno why Eric didn't just say they weren't, rather than all this maybe crap. And if they do come, what's all this about staying at a different hotel? Have we all got the plague or summat? What's the matter with 'em?'

'They probably have the same reservations as last time,' said Nigel, 'A boy's night out might not be much fun for a couple.' He took a pull at his beer and grimaced slightly.

'Then why the fuck doesn't Eric come by himself?' Jim continued to worry at the subject. 'We've left all *our* partners behind, haven't we?'

'But our partners weren't at Leeds with us, were they?' said Alan, 'Anyway Jim, I'd have thought you of all people would want to see Viv again.'

'What'd'ya mean by that?'

'Well, you and she were quite close, weren't you, mate? I mean, it was always her that helped …. I mean, who could speak to you when …..'

'When I was going doo-lally you mean? Why don't you come out and say it? Christ, it was depression, an illness; I aren't ashamed of it.'

'I'm not suggesting you are. Look, we all liked Viv, she was fun and a crackin' looker, I just thought –'

'I'm getting a bit peckish,' Nigel intervened, 'Where are we planning on eating? Not in here, I hope.'

He peered fastidiously at the array of crusty sauce bottles on the table. The pub was now in any case too full and too hot for comfortable eating. A few younger people had secreted themselves amongst the greying and balding heads, including a couple in full Goth regalia sitting at an adjacent table who were being served greasy bacon baps. Before Nigel's question was answered the male half stood and approached them to ask politely if he could take their tomato sauce.

'Go ahead, mate,' said Alan.

'Christ, those two look old enough to know better,' muttered Jim as the Goth resumed his seat, 'They must be about well over thirty, silly buggers. Why do people all want to be teenagers these days? Don't people in London get old any more?'

'Oh, lighten up, Jim.' Alan was still smarting from Jim's earlier outburst. 'You've got to accept the modern world even if you don't like it. If you don't you'll turn into an angry old git ranting against everything that's happened since you were twenty-one. Remember what *we* were like? How we said never trust anyone over thirty?'

Nigel, ever the peacemaker, intervened. 'Sometimes I think the secret of contentment in old age lies in pretending some things just don't exist, or ignoring them altogether.'

'What sort of things?' Jim asked

'Oh, things like hoodies, reality shows on TV – most things on TV in fact; why do all the audiences have to whoop and scream all the time? – and the Daily Mail, and petrol-heads, and semi-literate officialese, and George Bush: I could go on ad-infinitum.' He took a sip from his pint. 'But where *did* you intend us eating, Alan? I assume we are having some sort of lunch?'

Alan had been so concerned to plan the day's itinerary and to take in the best drinking establishments that he hadn't given a thought to eating, beyond a vague supposition that in the evening they'd return to Soho and find a pizza house or maybe a Chinese. A feeling of unease assailed him: the day seemed on the verge of unravelling already – everybody was being late; where was Tony for God's sake? Nigel had said there'd been no sign of him at the hotel. And why hadn't Eric phoned? Surely if the Jacksons were coming they'd have arrived in London by now? His unease began to develop into something approaching panic, accompanied by anger at the way he now got so uptight about such little things, he, who had always been seen as the most laid-back of the group. Laid-back, but without the cool connotations that the term implied.

'What's wrong with eating here?' said Jim, 'Seems ok to me.' He drained his pint and looked at Nigel expectantly.

'I'd prefer to find somewhere a little more roomy,' said Nigel, 'and bacon baps aren't to my taste these days.'

This was an understatement. Over the years Nigel had acquired a finely developed palate for Italian and French cuisine accompanied by fine wines. He learned to pigeon-hole his tastes: the consumption of good food and wine had been confined to expensive restaurants in England and to intimate family-run bistros on the continent. Beer on the other hand he'd preferred to imbibe in unpretentious pubs with raffish clientele. The Coach and Horses had been one of his favourite boozers during his years in London, but he would no sooner have eaten there than to have ordered a pint of bitter in the Savoy, not that he'd had the opportunity to contemplate doing either in recent years.

'Reverting to type, aren't you, Templeton,' said Jim, 'Once a toff, always a toff.'

'You might very well say that,' said Nigel, 'and I might reply once a Stokey always a Stokey, though I hope I'm not so bigoted ever to think such a thing.'

His companions were stunned into silence by the acid response, totally out of character with the Nigel whose politeness had been legendary. Alan felt another lurch of dismay – this was not being the comfortable, nostalgia-tinged gathering of old friends that he'd been so long anticipating. He had to say something to pre-empt the foul-mouthed rejoinder that would inevitably come from

Jim, and blurted out that the next pub would be better to eat in.

'Well, are we going there, or are we gunna have another one here first?' Jim tapped the side of his empty glass.

Alan, in his head still frantically revising the planned itinerary to ensure that the next pub would be gastronomically acceptable, was grateful for Jim's evident desire for an immediate refill.

'We'll have one more here,' he said, 'give Tony a chance to arrive.'

'In that case it's my shout,' said Nigel, standing up. 'Same again for you both?' He pushed his way towards the bar.

'Bloody hell,' said Jim, 'What's got into him?'

'It's probably his kid that's worrying him. He's probably got a conscience about leaving Melanie while he's out enjoying himself. Go easy on him, Jim, he's having a hard time.'

'He aren't the only one. At least he's got money behind him. Barn conversion in the Cotswolds! Bet he's got enough dosh to pay for care for the kid. We've all got problems, but the rich can always pay to ease theirs.'

'Oh for God's sake, Jim, give it a rest. Just for a few hours can't you spare us the polemics?'

Jim glowered, but decided against a response. The two sat in uncomfortable silence, their shared pasts no longer sufficient a bulwark against the intrusion of the present. They stared round the room, avoiding each other's eyes, both in their different ways aware that their memories of each other had been filtered by wants, needs and beliefs acquired over forty years of diverging life experiences. They each remembered in their own favour. When you pass so you become part of the me generation, no longer so concerned what others think of you: they have to accept you as you are, and that applies as much to old friends as to new acquaintances.

Nigel's arrival with the drinks coincided with the ringing of Alan's phone. He glanced at the screen – an unknown number.

'Hello …. Tony! At last! ……… I couldn't, you didn't give me your number. …….never mind that now; where are you?............ what are you doing there, for God's sake? ………… no, I never said that. …….. listen, we're in the *Coach and Horses*, but by the time you get here we'll have moved on, ……. listen, head for the *Princess Louise*, it's on High Holborn, near the tube …….. well, look at the underground map ……… keep your phone on, we'll be there in about half an hour.'

Alan looked at his phone. 'That was Tony. He's rung off.'

'Where is he?' asked Nigel.

'In one of the bars at Euston. He hasn't even made it to the hotel yet. He claimed I'd said we'd meet at the station.'

'I bet he's pissed,' said Jim.

'No, he didn't sound pissed exactly, just a bit strange.'

'What sort of strange?'

'Hard to describe. A bit manic to start with, then vague, and at the end he sounded, well, almost ……..'

'Almost what?'

'If I didn't know it was Tony, I'd have said he was tearful.'

Chapter 3

MARYLEBONE

'Where are you *going*, Eric?'

Staggering under the weight of the suitcases, Eric turned. 'Down to the tube. It's only a couple of stops, and – '

'Four stops and one change at Oxford Circus. It'll be intolerable in this heat. Let's get a taxi.'

'Okay, okay.' Eric deferred to Vivienne's knowledge of the London Underground, remembering that she'd probably become well acquainted with the capital's transport system during the frequent visits she used to make to her friend Belinda who lived in Bayswater. He followed her out through the exit into the glare that penetrated the Victorian cast-iron and glass canopy at the front of the station.

Looking around at the carefully restored brickwork and the freshly painted ironwork he felt suddenly transported to the stations of his train-spotting childhood: despite electrification, Marylebone had about it the gentle air of steam-train romance no longer found in the frenzy of Euston or Kings Cross or Birmingham New Street, all of which had come to resemble characterless airport concourses. It evoked setting off on summer holidays with his parents in the days before his father had scraped enough together to purchase a second-hand Morris. There was something else nagging at the fringes of his memory – what the hell was it? Suddenly it came to him and he hurried to catch up with Vivienne who was striding towards the taxi rank.

'Viv! Viv! Wait a minute!'

'What is it?'

'This station. Something about this canopy struck a chord with me, and I've just remembered what it was.'

His wife sighed. 'You spotted trains here, presumably?'

'No, not here. Always went to Kings Cross, to see the Eastern Region locos, you know, the Pacific Class. No, it was a hard day's night.'

'What was, train spotting? What do you mean? Surely even you weren't silly enough to go train spotting at night?'

'No, no, it was the film, *A Hard Day's Night*. You know, we went to see it in our first year at Leeds, at the Odeon in City Square it was, and you – '

'Eric, what *are* you going on about? Look, we've just lost a taxi.'

'I'm telling you. Remember the scene at the station, when the Beatles were running the gauntlet of fans, trying to catch the train? Well, it was filmed here! Just think! John and Paul running through that very entrance!'

Vivienne raised her eyes heavenward, then turned towards the taxis. Eric sighed and fell in behind her.

'Hilton Hotel, Upper Woburn Place, please,' Vivienne instructed the cab-driver. 'It's just opposite the BMA headquarters.'

'He probably knows that, Viv,' Eric ventured, 'I reckon every Londoner knows where Upper Woburn Place is, you know, after 7/7.'

'I'm just trying to be helpful, for God's sake,' snapped Vivienne, rummaging in her suitcase for the book in which she'd been immersed on the train.

Eric glanced towards the driver's mirror and caught the cabbie's sympathetic grin. Hastily, he turned to observe the passing scene as the cab stop-started its way through the traffic. White vans, black limos, red bendy buses, suicidal motorcyclists, masked cyclists: and the pedestrians – all ages, races, statures, sexes; eclectically dressed – and all hurrying. And the noise! Horns, sirens, thumping car stereos. The most exciting city in the world, it was said, but Eric could do without excitement. He'd come to relish a slower pace of life since his retirement. When still working he'd attended occasional meetings of the Secondary Heads Association held in London, but was always relieved to get home to the relative peace of Leamington Spa. Vivienne had always enthused about the cultural life of the capital on returning from her visits to stay with Belinda, though these had abruptly ceased some ten years ago, for some reason which she'd never fully explained.

He sneaked a glance at his wife. They'd spoken little since leaving the house that morning. Her lips were pursed slightly as they had been throughout the entire journey, but he couldn't be sure if this was an indication of her continuing reluctance to participate in the reunion or whether she was merely concentrating on her novel. He felt a renewed welling of irritation with her. Disagreement had festered between them for the past three months, ever since they'd first been invited. He had been eager to attend; she was adamant that they should not. They'd had the same disagreement over the same issue ten years previously, and on that occasion he'd deferred to her wishes. This time he'd been determined not to give way. Eventually she'd agreed to come on condition that it was London not Leeds, that they didn't join the others until mid afternoon, and that afterwards they stay at a different hotel. When he'd reluctantly agreed to the compromises, she'd hurriedly added a further condition – that he inform Alan that they would not be able to confirm their attendance until the very day of the reunion. 'Why?' he'd asked. 'In case I change my mind,' she'd said, meaningfully.

The cab pulled up outside the Hilton. Vivienne paid the fare, Eric grappled with the luggage. He mounted the steps to the hotel entrance and stopped, confronted by revolving doors which prohibited entry to one carrying two suitcases. He waited for assistance from Vivienne: it was not forthcoming; she pushed through the doors leaving him to make two entrances, each with an individual case. His irritation was blunted by a sense of déjà vu; something involving revolving doors. He dredged his memory, to no avail. No doubt recall would come when he was thinking of something else.

Inside the lobby it was blessedly cool. The necessary formalities at the reception desk completed, they entered the lift and ascended to the fourth floor, Eric trying to avoid glancing in the mirrors that formed the walls on two sides. He didn't care for full-length mirrors these days. A large pot belly protruded from his slight frame, and he was always undecided whether to pitch his belt above or below it. He noted his wife examining her reflection appraisingly: for a 61 year old she had a trim figure, still able to wear close-fitting jeans.

Vivienne pronounced herself satisfied with the room and set about unpacking. Eric sat on one of the twin beds, debating whether he dare take an initiative. Now they'd arrived in London Viv might be more amenable to an early start – it would be silly to hang about with the others so close; surely she would see that? He decided to take the risk, walked over to his linen jacket which he'd slung over a chair and extracted his mobile phone from the inside pocket.

Vivienne was on to him like a shot. 'What are you doing?'

'Oh, I thought I'd give old Al a ring, find out where they are.'

'Why? It's only just after twelve.'

'I know, but why hang about? Now we're here we might just as well join them. They'll probably be eating soon.'

'The last thing I want to do in this heat is eat ghastly pub food in a bar jam-packed with workers taking their lunch break. I thought we'd agreed that we'd eat here, in the hotel bar. It's bound to be air conditioned.'

'But that'll take ages, Viv. Look, we haven't seen them for nearly forty years. We need a few hours with them to catch up. They'll be talking about old times already; I don't want to miss out on any of it.'

'Old times!' Vivienne was scathing. 'That's all you can think about. You'll be disappointed, you know: when we get to meet them we'll probably find we've got nothing to say to each other.'

'Why did you bother to come, then?

'That's something I've been asking myself all day. Look, I'm going to freshen up and change before we eat. If you're in such a hurry why don't you go down to the bar and get a menu?' She turned and entered the bathroom, locking the door behind her.

Eric sank back on the bed, deflated. Vivienne's reluctance ever to revisit the past was one of several disappointments he had suffered during their long marriage, a union which, like many that manage to survive, had settled eventually into the sort of semi-contentment that derives from resigned acceptance of each other's foibles. They'd met as freshers at university in 1964, had become a definite item in their final year and had married eighteen months later after he'd qualified as a teacher and she as a librarian. The decades since had passed for him in a flurry of career advancement, and for her in child rearing, home making and part-time employment in the county library. But he'd never forgotten the heady days of their youth – even as a staid, responsible head-teacher, waging a constant rearguard action against adolescent excess, he'd continued when alone in the house to listen to 'Sounds of the Sixties' on Radio 2 on Saturday mornings and to wallow in nostalgia for his own time of freedom and irresponsibility, and for the company of the friends who'd shared his rites of passage.

Vivienne, however, once married, had cast aside youthful things with scarcely a backward glance, even before the arrival of their first daughter. She'd set her face against gatherings of their university friends, saying the cottage was too small to accommodate them all, that they had neighbours to consider, professional reputations to safeguard. He'd persuaded her to invite them singly, and for a year some had thus attended, Nigel twice, Alan and Jim once, but Tony never. Vivienne had entertained them well; too well, Eric had thought, as they sat politely round the dinner table complimenting her on her cooking and afterwards decorously sipping a nightcap before retiring to bed before midnight. Their visits ended when Eric no longer had the energy to persuade Vivienne to let him issue further invitations.

'Bugger getting the menu,' he said to himself rebelliously. Viv would no doubt occupy the bathroom for her customary ages: he didn't see why he should be confined to the room waiting for her. In any case, he could do with a beer – the idea of a solitary aperitif before being joined by his wife was suddenly very appealing.

'Viv!' he shouted at the bathroom door, 'I'm going down to the bar. I'll wait for you there.'

'Aren't you going to bring up the menu?' Her clear, well-modulated tones penetrated the door without her having to shout.

'It won't take you two minutes to choose from a bar menu.'

'Oh, all right. But don't start drinking this early, *please.*'

Eric chose not to respond, grabbed his jacket and left.

Viv had been right about the bar, of course: it was air-conditioned and pleasantly cool. It was a spacious room; deep easy chairs were grouped round low tables, but with ample circulation space between them. Eric stood at the entrance, peering round to find a vacant table. Most were occupied by youngish people, mainly men but with a scattering of females amongst them. All were conservatively dressed, the men wearing ties, the women in crisp white blouses and tailored skirts, and most were chattering animatedly either to each other or into mobile phones, apart from a few who were intent on tapping the keyboards of their laptops. There were a few middle-aged couples, distinguished by their casual dress and the absence of any conversation: they were staring at a large TV attached to wall which was silently broadcasting Sky 24 Hour News.

Eric was comforted by the scene: sensible business people and tourists, he thought. No evidence of the uncouth loutishness which seemed to him to be permeating all levels of society and which might even, he'd thought, have penetrated the portals of a four-star hotel. As a head-teacher he'd sadly witnessed a gradual decline in manners, standards of behaviour and respect for learning amongst pupils, their parents and even some junior staff. It was this, together with an increasing propensity for his pupils ('students', they called themselves) to resort to the threat of violence when confronted with discipline, that had prompted him to take early retirement.

He ordered a half of bitter at the bar. The young man behind it was foreign and didn't appear to understand the term 'bitter' and Eric had to resort to pointing at the Sam Smith's pump. Seeing a chair become vacant he grabbed the beer and a menu and rushed to secure it, the two suited young men seated at the table not giving him a glance when he sat. They were talking enthusiastic gobbledegook about information technology, and Eric noted gloomily that their evident technical expertise was not matched by an ability to express themselves in English. Glottal stops abounded (Eric blamed Tony Blair for their increasing prevalence) along with 'innits' and 'likes'. Blokeishness, it seemed, now ruled even in four-star hotels; everyone now was desperate to disavow elitism. Eric began to feel depressed, a depression which deepened when he found his Sam Smiths to be ice-cold.

In an effort to shake himself out of his mood he thought of meeting his old friends. He'd been looking forward to it for months. But the omens were not good for the remainder of the day. Any chance there might have been to jolly Vivienne out of her reluctance to attend seemed to have evaporated. Surely she wouldn't stay sour once she was with the others? Perhaps when she was reminded of old times she might even start to re-live them? She'd been popular with them all, not just for her gamine looks and inviting figure (she was one of the first in their year to wear mini-skirts) but for her vivacity and her acerbic wit. Maybe she didn't want them to see her as she now was? Women were sensitive about ageing. But then she'd always set her face against revisiting the past, even when in her twenties.

Perhaps she'd never liked the others as much as they'd liked her? Maybe she had a never-revealed longstanding antipathy towards one or more of them? In the frantic enjoyment of their final year at Leeds he'd not had time to nurture any small reservations that he might have had concerning his fellows; they'd had all been caught up in the unthinking pursuit of pleasure. That was how he remembered it, anyway. But her reluctance to attend probably had nothing to do with their fellow-alumni. It was something in her nature, something he'd never understood and was never likely to. There was much that he didn't understand about his wife. Where the bloody hell had she got to, anyway? He was tempted to get another beer, but Viv was right, as usual: once they were with the others he'd be honour-bound to keep up with the rounds. He wasn't used to drinking, these days.

Chapter 4

TOWARDS THE PRINCESS LOUISE

Their departure from the Coach and Horses was delayed by the queue for the cramped and noisome toilet in the pub's basement where Nigel had been disappointed to find that the 'Albert Tatlock was here' graffiti had been erased from the wall. Outside, the sky had turned milky but a hazy sun still beat down on the crowded pavements. The street was airless with no breeze to disperse the acrid wafts of cigarette smoke, the more noticeable after its absence in the pub. The three began by sauntering side by side, but the polyglot crowds seemed unwilling to compromise and barged into them without apologies. Nigel in particular seemed to be on the receiving end of pushes and shoves, the result perhaps of his height and debonair appearance.

Jim was all for challenging such behaviour. 'Why don't you give as good as you get?' he asked after Nigel had been eyeballed by a swarthy youth jabbering in a middle-eastern tongue into a mobile phone and who resolutely refused to make way for them despite there being enough room for him to pass: Nigel had been forced into the road.

'It's not worth it, old boy. It's all to do with the transfer of embarrassment that seems to have occurred recently.'

'What d'you mean?' Alan stopped to listen to Nigel's explanation and was immediately pushed into by a young woman who'd been following close behind. He offered apologies but these were evidently not accepted, 'Get a fuckin' move on, can't you,' being the response.

'Well, it used to be that people were embarrassed to do things that might offend others. Now it's us, we who are offended, who are embarrassed about making a scene. If I challenged people who push into us it would be met by blank incomprehension. It's not just London, y'know. I've even come across that sort of behaviour in Stow, and – '

He was cut short by yet another exhortation to get out of the way, this time delivered by a smartly-dressed man whose glottal-stopped delivery belied his svelte appearance.

'Perhaps we are being a bit anti-social,' said Nigel, 'This isn't really a tourist area, not at this time of day anyway. Everyone's desperate to find somewhere to eat and get back to work; can't expect them to be tolerant of old codgers like us cluttering up the streets.'

'You don't find folk in Stoke charging about like this when they're on their lunch hour,' said Jim. The remark was made over his shoulder: he'd had to accelerate smartly to avoid entangling with two elegant black girls who strode towards them, immersed in noisy conversation and oblivious to their surroundings.

Alan briefly appraised their finely sculptured Nubian features as they passed. He had been about to inform Jim that in London an hour for lunch was a thing of the past, but the two girls distracted him. Though stunningly attractive, they aroused no desire in him. As with all young women he could appreciate their unlined flesh, their firm bodies, their coltish movements, but it was an aesthetic appreciation, devoid of erotic urges. He wished he'd had the opportunity to explain this to the East European in the

Pillars of Hercules. He'd never understood the predilections of dirty old men, but nevertheless felt a twinge of regret that he'd been born too soon to experience the exotic delights afforded by being young in a multicultural society.

'Look here, you chaps,' said Nigel, 'We can't go on walking three abreast. You two go on ahead, I'll follow.'

He fell back. He knew the way to the Princess Louise, it had been another of his old haunts. He approved of the venue; the pub offered good basic lunchtime fare and ample seating space. He'd been surprised by Alan's evident distress at the change to his planned itinerary: things like that never used to bother him, in fact as a student he'd lived so much for the moment that planning itself was an alien concept. Such was his disorganisation that, unlike most of his peers in Leeds, he'd not got it together to share a flat, choosing to live in digs with a motherly old landlady in Providence Avenue. But he'd never seemed to be lonely – his sunny disposition and tolerance of the foibles of others resulted in his having a complex network of friends across a wide spectrum of university society. He'd been as at home in the Mouat-Jones coffee lounge chatting to the Union elite as he was in Caff listening to the rantings of the Marxists, or in the Union Bar chanting obscene songs along with the university Rugby club. Everyone had liked Alan, though Tony, it would have to have been Tony, had once referred disparagingly to his character as being chameleon-like.

Nigel had other reasons to walk by himself. He needed some moments of introspection. He wasn't sure that he was enjoying himself. He felt guilt laced with anger for what he'd left behind in Stow. It was the school holidays and Melanie was alone with Oscar. She never gave herself a break: she accepted her lot with all the dour stoicism

47

of the family from which he thought he'd rescued her, seemingly wishing to atone for the sin of risky procreation by a stubborn insistence on coping without the outside help that was well within their means. Nigel had begun to be increasingly exasperated. The years of mutual support when visiting hospitals, clinics, social services, support groups and even faith healers seemed to count for little, for as soon as he'd tentatively suggested residential care, Melanie had immediately withdrawn, and now seemed to have little affection left over for him after expending all her love on Oscar. When he'd hesitantly mooted the idea that he might spend a day in London with his old friends, mentioning that he was particularly keen on seeing Eric and Vivienne again, her response had been 'For God's sake go and see them, then, since they're obviously so important to you'.

Now a good ten yards behind Jim and Alan, he began to negotiate the traffic, pedestrian and vehicular, that swirled around Cambridge Circus. Here, he needed more than ever to be alone. He looked at the Palace Theatre – when was it he'd seen *Les Miserables* there? Must have been 1986 or thereabouts – yes, he'd just returned from a gruelling stint in Prague, he'd attended the show with his then lover after an afternoon of tender reunion in his flat. Stolen moments. Her visits to London were so infrequent that he resented any time spent not alone with her: it was she who insisted on trips to theatres or restaurants. She'd liked the passion of their assignations to be leavened by activities where they could just hold hands or walk arm in arm, and engage in all the simple expressions of everyday affection employed by what she called 'normal' couples. When he'd said that normality could be achieved by her coming to live with him, she'd reminded him this wouldn't be possible for years, and begged him not to spoil their short time together. She never had come to live with him. Lonely, and with early retirement looming, he'd turned to Melanie for comfort.

He stood gazing at the Theatre. The hoarding at the front proclaimed a show called *Spamalot*. He'd never heard of it. I've become provincial, he thought, I'm out of touch with London life, and I avoid media accounts of it lest I be tortured by regrets at having left. He turned his head slowly, taking in the narrowing perspectives of the streets that radiated from the Circus. He grinned wryly as he remembered how le Carre had had placed Smiley's HQ in one of these pleasing Victorian buildings, when the reality was a grim modern block in Lambeth. Smiley's certainties had long since evaporated. It had been when the Cold War seemed finally to have ended that Nigel had realised he was becoming one of yesterday's men and began seriously to consider retirement. Looking back, the 1990's had been a brief golden age of optimism when his generation were at last free from the nagging fear of nuclear oblivion that had haunted them all their lives, before the 21st century had ushered in new horrors. Terrorism, given its random nature, didn't worry him too much: it was the threat of global warming that sometimes kept him awake at night. Perhaps it would have been better for the world to have ended with a bang rather than to wait for civilisation to crumble with a protracted whimper. There were times when he was glad that Oscar would not live long enough to see it.

Chapter 5

Hilton Hotel

Refreshed from her shower, Vivienne put on her new summer dress and examined herself in the mirror. Not bad, not bad at all: she could still get away with skirts just above the knee. She sat to apply her make-up. She thanked providence for having the pale skin that accompanied her once-auburn hair, skin that she'd always taken care to protect against the sun with the result that it was relatively unlined compared to her contemporaries. She supposed she could be described as well-preserved, a term she'd once regarded as derogatory but which had lost its stigma now she was in her sixties. The same could not be said of Eric; he'd begun to let himself go as soon as he began climbing the career ladder.

She felt a sudden twinge of conscience as she remembered her husband's years of toil. Were she not a 21st century woman she might have acknowledged that he'd been a good provider, but the phrase was not part of her vocabulary. She could, however, concede that he'd been a dutiful partner and a caring, sometimes over-indulgent, father. The sudden responsibility of having to provide for a young family (the result of her abandoning the pill because of the burgeoning health scare) had prompted Eric to immerse himself in his work, and he'd moved from school to school in the pursuit of promotion. Vivienne had been relieved by his belated commitment to the future, and grateful for the salary increases which permitted them to move from the cramped cottage to a semi in Alcester, then to a four bedroom detached in Leamington in which they still remained. Their upward mobility had been accompanied by the expansion of Eric's waist, the retreat of his hair and the cultivation of a rather inadequate beard which he persisted in stroking thoughtfully, much to her annoyance. He'd become a reluctant workaholic, too tired and too absorbed by the demands of his job to do much more than slump in front of the TV on the few evenings when he was not in his study or attending a meeting. She'd begun to build a social life of her own based on her intellectual and artistic interests, and visiting Belinda in Bayswater, of course.

She'd hoped that when he retired there'd be a re-awakening of his former academic interests, but it had not happened. Years of grappling with the daily demands of pupils, staff, the school budget and the inquisitorial visitations of OFSTED had extinguished his intellectual curiosity. He seemed content to potter in the garden, to attempt the *Guardian* crossword, and to watch news and current affairs programmes, the latter usually provoking him into prolonged impotent rantings about the modern world. It apparently never occurred to him to break out, to explore new horizons, to seize the chances that freedom from responsibility could bring. She complained about this to her friends in the Book Club many of whom were similarly burdened with a permanent husbandly presence and who had in varying degrees explored new paths once the shackles of child-rearing (which today seemed to last until late adolescence) had been unlocked. Women of her age seemed to realise they could find themselves through alternative endeavours; they were far more open to change than their menfolk.

She began to brush her grey hair. It required little attention, being a short-cut cap, but she wanted to delay joining Eric in the bar, to linger over lunch, to put off for as long as she could that moment when she'd be confronted with the others. Try as she might to re-assure herself that they were now all in their 60s and different people from those that they'd once been, she was aware meeting former friends sometimes had the effect of nudging one back to the past, a past that often seemed more brightly lit, more detailed and immediate than anything that had happened in the intervening years.

That was how it was for Eric, she supposed. Thinking of him as he was now, she knew that that final year at university had been, for him as for her, an aberration: his nostalgia for that time was misplaced, past events and emotions had built in his memory. Arriving in Leeds in 1964 had been a culture shock for them both. They'd met in their first year whilst taking a cigarette break outside the Brotherton Library (she was persevering with No. 6 Tipped in an effort to be cool), and had after a few stumbling sentences recognised each other as being fellow southerners trying to adapt to life in a sulphurous industrial city and to a university where most of the students were not only northern but, in their eyes, aggressively so. They had drifted, firstly into each other's occasional company, later into unconsummated coupledom. Thus mutually fortified, they began to participate, first hesitantly, then with growing confidence, in the explosion of youth solidarity which by the mid 1960s had begun to transcend differences of class or region.

She remembered how Eric, after a few experiences at the Saturday evening Union Hop, had become an enthusiast for rhythm and blues, and how he'd embraced short jackets, hipster trousers, tab collars and slim knitted black ties. She'd held out for a while, but then also succumbed to the prevailing mood, and adopted the pale make-up, black mascara and Mary Quant hairstyle worn by her more adventurous peers. She could still remember the shock at first seeing herself in the boutique mirror, wearing white knee-length boots and a skirt a few inches above her knee – she was, suddenly, sexy. She'd never thought of herself as sexy. Gradually, they'd begun to move easily amongst the trendier members of the University union, on the fringes of that admired elite that held court in the Mouat-Jones coffee lounge. By their final year Eric had adopted flowered shirts and flared jeans, while she had a Marianne Faithful hairstyle and wore mini-dresses that left little to the fevered imagination of her male fellow-students.

Thinking of Eric as he once had been and how he was now, she felt a wave of something akin to affection, tinged with pity. He was fundamentally a decent man; he had no real vices apart from pedantry and sentimentality, he didn't smoke, drank rarely, never lost his temper, never really argued back. He was so bloody *moderate*. Maybe that was his problem. Also, he had no real friends. He wasn't clubbable; his social life, such as it was, had revolved round his colleagues, and now he no longer had even them. It occurred to her that he might be lonely, that this was why he was so eager for contact with the old crowd, forgetting how they'd so often teased him for his lack of cool. He had never been the hedonist of his memory, had never really been able to cast off the inhibitions of his upbringing.

Back then she'd been secretly frustrated by his gentlemanly acceptance of her rejections of his sexual advances: in those days a girl of her background had been indoctrinated to say 'No' even when she didn't mean it. She, in that final year, had sometimes been tempted to break out, be wild, live for the moment – and God knows she'd had enough offers of assistance for such an escape.

She hastily applied the brakes to these thoughts, and realised she'd been brushing her hair for nearly five minutes. There were no more displacement activities to hand; she'd have to join Eric in the bar. She applied liberal splashings of perfume, picked up the room's swipe-card, and made her way to the lift, resolving to be more sympathetic to her husband. She felt she'd been fully justified in vetoing their attendance at the 1997 reunion given that it was to have taken the form of a pub-crawl along Headingley Lane, retracing the steps of their final night as university students. Couldn't he remember what a disaster that had been for him?

But this time – well, perhaps the London venue might be tolerable, given that their separate hotel booking would give them the opportunity to opt out of the proceedings if things became too noisy, or if other embarrassments raised their heads. Belinda's geographical proximity was a bit unnerving though, not that there was the remotest chance of running into her. Yes, the conditions she'd imposed were probably sufficient: she shouldn't keep punishing Eric, poor old bugger. She resolved to make amends by discussing the details of the forthcoming event, something she had resolutely refused to do ever since the day it had been mooted.

Eric's irritation at being kept waiting was verging on self-righteous anger when Vivienne finally appeared at the door of the bar. There was a brief moment when he failed to recognise her – she'd changed into a dress, a new one, he supposed, at least he'd not seen it on her before. It was short, well, just above the knee, and showed her legs to advantage. She still had good legs, not just long and shapely, but sufficiently blemish-free to enable her to dispense with tights. The dress was close fitting and she wore it well: she was still boyishly-hipped, with a supple waist. Not having spotted him, she turned towards the bar. From behind she could pass for a thirty-five year old, apart from the grey hair, of course. He'd once tentatively suggested that she restore it to its former auburn glory, but the response had been dismissive. Her responses to his suggestions often were.

He hailed her. She turned and graced him with a smile, the first she'd bestowed on him that day. There wasn't a vacant seat at the table, the young technologists were still in occupation, but as she approached one of them stood and offered her his chair. She thanked him graciously and sat, crossing her legs at the knee.

'A pleasure,' the young man said, his eyes swivelling between her face and her legs. His companion muttered 'Not bad,' in a voice that she was obviously meant to overhear.

'Let's have a look at the menu, then,' she said, 'Have you decided what you're having?'

Eric had elected for a Caesar Salad, and after due consideration she chose the same, and asked for a mineral water. He went to the bar to order. As he waited for the attention of the barman, he noticed that Vivienne was in conversation with the two young men. Something was said to amuse her: she threw back her head and laughed. She seemed to be in good humour, suddenly. Was it the obvious appreciation shown by the two men that had caused her sourness to evaporate? Weren't such expressions of appreciation condemned by feminists as sexist? Or was it now acceptable, in these post-feminist times? Not that he really understood what was meant by post-feminism; he'd found it hard enough to comprehend the ideology of the original Greer generation by whom he'd stood accused of being a chauvinist oppressor simply by virtue of his gender. In the early years of his career advancement he'd had some uncomfortable moments with female colleagues, who though his contemporaries, seemed a generation away from the sweetly submissive girls he thought he remembered at university. Then, just when he'd finally learned to disguise every managerial directive as a request, never to use terms of endearment and at all costs to avoid physical contact, the dungareed harridans transmogrified into a new race of women, skirted, heeled and made-up, who scorned his mild-mannered suggestions and told him to make a decision for God's sake, yet had no compunction in putting their arms round his shoulders in times of stress, or even, post-Diana, in hugging and kissing him. It could all have been done ironically of course, so he never reciprocated. Far too risky. He'd never really understood women. Even parts of Viv were a closed book. She'd never been a strident feminist, had seemed content to do the childrearing thing despite her good degree and her creative interests. Though she could be scary when roused, mostly she was cool, almost aloof. If asked to sum her up he would have replied 'quietly assertive'.

When he rejoined her the young men were on the point of leaving. They said it had been, like, great chatting to her and hoped she'd have a cool day. As they left they nodded to Eric respectfully.

'What pleasant young men,' Vivienne said as Eric sat down, 'You see, some young people still have good manners.'

'Pity they can't string a sentence together,' Eric grunted.

'Old grump,' said Vivienne, not without affection. 'So, where are we meeting the others, then?'

For a moment Eric was silent. Was this sudden willingness to talk about the events of the day, he wondered, an implicit apology for her prolonged churlishness? It was, after all, the way both of them always signalled an armistice after a disagreement. Neither of them ever conceded they'd behaved badly, said hurtful things, been in the wrong. Rows had never ended in a cuddle, even as newlyweds. An end to hostilities came when one or the other of them, in a light, neutral tone of voice, introduced a new topic for discussion. Yes, this was definitely an apology. He decided to be magnanimous and not remind her that, at her insistence, the others were still unsure if the two of them would be attending at all.

'Depends on when we've finished eating. I'll phone Al as soon as we're ready to leave to see where they are.'

'How is Alan? Ebullient as ever?'

'He seemed to be when he first phoned. After that we communicated by email.'

'Well, what else? What's he doing with himself?'

Eric decided against reminding her that she'd shown steadfast indifference to his previous attempts to engage her in discussions about Alan and the others.

'He's retired. Didn't get much further than a basic grade teaching. He lives in Ealing. Got four kids; seems happy enough.'

'What about the others?'

'I haven't been in contact with them. All I know is what Alan's told me.'

'Well, what *did* he tell you?'

Eric decided on a mild challenge. 'Why the sudden interest, Viv? You've not shown any before, quite the opposite in fact.'

There was a furrowing of her brow, and he tensed, waiting for the outburst. It didn't come: she stared over towards the bar for a few moments before resuming eye contact with him.

'Look,' she said quietly, 'You know I don't like living in the past. Against my better judgement I've agreed to come on this jaunt, since it seems so important to you. But as I'm soon going to be meeting them all again I need to know a bit about how life's been for them, if only to avoid making a gaffe.'

'What do you mean? What sort of gaffe?'

'Oh, anything. If any of them are divorced, or have gone gay, or are living in abject poverty, or have been in prison – the sort of thing they wouldn't write about in a Christmas card or want to talk about. Are there any subjects I should steer clear of?'

'Oh, I see. Well, Alan hasn't told me much; things seem to be the same as they were when they had their last reunion in Leeds. Jim's still working, still in Stoke –'

'How is he?'

'OK I think. Not married. Tony's still in Leeds, still wheeling and dealing, probably as rich as Croesus. I reckon he –'

'Never mind Tony, he was bound to come up smelling of roses. What about poor old Jim, his state of health, I mean?'

'No more breakdowns, if that's what you mean. You always had a soft spot for him, didn't you?'

'It wasn't a question of having a soft spot. I was the only one prepared to spend time with him when he was down. All you lot did was try and jolly him out of it, and as for Tony, the unfeeling –'

'Hang on, Viv, that's not fair. Men didn't do that sort of touchy-feely sympathy back then. You had to be a woman to be able to hold his hand and give him a cuddle, which you did, didn't you?'

'Metaphorically speaking, yes,' said Vivienne. She flushed slightly and Eric felt he had a rare tactical advantage.

'Don't you want to know about Nige, then?' he asked.

'What about Nigel? What's happened to him?' Her response was sharply interrogatory.

'Well, after he married he moved to the Cotswolds, Stow-on-the-Wold.'

'We know that, for God's sake.'

'Do we?'

'Of course you did. He told us on a Christmas card.'

'Did he? I didn't think we'd had a card from him for years.'

'Well we have.'

Eric decided not to pursue the issue. Christmas cards were Vivienne's responsibility. The ones they received were always suspended on the walls of the lounge before he had time to read them. The only thing he'd noticed was that over recent years the number of cards had begun to decline.

'So, is that all you can tell me about them?'

'I think so, yes. Now if we'd have met up with them all in Leeds ten years ago –'

Vivienne sighed. 'Oh, let's not go over all that again. You *know* why I didn't want to go. Why on earth you wanted to replicate that pub-crawl I've no idea, after the way you disgraced yourself the first time. And I certainly didn't want to be reminded of your behaviour, which the others would no doubt have taken great delight in doing. I just hope they've got all that re-living old times stuff out of their systems.'

Their salads were delivered with an 'Enjoy!' from the microskirted oriental waitress. Eric hardly registered the misuse of the transitive verb, something which usually outraged him. He was wondering why the events of forty years ago were still held against him. If you couldn't get pissed out of your brains on your last evening at university, when could you?

*　　*　　*

He was surprised when she agreed to join them all on that last Headingley Lane pub crawl. She didn't really care for boozing. They started out at the Eldon of course and moved on after one pint to the Packhorse. Both places were heaving, not only with students but with older locals, former residents of the maze of back-to-back houses that had until a few years previously formed an impenetrable hinterland clinging to the main road leading down to the city centre. The pace of consumption began to quicken in the Packhorse, Tony downing his pint in three swallows and urging the others to drink up so he could get another round in. Jim and Alan needed little encouragement: Nigel said he was happy with what he'd got, and Eric, mindful of Vivienne's presence, made do with a half. They stood in the crush by the bar; conversation being reduced to shouted asides in an attempt to be heard over the drunken rendition of *A Whiter Shade of Pale* coming from the snug. Tony was soon ready to move on to the Hyde Park, but Eric wanted to visit the Bricklayers Arms. He wanted, for one last time, to hear the elderly Irishmen who gathered there sing the songs of home. Despite his neophilism, Eric retained an affection for the traditional. Jim and Nigel supported him, Alan said he was easy, and Tony eventually agreed with ill-disguised bad grace.

It was in the Bricklayers that he began to feel drunk. He was chatting to Alan and Nigel, at the same time keeping half an eye on Vivienne conducting a sotto-voce conversation with Jim, when, on his second pint, he suddenly felt the surge of euphoria that usually set in after the fourth or fifth. He stood up, moved over to the bar and joyfully began to join the Irishmen in a spirited rendition of *I'll Take You Home Again Kathleen*. After a few bars he was dimly aware that his participation was less than welcome, and foggily remembered that the locals had recently developed an antipathy to flowered shirts and collar-length hair, in contrast to the tolerance they'd previously shown towards donkey jackets, jeans and Beatle fringes. Alan and Nigel moved quickly to prevent a fracas, and they were all suddenly walking back towards Headingley Lane, Vivienne berating him for his stupidity and demanding that he stick to soft drinks from then on.

He remembered entering the Hyde Park (he'd got spectacularly entangled in the revolving doors), and sitting at a table by the rear wall near where the piano used to stand, and Alan and Tony going to the bar, and his receiving his orange juice to the jeers of the tables around them, and Vivienne pointedly ignoring him, and then …. little else, beyond feeling very ill, and waking up late the next morning feeling even worse, not knowing how he'd managed to get home. After his third bile-heaving visit to the toilet he shakily joined Nigel who was reading the *Manchester Guardian* in the kitchen-cum-living room, seemingly unaffected by the previous night. It seemed that Nigel had half-walked, half-carried him the short distance from the Hyde Park to the flat they shared in Brudenell Road, put him to bed, and then hurried back to join the others in the Original Oak.

'It must have been something I'd eaten, man,' he said.

'If that's what you say, Eric old boy,' Nigel replied, 'but I think you'll have a hard time convincing Viv of that.'

'Did Viv finish the pub crawl with you?' he asked.

'Yes, all the way to the *Woodman*. She was in quite high spirits towards the end. She was certainly giving Tony as good as she got.'

'What happened afterwards?'

'We caught a Number One back down to Sweaty Betty's, but Viv said she didn't fancy fish and chips. She went back to her flat. Wise girl: we all got a bit queasy faced with Sweat's mushy peas. In fact Tony only managed a few mouthfuls and left for home almost immediately. Al and I stayed to keep Jim company; he'd started to get a bit maudlin again.'

After Nigel's disclosures he moped about his flat for most of the day, dreading the visit he knew he had to make to Vivienne, uncertain whether to be humbly apologetic or to brazen it out, and fearful of her reaction whatever he did. He still couldn't believe his luck in having her, was always fearful that she'd find someone better looking or more exciting. His behaviour could well have provided her with the thing he sometimes suspected she might be seeking, an excuse to end the relationship. In the event, she was strangely muted: after enquiring as to his health she said mildly that he only had himself to blame, that he was always led astray when in the company of that lot, and that it was perhaps a good thing that they were all going down the following day.

*   *   *

They were silent while they ate, but when Vivienne pushed away her plate with praise for the wholesome simplicity of the meal and a suggestion that he might wish to freshen up before joining the others, Eric knew that she was signalling her willingness to forget their disagreements. He decided that magnanimity would be in order by offering her an opportunity to escape from all-male company.

'Course, if you really don't fancy meeting up with the others, you could always visit Belinda, couldn't you? I suppose she still lives in Bayswater?'

'Why on earth do you imagine I should want to do that? Vivienne's indignation verged on the strident.

'Just a thought. She's your oldest friend after all. You used to see such a lot of her.'

'That was years ago. There's no way I could call on her at such short notice, even if I wanted to.'

'Viv, what was it that happened between you two? You never really explained why you suddenly stopped seeing her.'

'I told you. I didn't like the way she was starting to live her life. Friendships can *end*, you know. People grow apart. Are you going to phone Alan or not?'

Eric shrugged, pulled out his mobile phone, and began keying in Alan's number.

Chapter 6

TOWARDS THE PRINCESS LOUISE CONTINUED

Nigel shook himself. Jim and Alan had disappeared along Shaftesbury Avenue, and he set off after them. For all his 62 years he was nimble enough to avoid collisions with his fellow citizens by taking swift evasive action. In this he was assisted by his height, which gave him the advantage of spotting the next encounter-but-one, and by his training, which helped in anticipating the moves that potential assailants might make. That he should think of the early-afternoon crowds as being the repository of violence was, he thought, less a measure either of his age than of the fractured nature of the society in which he lived. What the hell had happened over the past ten years? He remembered the television images of that glad May morning in Downing Street, the euphoria that he and Alan had shared a month later in Leeds: even Jim had grudgingly accepted that things could only get better. Tony, of course, had been scathing, forecasting punitive taxation and the end of life as he'd known it, but then that was probably an act to impress the blonde bimbo who accompanied him. Or was it? Even as an undergraduate he'd voiced reactionary opinions, usually when drunk and ostensibly in jest, but Nigel had not found it amusing.

Nigel had reservations about Tony from the time he first met him in his final year at Leeds, when he'd made it abundantly clear that his motivation for joining the Entertainments Committee was to gain access to the girls who flitted around its periphery. He evidently had no real love of the music apart from utilising its aphrodisiac potential at parties. Nigel found particularly irritating his insistence on emphasising their shared Yorkshire heritage; Tony had never appreciated the gulf between those raised in the Wharfedale countryside by professional parents with liberal inclinations, and those who inherited the brash right-wing entrepreneurialism of the Leeds business classes.

Nigel, with the acquiescence of his solicitor father, had deliberately elected to read History at a provincial red-brick university rather than take up the place that had been offered at Oxford. He'd been lonely at his public school, and in the sixth form had developed a social awareness which prompted him to reject further exposure to the ranks of the privileged at Oxbridge. However, Leeds had come as much as a shock to him as it had to Eric, with whom he became acquainted by virtue of their both opting for Economic History as a subsidiary subject in their second year. The two had rapidly developed an accord which led to their sharing the Brudenell Road flat. Theirs was an easy-going, mutually supportive relationship, made the more satisfying for Nigel by his introduction to Vivienne, the first girl of his own age with whom he'd had anything approaching a friendship. She'd proved an ideal ice-breaker for the shy product of an all-male education in his initiation into the arcane world of femininity: though attractive and affectionate towards him, she was spoken for, his flat-mate's girl, and he was thus spared the pressure to embark on what seemed to be expected of young men at university in the era of sexual revolution.

It was Eric and Vivienne who'd introduced him to the music-loving cognoscenti of the Union in-crowd. He'd never been part of the rock-aficionado minority at school, his tastes inclining more to the New Orleans jazz beloved of his father, but, tutored by Alan, he began to appreciate the sounds of the mid sixties, recognising the shared blues heritage of both genres. He realised he'd been on a similar journey to that experienced by Jim, who'd arrived at the same point via the Mississippi bluesmen, Woodie Guthrie and Bob Dylan.

By his final term he'd found himself to be part of a group of friends, friends who accepted him for what he was and who teased him but gently for his adherence to the clothes, hairstyle and speech pattern of a generation passing into history. All except Tony, who had begun to make snide references to Nigel's celibacy. By the time they came to celebrate the end of Finals, Nigel had known that his reservations about Tony had turned to active dislike.

*   *   *

Nigel liked his drinking to be accompanied by conversation, and talking was an effort in the crowded pubs near the University. Neither did he care for the insistence on buying in rounds, which put pressure on him to consume more than was comfortable, and the mockery that ensued from Tony if he elected to have a half pint. It was a relief, therefore, when Vivienne entered the Eldon with Eric, for her presence often had a restraining effect on Tony. It was impossible to get a seat of course, and even worse in the Packhorse where they were forced to stand in the crush by the bar, shouting at each other in an attempt to be heard over the singing coming from the snug. For once Tony seemed uninhibited by Vivienne's presence and cracked several risqué jokes before urging them all on to another pint, which Nigel refused. The resulting invective had then been turned on Eric when he suggested that they call in at the Brickies instead of moving straight on the Hyde Park.

'What the fuck do you want to go there for?' he demanded, 'It's full of old men.' Eric replied that they'd had good times there and that he wanted to visit it one more time. Tony forcefully reminded him that this was supposed to be a rave-up and that things would be swinging in the Hyde Park with lots of spare chicks.

'I'm not interested in spare chicks, man,' Eric retorted, 'I've got Viv, in case you'd forgotten.' He gestured towards Vivienne who was standing with Jim and Alan in the snug doorway.

Nigel observed the look of loathing that passed across Tony's features, somehow made the more menacing by the moustache that he'd recently affected, and the venom in his voice when he observed that Vivienne spent more time snuggling up to Jim that she did with Eric, and that she probably fancied a bit of Stokey rough.

Eric blanched at this remark and Nigel intervened, calling on the support of Alan and Jim for a visit to the Brickies, and Tony was forced to concede. Once there he seemed reconciled to his defeat to the extent of accompanying Nigel to the bar to help carry back the drinks to their table, saying that he'd get in a whisky chaser for himself while there. He did the same half an hour later when it was Jim's round, after which Eric lurched from relative sobriety to drunkenness within the space of a few minutes and they'd had to drag him from the pub to rescue him from affronted Irishmen. Nigel began to have his suspicions about the cause of Eric's malaise when, on their way to the Hyde Park, he noticed Tony smirking as Vivienne quietly berated her partner for his stupidity. His suspicions were confirmed when, once in the pub, it was Alan's turn to receive Tony's assistance in getting in the ale. On the excuse of visiting the gents Nigel lingered near the bar, hidden from his mates by the crush, and watched Tony wait until Alan returned to the table with half the order, and then purchase not just a scotch but a double vodka. Nigel wasn't able to break cover to witness what actually happened to the vodka, but he didn't need to.

To challenge Tony, or warn Eric, or tell Vivienne, would risk an acrimonious end to their last evening together. In the event, it was too late: Eric quaffed his orange juice and in the space of a few minutes lurched from mere drunkenness to total incapacity, his head lolling over Vivienne's shoulder, his arms flailing and in the process knocking over Jim's pint. An ironic cheer came from the tables around them, redoubling as Eric slid slowly from his chair, only being saved from total collapse by Alan grasping him under the armpits.

Vivienne was furious, but her anger soon turned to distress and embarrassment when the state of Eric's incapacity became apparent. Nigel knew he had to do the gentlemanly thing, feeling a measure of responsibility for his flatmate, as well as sympathy for Vivienne, but was surprised when she refused to accompany him and his charge back to the flat in Brudenell Road.

'If you think you can manage him, Nigel, then I'd prefer not to,' she said, 'Why should my evening be spoiled just because of his stupidity?'

Nigel cursed his flatmate as he half-carried him back to the flat. Once there, with Eric insensible on his bed, he considered remaining with him, before deciding that Tony was in such a malicious frame of mind that he ought to be watched. Jim and Alan were slightly in awe of him, and Nigel had felt that only he could offer the support that Vivienne might need as the evening progressed. He made a final check that Eric was still breathing, then left the flat and ran through the midsummer twilight towards the Original Oak.

He found the four sitting in the upstairs lounge; they all had full glasses so he went to the bar to order his pint. As he waited for service, he watched the quartet. Alan was talking to an unsmiling and apparently unresponsive Jim, Tony was evidently entertaining Vivienne, for she kept throwing back her head and laughing. Vivienne was usually restrained in such situations, permitting herself only the briefest of smiles when her companions engaged in half-inebriated inanities. She suddenly gave a loud belly-laugh, audible above the hubbub in the room, and Tony's response was to touch her briefly on the knee. She appeared not to notice. Her mini-dress had ridden far up her thighs: she seemed unaware of this as well.

Nigel hurried across to join them. He reported that Eric was okay, and, staring meaningfully at Tony, observed that it was strange he'd got so drunk after only a few pints. Tony retained eye-contact and said that Eric never could take his ale, that he hadn't had enough practice.

'He's always been a bit straight, hasn't he?' He turned to look at Vivienne. 'Not like you, Viv; I reckon you're a frustrated raver.'

Vivienne flushed, then grinned. 'Who are you calling frustrated, Tony?'

Tony leered at her. 'I reckon you're one of these quiet ones, aren't you? It's always the quiet ones.'

That exchange set the tone for the remainder of the evening as they progressed from the Oak to the Skyrack and then to the Woodman. Nigel had never before seen Vivienne as a coquette, but then he'd never seen her without Eric in tow. The evening was spoiled for him: on this, their last night together, he wanted everyone to behave in character so that in the years to come he could remember them as they had always been. Jim was true to form of course, sinking further into gloom as it became evident that Vivienne was intent on verbal sparring with Tony and no longer receptive to his outpourings. Even Alan was less sunny than usual.

By closing time in the Woodman they were all in various states of inebriation, but it was not their usual ebullient tipsiness. Vivienne became more restrained, evidently regretting her earlier behaviour. Tony was quiet for a while, then announced that he was bloody starving and fancied fish and chips at Sweaty Betty's, did anyone else? They seized the opportunity for displacement activity, and hurried out of the pub to catch a No. 1 back down towards the University. On the bus Vivienne sat next to Nigel, saying little.

At Sweaty Betty's there was the usual rowdy queue for the small back-room sitting area. The smell of cooking fat was overpowering. Vivienne stopped outside the door, and said that she was sorry, she couldn't take greasy chips after all that drink, and that she was going back to her flat to crash out.

Nigel offered to walk her back, but she declined, saying it wasn't far; indeed, the Henry Price student flats were only a few hundred yards away. She said goodnight hurriedly, adding that she expected she'd see them all again before they all went down. She then turned and quickly walked away, her long legs flashing yellow in the sodium street lights.

As they joined the queue Tony observed that Viv was wasted on Eric, and that what she needed was a good screwing. Jim, roused from a long period of introspection called Tony a fucking bastard, and it took the combined diplomatic efforts of Nigel and Alan to prevent further outpourings of rancour. By the time they were at last seated at the formica-topped tables Jim had reverted to taciturnity and Tony was commenting loudly on the breasts of a girl standing in the entrance waiting to be seated. When the fish, chips and mushy peas arrived, Jim and Alan began to devour theirs with relish. Nigel, wishing he'd not ordered the peas, started when Tony suddenly threw down his cutlery and announced that Christ, he thought he was going to puke.

'But it was you who suggested coming here,' Alan mumbled, his mouth full.

'Well, I've changed my mind. I'm going home.'

'You're not going to drive, are you?' Nigel asked, 'You're in no fit state.'

'Well I'm not getting a fucking bus out to Roundhay. I'll be all right. I'll see you lot tomorrow.' He stood up and walked out, none too steadily, leaving Nigel, Alan and Jim to conduct a rather sorrowful post mortem on the evening's events.

*　　*　　*

Recalling the evening forty years on, Nigel realised that it had been the last time that all six of them had been together, for none had felt inclined to seek out the others in the days following. Eric vacated the flat after a week to return to Henley and in those seven days Vivienne didn't show her face there. He'd had a farewell drink in the Union bar with Jim and Alan, but Tony failed to appear. Their university days stuttered to an end.

Thoughts of the past had caused him to dawdle along Shaftesbury Avenue. He quickened his pace and turned into High Holborn, expecting that Alan and Jim would already be in the Princess Louise, but approaching the pub he saw them standing outside, Jim looking disconsolate and Alan distraught.

'It's bloody closed!' Alan seemed on the verge of tears, 'Closed for refurbishment. It was open in February, and no one said anything then about it closing. Bleedin' hell, Nigel, I'm sorry mate, shit, what shall we do? Where shall we go to eat?'

'Does it bloody matter?' said Jim, 'lets just find a pub, I don't care what it's like just so long as it does food.'

'Nothing to worry about, Al,' said Nigel, 'the Cittie of York is just a bit further down the road; it used to serve good lunches.'

'But we can't go there yet!' Alan almost wailed, 'It would be out of sequence.'

'What do you mean, out of sequence?' said Nigel.

'We were supposed to go there *after* the Lamb and Flag and the Princess Louise.'

'Fuckin' hell, Al.' Jim was exasperated. 'What does it matter so long as we get to visit them all at some point?'

'But it does! I wanted you to see a Covent Garden pub before we headed off toward Fleet Street. Let's go to The Lamb and Flag now, then go to the Cittie of York after that. Then we'll be back on track.'

'But that means quite a trek,' said Nigel, 'are you sure you're up to it in this heat?'

'What do you mean by that?' Alan rounded on him. 'Of course I'm up to it, what are you getting at? Just because none of us are as bloody well-preserved as you are doesn't mean we can't walk a few yards round London.'

'But you look knackered,' said Jim, 'Are you sure – '

'OK, Al,' Nigel interrupted. 'It's your party, come on, let's get going. The food's not up to much in the Lamb, but we'd better get there before they stop serving.'

Alan turned without a word and began marching back towards Shaftesbury Avenue.

'What's got into him?' said Jim, 'I've never seen him so uptight. He never used to worry about plans going wrong. Come to think about it, the old bugger never used to *make* any plans.'

'He certainly seems to have a lot invested in this reunion,' said Nigel, 'I was a bit surprised when he first mooted it; after all, our last meeting in Leeds wasn't a great success.'

'That was down to bloody Tony. Don't know why Al bothered to ask him this time.'

'I think he may have invited him on the assumption that the Jacksons wouldn't be coming: just the four of us would hardly be worth all this planning. But you're right, Jim, the old chap certainly looks unwell. Come on, we'd better catch him up. He might need reminding to tell Tony not to go to the Louise.'

'I could do without all this fuckin' charging about, especially in these crowds.'

'That's another reason to catch him up. We don't need to go back down Shaftesbury Avenue. Old Al doesn't know London as well as he likes to make out.'

Chapter 7

The Lamb and Flag, Rose Street, Covent Garden

They arrived in Rose Street to find the cobbled alleyway outside the Lamb and Flag crowded with drinkers, an incursion into public space evidently tolerated by the authorities, though chairs and tables were absent.

'You two wait out here,' said Nigel, 'I'll go and see if they're still serving food. There's no point our hanging round here if they're not.'

He made his way through the throng with his customary *excuse mes* and *thank yous* and pushed through the open door.

Jim glanced around, noticing the profusion of garish hanging baskets on the outside wall, such a display apparently a standard feature of inner London pubs, as though they were trying to pass off as country hostelries. The drinkers, perhaps a consequence of the need to stand, seemed younger than those they'd encountered hitherto. A circle close to him, a mixed collection in their late twenties perhaps, were jabbering away loudly and excitedly, laughing, interrupting each other, totally group-absorbed. They were smartly but casually dressed, the men without ties, most of the women in tight black trousers, but all leather shod. The absence of tee-shirts and trainers pointed to their being office workers taking advantage of dress-down Friday, a metropolitan convention of which Jim had read with some bemusement, for in the Social Services Department in Stoke every day was dressed down, except when court appearances dictated a degree of formality.

He began to eavesdrop on their conversation. There was little he could understand – it wasn't just the accent (which had an antipodean twang overlaying a debased form of cockney), nor the arcane slang, but the subject matter under discussion. It seemed to about some form of entertainment, but the jargon was incomprehensible, peppered with the 'likes' and 'whatevers' which now seemed to be a universal lingua franca for those under 30. Sometimes they broke off and exchanged cheerful insults, each followed by a bellow of mirth, the girls laughing as raucously as the men. There was no evidence that any of them were couples, no handholding, no surreptitious circling of waists or covert caressing of bums, yet they were all as attractive as only young people can be. Surely, Jim thought, there must be some sexual frisson between some of them? Perhaps their generation had sex so often, took it so much for granted, that they were freed from the need for public displays of lust. Three of the women drained their glasses and made reference to getting back to work: they exchanged embraces with their friends, both male and female, showing the easy affection that would have embarrassed Jim's generation back in the 60s which were, he was only too painfully aware, by no means as liberated nor as tolerant as the nostalgia industry liked to paint.

He turned to share his observations with Alan, to find his companion in the process of carefully lowering himself to the ground. He sat down on the pavement, legs in their baggy fawn trousers stuck straight out in front of him and protruding between the feet of the drinkers.

'Are you ok, Al?' Jim made to squat beside him, but his thigh muscles were unequal to the task and he rose unsteadily, using Alan's shoulder to support him.

Alan winced. 'Yeah, I'm ok, least I was until you started using me as a bleedin' banister. Just fancied a sit down, that's all. Been on me feet a long time: they're killing me.'

The drinkers on either side of his outstretched legs shuffled sideways to distance themselves from embarrassing proximity to an elderly man sitting bolt upright on the ground. Jim had to acknowledge that Al did present a bizarre figure: it might not have been so bad had he been wearing jeans, or had chosen to support himself casually on one elbow and maybe crossed his legs at the knees, but his position was uncompromisingly that of an old git who was knackered. The distaste of the young for the old is overwhelmingly physical.

'Hadn't you better try phoning Tony again?' he said to the top of Alan's head, 'He'll be pissed off if he's made it to that pub that was shut.'

Alan had tried to phone while walking from the Princess Louise, but the co-ordination required to walk, dial and dodge traffic had proved too much.

'Suppose so.' Alan's enthusiasm for having all the old gang together again seemed to have waned. Nevertheless he keyed in Tony's number and began a protracted but evidently frequently interrupted explanation of how he could get to the Lamb and Flag. While he was thus engaged, Nigel emerged from the pub, looking flushed and slightly less dapper than usual.

'Is he all right?' he mouthed at Jim over Alan's head.

Jim nodded. 'Is there any room in there?' he asked.

'It's chokka,' said Nigel, 'At least it is in the bar. There are some seats in the Dryden Room upstairs, but they only serve hot meals. If it's a snack we want then we'll have to wait down in the bar.'

'Fuckin' hell,' Jim exploded, 'I'm starving, *and* I need a slash: where are the bogs?'

Nigel explained and Jim pushed his way towards the entrance, asking over his shoulder whose bloody round it was.

Nigel lowered himself easily onto his haunches beside Alan, whose phone conversation was stuttering to a conclusion. 'Tony's on his way,' he said as he fumbled his mobile back into his shirt pocket.

'Where is he?'

'Hard to tell. He's not very coherent. I told him the name of the pub and the name of the street and told him to ask for directions. Easier than trying to explain on the phone.'

Nigel, still squatting, had begun to register the glances, some amused, others slightly hostile, that were coming their way. The lunchtime crowd was gradually being replaced by afternoon boozers, who could be unpredictable. It was time to become less conspicuous.

'Come on, Al. Let's go inside, so when people leave we can grab a free table. In any case I want to get out of the sun. It may be sweaty in there but at least we can avoid sunstroke. You need…. I mean we all need more liquid inside us as well.'

He put his hand under Alan's elbow. Alan shook him off with an impatient shrug, and staggered to his feet unaided. As they walked towards the entrance the sun was suddenly obscured by a small black cloud, a solitary blemish in a sky that was now not so much milky as ochre. The temporary shadow brought no relief from the heat.

They forced their way inside. The small bar by the entrance was crammed with standing drinkers, the only concession to those wishing to sit being a few high stools jammed against the walls. They pushed their way though the crowd and wedged themselves against the wall that ran parallel to the bar. The space was little more than a corridor, and the drinkers who occupied it formed an uncompromising phalanx against access to service. Nigel's height permitted him a view over the heads of the crowd by the bar: one thing that had changed since his last visit was that some of the staff were now young and female. Other than that the pub, with its low beams, wood panelling and bare pine floors seemed, like the clientele, to be largely unreconstructed.

Jim emerged from the door leading to the toilets.

'Bloody hell, Al, don't any London pubs allow you to have a piss in comfort? The bogs here are even more rank than in the last boozer.'

There was sudden movement amongst the throng standing at the entrance to the back room as a large party drained its glasses in unison and began to shout bawdy farewells to the young women behind the bar. Nigel moved swiftly to occupy the space that became available as the group began its unsteady evacuation, and shouted to Jim to come on, assuming that Alan would be incapable of the necessary speed.

Eventually Alan shuffled across to join them. He leaned gratefully against the bar.

'What are we drinking?' said Jim, 'What's all this stuff?' He pointed at the pumps which offered a choice of Youngs, Courage and Directors ales.

'Directors is a good pint,' Alan replied.

'I think it's time we slowed up a bit,' said Nigel, 'Just a half for me, Jim, if you're offering, and I'll get the food in. Looks like a choice between sandwiches, jacket potatoes or hot dogs. What do you fancy?'

Jim opted for a sandwich. Alan said he didn't really feel very hungry. Nigel said that he ought to get something inside him. Alan said that Nigel sounded just like Sheila in one of her fussy moods. Further exchanges followed which began to verge on the ill-tempered, but eventually three halves of Directors and three rounds of ham sandwiches appeared on the bar before them. They began to eat and drink in silence, apart from Jim's grudging expression of appreciation for the quality of the beer. Nigel, ever vigilant, continued to glance around him, ready to execute a rapid transfer to one of the tables in the back room should one become available. However it was Jim who observed that a stool further down the bar had been vacated, and he quickly grabbed it and carried it over.

'Well spotted, Jim,' said Nigel, 'There you are, Al, take a seat.'

'Don't need it,' said Alan, 'Jim fetched it: he can have it.'

Jim said that he didn't like perching on bar stools.

'Go on, Al,' said Nigel, 'Take the weight off your feet.'

'For Christ's sake!' Alan exploded, 'You're not my bloody carer! *I'm* not disabled!'

Nigel recoiled as though he'd been slapped across the face. He remained silent for several seconds, a vein pulsing in his temple, before saying quietly that he needed to visit the toilet, and would they excuse him for a moment.

Left alone with Alan, Jim was at a loss. He was accustomed to dealing with outbursts of inarticulate rage amongst his clients and was adept at counselling and cajoling the angry teenagers, violent fathers and despairing mothers in the dysfunctional families that made up his case-load on the Stoke estates. In those situations he could remain professionally detached, could act out the lines he'd honed in countless similar performances to such an extent that he was able in his mind's eye to monitor his effectiveness even as domestic mayhem raged about him. But he'd never been able to cope with emotionalism in his family nor later amongst his friends – it was too close to the bone, too raw: he shrank from it. Never had he imagined that Alan, jovial, laid-back Alan, could have resorted to such cruel invective. He had no idea what to say; he couldn't bring himself to look at his companion. He was embarrassed. He dreaded Nigel's return. For the first time that day he found himself wishing for Tony's arrival.

'Christ, what's got into me?' he heard Alan mutter, 'I can't believe I said that.'

He forced himself to face Alan.

'Aye, what *has* got into you? It's me that's supposed to be the tactless twat. Fine bloody reunion this is turning out to be.'

'It's just that Nigel's so bleedin' …. so bleedin' *good mannered.* Just 'cos I'm not as fit as he is he seems to think he has to look after me all the time. Christ, I had to stop him taking my arm when we were coming here, as if I wasn't as used to London traffic as him, more so now, probably.'

'I know what you mean,' said Jim, 'He's always the perfect gentleman. But did you bloody *have* to mention caring and disabilities?'

'I know, I know,' Alan groaned. He took refuge in his half pint glass as Nigel re-entered the bar. He had evidently regained his composure, remarking, as he reached for his sandwich, that it was indeed time that the toilets had some refurbishment.

'Nige,' said Alan, 'I'm sorry, mate, I just wasn't thinking, I only meant –'

'Forget it, old boy, I already have. We're all getting a bit overheated, I think. Just imagine what'll happen to social niceties when global warming really does start to set in.'

'I reckon social niceties'll be the last thing we'll have to worry about,' said Jim, 'Not that it'll affect us, we'll be pushing up daisies anyway. It's today's kids who'll cop it. I'm glad I don't have ......'

He tailed off, conscious that Alan already had numerous grandchildren of whom he was inordinately fond and that Nigel would be unlikely to enjoy a conversation about his child's prospects. This gathering was becoming fraught with the need to leave things unsaid. The years they'd accumulated were heavy with the baggage of experience, not all of it pleasant. He glanced at his watch: two-thirty; unlikely that Eric and Vivienne would be coming at this late stage, and it was the prospect of seeing Viv again that had been the main reason for his deciding to attend. He felt a sudden longing to be back in Stoke with Nicky.

'That table in the corner over there's going to be free any minute,' said Nigel.

Jim peered across the room at the quartet sitting there.

'What makes you think so?' he asked, 'They look pretty settled to me.'

'I grant you the two chaps want to stay, but the ladies' glasses are empty and the one nearest us keeps looking at her watch, and from her body language I reckon she's the queen bee of the group.'

Jim was wondering how it was that Nigel had developed such phenomenological acuity when, as if on cue, the men drained their glasses and stood up. Nigel moved to stand by the table even before the slower of the women had risen, and within seconds the three were sitting, beer and sandwiches in front of them, the fourth chair draped with Nigel's jacket.

Ten minutes later the pub had emptied further and had begun to exhibit the mellow ambience beloved of afternoon imbibers. The three friends gradually relaxed, and, encouraged by Alan, began to talk of their time at university – the hops, the bands, the parties, the frequent mismatch of their memories prompting gentle chaffing about the onset of senility. Nigel said this was because memory comprised a series of snap-shots, not continuous film footage, and that it was hardly surprising that each had different photographs in their mental albums.

'It's only when you see old film footage of that period that you realise how ridiculous we looked,' Alan said, 'All that long hair and beads and bells!'

'Speak for yourself, Al,' Jim protested, 'I never went for all that flower-power stuff, and neither did Nige here, did you Nige?'

'Actually, I think you'll find that very few of us did,' said Nigel, 'Societal memories are those of the activities of the avante-garde.'

'What the bleedin' hell are you on about?' said Alan.

'Well, what we think of as our common memories are often false, because we get them from the media, and the media always focuses on the activities of those in the vanguard of change. Take the so-called roaring twenties: they didn't roar for most people, just the spoilt children of the rich. But we have this idea that all our mothers were flapping around in short skirts with bobbed hair doing the Charleston and drinking cocktails. It's the same with the sixties.'

'How come?'

'Well, it was only a minority who adopted hippy clothes and smoked dope in 1967, mainly students, and most of them in London. It wasn't till the early 70s that ordinary youngsters caught up with it. And as for the sexual revolution – well, maybe it touched some of our contemporaries, but things didn't really start to swing for middle England until much later.'

'He's right,' said Jim, 'The closest I got to being trendy was a cord jacket. Remember what it was like when we first started at Leeds? All donkey jackets and jeans, then all that mod gear. I dunna remember you ever dressing like Mick Jagger, Al; the nearest you got to it was a flowered shirt.'

'But I distinctly remember Eric wearing a kaftan at one party,' Alan was insistent, 'and he had shoulder length hair, and a headband.'

'Oh, *Eric*,' Jim said dismissively, 'Well, he would have, wouldn't he? He was always a sucker for the latest trend. He wasn't half as cool as he thought he was. I always thought that underneath that 'let it all hang out, man' façade he was a bit of a prat. It was only because of Viv that he made it with the Union in-crowd. Now she really *was* cool. A girl like that could make it anywhere.'

'Yeah, she was a looker and no mistake,' said Alan, 'I never worked out how old Eric got it together with her in the first place, let alone fight off the competition. She had a sharp tongue when she wanted, did Viv. Remember how she used to let Tony have it when he tried his drunken come-ons?'

'Aye, except on the night of that last pub crawl,' said Jim, 'she showed herself in a new light then, didn't she? At one point that evening I thought Tony was beginning to get somewhere.'

'Well, she was pissed off with Eric for making a pillock of himself,' said Alan.

'And she'd pulled herself together by the time we got to the Woodman,' Nigel reminded them.

'Funny evening, that one,' mused Alan, 'Fancy ending up eating fish and chips.'

'That's what we did. No curry houses then.'

'No drink-driving laws either,' said Alan, 'Christ, remember the state Tony was in when he left? God knows how he managed to drive home.'

'But he didn't,' said Jim, 'not immediately.'

'What d'you mean?' said Alan, 'He said he was going to puke and headed off for his car. He'd parked it opposite the Parkinson.'

'Aye, but he didn't drive straight home. Funny, I've only just remembered this, after 40 years,' said Jim. 'I ran into him early the next morning, walking along Clarendon Road.'

Nigel, about to take a swallow of beer, suddenly stopped.

'What?' he said sharply, 'what time was that?'

'It was about five. I couldn't sleep as usual, so I got up at first light and went for a walk across Woodhouse Moor. I'd just got to the statue of Wellington and spotted Tony across the road. He said he was so pissed that he spent the night in his car, and was just stretching his legs before driving home.'

'Typical Tony,' observed Alan, 'He was lucky the cops didn't find him asleep: remember what bastards the Leeds police could be? D'you remember the time –'

He was interrupted by his mobile phone ringing.

'Speak of the devil; that'll be him. Silly sod's probably lost again. Hello, Tony …. What? Eric! Where are you? What are you doing? ……… Is that where you're staying? …….. Fantastic! …………We're at a pub called the Lamb and Flag, in Rose Street. Make for Covent Garden tube station ….. Have you got an *A to Z*? ……. Great! We'll get the ale in for you. Seeya soon.'

He pocketed his phone and beamed at his companions.

'Eric and Viv! They've made it!'

'Why so late?' asked Jim.

'They've already had lunch at their hotel. They're staying at the Hilton, just round the corner from us.'

'Why? Isn't the Tavistock good enough for 'em?'

'Oh, come off it, Jim,' said Nigel, 'they weren't ever like that.'

'But who knows how they've changed in 40 years? They were getting a bit bourgeois even a couple of years after Leeds, when they were in that cottage. Bloody four course meals and wine, and music played only as background. I only got invited once. I bet you went more than that, Nige, you knew which knife and fork to hold.'

'We discussed all this ten years ago, Jim,' said Nigel, 'and as I said then, I was invited just twice. Why do you keep on about it? None of the rest of us issued invitations to our respective homes, did we? Why did you have that expectation of the Jacksons?'

'Because they were bloody married and had a house, of course. Couldn't see any of you dossing down in my bed-sit in Hanley. You didn't invite us to your place, either.'

'I was very rarely at home at weekends early in my career,' Nigel replied, 'Lots of training courses to attend.'

'Yeah,' Alan interjected, 'what exactly was that career of yours? You've never been very forthcoming about it. What's so bleedin' secret about a job in the civil service? Hob-nobbing with cabinet ministers were you?'

'And how come you walked straight into a job immediately after graduating?' said Jim, 'I don't remember you ever going for an interview. Was it the old-boy network? Or were you headhunted? You were always known as a clever bugger'

Nigel smiled his benign smile. Little ever appeared to ruffle him.

'This clever bugger could do with a refill. Mine's another half, if you're getting them, Al.'

Alan eased himself onto a stool to await the attention of a barmaid. He was beginning to feel better. Nigel had evidently forgiven him his outburst. It was a bit cooler now the crowds had left, the sit-down had refreshed him, and at last they'd started to talk of old times. Best of all, Eric and Viv were on their way. Whatever sort of mood Tony was in could be neutralised through strength of numbers. This was the reunion as he'd planned it. Pity about the Princess Louise being closed, but they were back on track now.

The barmaid seemed intent on avoiding his eye, and as most of the staff had shown evidence of speaking English as a second language Alan doubted that his customary shout of 'when you're ready, darlin'' would have the desired effect. In any case you had to be careful how you addressed young women these days. He wasn't too concerned about the poor service; he welcomed the chance to have a few moments alone. At all costs he must try to avoid becoming emotional as the day progressed. He'd have to steer the conversation towards remembrance of the fun they'd once all had so as to pre-empt exchanges about present circumstances. Nigel would appreciate that, he was sure.

He looked over at his friends. Despite the thinning hair and wrinkles (not that Nigel suffered much from the former) a palimpsest of them as young men emerged. Nigel still crossed his long legs at the thigh and again at the ankles, a posture which always used to provoke mocking accusations of effeminacy. Jim still constantly rubbed his hand round his jaw, raising it to cover his mouth when he spoke, even though the stained teeth of which he once been so conscious had been replaced. Conversation seemed to have stalled; both looked rather miserable, but suddenly Nigel made a remark which amused Jim, who laughed, and Nigel smiled companionably. Alan realised they'd not been miserable, it was just that they'd reached the age where their facial muscles were unequal to the task of demonstrating any emotion except joy or grief: when one is pensive one looks unhappy, when feeling benevolent one merely looks stupid. No wonder ageing film stars took such pains to adopt manic grins and wide-open eyes when photographed.

'Yes?' His reverie was interrupted by the barmaid.

'Same again, please.'

'What?'

'Three halves of Directors.'

'Which drink you want?'

The question was framed almost aggressively; not the merest hint of a smile graced her undeniably winsome face under its spiky blonde hair, and her gaze was directed at a point somewhere above his head. Alan eased himself off the stool and moved up the bar to position himself opposite the pumps.

'Directors,' he said, pointing, 'three half pints.' He enunciated clearly but did not feel inclined to add 'please'.

He watched the young woman pulling the beer. She showed little regard for the technique required to deliver a full glass with the correct measure of head. Appalled by the barmaid's total lack of concern for the most English of rituals, he was unaware of the door opening and of the passage of new entrants behind him, until a shout of 'Eric! Viv!' came from Nigel.

He turned. They'd arrived. They stood with their backs to him, facing Nigel who was already on his feet, and Jim who still sat, staring up at them, a delighted grin lighting his face. He was able to watch unobserved the enactment of contact re-established after four decades. The men shook hands, of course, Nigel with his other hand on Eric's elbow. As Eric turned sideways to greet Jim it was evident that he'd put on weight round the gut, and he'd grown a beard. Nigel extended his hand towards Vivienne: there was a moment's hesitation, then he kissed her cheek briefly. Viv turned towards Jim – my God, she was still an attractive woman – and bent to kiss him, placing her hand on his shoulder as she did. Jim blushed. It occurred to Alan that throughout their time at university none of them, with the exception of Eric of course, had ever exchanged kisses with Viv. At that age, and in those times, there were sexual undertones in any physical contact, and you didn't kiss a mate's girlfriend. Was the scene he'd just witnessed a reflection of the new times, or simply an indication of the acceptance of the loss of libido?

'Now then you two,' he shouted, 'what do you want to drink?'

The couple turned, smiled broadly on seeing him and advanced towards him. It was his turn to receive a handshake from Eric and a peck on the cheek from Vivienne. They stood exchanging banalities – you haven't changed a bit, I'd have recognised you anywhere, you're looking well. But even in his pleasure Alan noticed Vivienne's appraising stare; oh yes, Viv, I've changed, I've changed more than any of you, certainly you. Vivienne, still trim, still with those wonderful legs, could have passed for forty-five, except for the grey hair. He was ashamed to find himself comparing her with Sheila who could best be described as comfortable.

They sat round the table with their drinks, and compared notes on their respective journeys and the heat.

'How's your family, Al?' Eric asked.

'Thriving, six grandchildren, another on the way.'

'And Sheila?'

'She's fine. Loves being a granny. How about you?'

'No grandchildren yet. Career women, our girls.'

'What about you, Nige?'

'Just one son.' Nigel's face was shuttered.

'How's Melanie?' Vivienne ventured.

'She's well, thanks.'

There was silence for a moment, broken by Vivienne.

'So you haven't retired, yet, Jim?'

'Fat chance. Can't afford to, can I?'

'It's social work isn't it? Must be interesting.'

'Has its moments.'

Another moment of silence.

'London's incredibly busy,' Eric said. 'I bet you've seen some changes, Al. It's Ealing you live, isn't it?'

Conversation continued to stutter. Christ, thought Alan, how do you pick up after 40 years? We'll be talking about cars and house prices next. He cast around for a topic with which they could all connect, and asked Eric what sort of music he was into these days.

'Oh, mainly classical now,' Eric replied.

'When was the last time you listened to classical music?' Vivienne said sharply, 'You prefer Radio 2 and you know it. He's still locked in a 1960s time-warp,' she said to Alan, 'He leaps around to Sounds of the Sixties when he thinks he's alone in the house.'

Eric looked down into his beer. Alan, Nigel and Jim exchanged glances.

'Well, sometimes I think that when you reach our age the only dream you can have is to be young again,' said Nigel.

Vivienne glanced at him. 'You don't really think that, do you?'

'Well, maybe not young. But I'd certainly like to be the right side of forty, young enough still to have options.'

'Oh yes,' Vivienne said quietly, 'I remember options.'

Another silence fell over the group.

It was broken by a bellow from the bar. 'Have I got to get my own booze in then, you fuckers?'

It was Tony.

Chapter 8

The Cittie of York, Holborn

They walked, in two groups, back towards Holborn. It was that hiatus that occurs after the lunchtime rush. The solicitors and barristers were back in their offices and in the Inns of Court, the area was off the tourist trail, and the pavements were relatively empty. The traffic however was frenetic, if anything faster since the introduction of the congestion charge, and exhaust fumes hung in the flaccid air. The sky now verged on the overcast, but a blood-red sun brooded through the murk. It was still stiflingly hot.

Alan had urged the others to move on to the next pub only a few minutes after Tony's arrival when it became evident that the Lamb and Flag was too small and intimate to accommodate him. He'd lurched towards them, swearing his greetings loudly in an exaggerated Yorkshire accent, and circled round the group, all of whom were too startled to rise, clapping each one on the shoulder until he reached Vivienne whose waist he'd encircled, attempting to pull her to her feet while at the same time trying to land kisses on her mouth. She was the only one whom he'd addressed by name, to little avail because she shrank from him with a visible shudder. Jim had eventually risen and asked what Tony wanted to drink, but the barmaid had already summoned a burly helper from the recesses of the bar whose demeanour suggested that not only was service unlikely but that the presence of the group had become unwelcome. Alan had led the evacuation, hustling Tony who protested loudly that he'd only just fuckin' arrived and he needed a fuckin' drink.

'Make for the Cittie of York', Alan had hissed at Nigel, 'I'll go with Viv and Eric, you and Jim take Tony, and for God's sake try and get the bugger to calm down before we get there. Give us a few minutes start.'

Thus Alan, Vivienne and Eric walked together, Vivienne between the two men.

'My God, Alan,' said Eric, 'What's got into him? Is he drunk already, d'you think? Was he like that when you last saw him in Leeds?'

'No, not like that, but he was with a young woman, and —'

'Well thanks very much.' Vivienne was indignant, 'So my advancing years rule me out when it comes to moderating male behaviour, do they?'

'You know I didn't mean that, Viv,' Alan said reproachfully, 'Anyway, I don't think he's drunk today, not like he used to get back at University; I mean his speech isn't slurred and he wasn't staggering, was he? Did he smell of booze, Viv? When he tried to kiss you, I mean?'

Vivienne's lips curled in disgust. 'I didn't need reminding of that. I averted my head, in case you didn't notice.'

'He looks quite smart, though, doesn't he?' Eric observed, 'And well preserved. Still got all his hair, the lucky bugger.'

Vivienne snorted. 'You're so unobservant. That suit may have been expensive, but it's dirty; didn't you notice the stains on his trousers? And he may have all his hair but I doubt he's washed it for weeks. And what about the bags under his eyes? Disgusting, foul mouthed man. And why's he carrying a briefcase? Trying to show he's a big-shot, I suppose.'

'Well, he is, leastways he was when we last met him,' said Alan, 'He had a property company in Leeds, making millions so he said, and he turned up with his woman in a bloody Porsche. His dad died soon after we left university; reckon he inherited a bundle from him as well.'

'I don't care how well-off he is,' said Vivienne, 'he's a lout. And why is he putting on that exaggerated Leeds accent? He never used to speak like that. And all that aggression and swearing! He'll get us thrown out of all the pubs; I don't think I can stand it.'

'I think we'll be all right in the next one, Viv, it's a big place with lots of private cubicles, and in any case he may have calmed down, I asked Nigel to –'

'No.' Vivienne suddenly stopped walking. 'I don't want this. I knew this jaunt was a bad idea. Eric, let's go back to the hotel.'

Alan felt a lurch of dismay. The well-being that had begun to creep over him in the Lamb and Flag before Tony's arrival evaporated, and he suddenly felt unwell again. And hot. He saw the disintegration of his long-awaited day, envisaged his sad return to Ealing, the effort required to put on a cheerful face for Sheila, the re-emergence of the miasma of depression which had been hovering over him for the past three months. He couldn't face that. Better that Tony should be cast aside than to lose the company of Eric and Vivienne.

'Viv,' he said, 'please don't do that. I haven't seen you for 40 years, we've got so much to catch up on. Eric, you don't want to go, do you?'

Eric glanced at his wife. 'Well, if Viv's feeling uncomfortable I'll take her back and rejoin you later.'

'No!' Vivienne's response was strident. 'What makes you think I want to spend the rest of the day sitting by myself? You come with me Eric, maybe later we can find a decent restaurant –'

'No, Viv, please!' There was a hint of desperation in Alan's voice. 'If you two leave the whole day'll be ruined. At least come to the next pub. Look, if Tony carries on being a pain in the arse I'm sure Nigel'll sort him out. Come on, let's get moving, otherwise they'll catch us up.'

Vivienne thought for a moment, then resumed walking. Her companions joined her, each with their own distinct and separate feelings of relief.

'I'm doing this just for you then, Alan, since you organised all this,' she said, 'but if Tony carries on like he has then we'll have to leave, won't we Eric?'

Alan had to be content with Eric's non-committal grunt.

Nigel, Jim and Tony were lagging many yards behind. Their progress since leaving the Lamb and Flag had been slow and uncertain. This was because Tony kept stopping to look about him, an action which bemused them the first couple of times, annoyed them on the third and fourth occasions, and then alarmed them when he'd come to a sudden halt in the middle of the road whilst following them across Kingsway, provoking an outraged blast on the horn of a taxi which screeched to a halt a few inches from him. He was chastised in no uncertain terms and in good old fashioned cockney by the driver.

They pulled him to the pavement, and, one each side of him, resumed their progress towards Holborn. Nigel kept a hand firmly under his elbow. He seemed not to notice, but began a rambling monologue, punctuated by sniffs.

'It's great to see you guys again, never thought it would happen, Christ I'm sweating like a pig, is it always like this in London? Why couldn't we stay in the last pub? It took me fuckin' ages to find you and when I do you don't even let me stay for a drink. Where are we going? Where's Viv? Is she coming as well? It's really grand to see you after all this years, how long is it, must be about 40, it was when we graduated wasn't it?'

Jim raised his eyebrows at Nigel.

'You saw us ten years ago in Leeds you pillock, are you going senile?'

Tony stopped in his tracks. 'Course I remember, what d'you mean? Viv was there, wasn't she? Couldn't forget that evening, could I?'

'But Viv wasn't there –'

'Come on, Tony, let's get going.' Nigel tugged at his elbow and shook his head at Jim. Progress resumed, somewhat uncertainly. Jim was becoming increasingly irritated by his knee coming into contact with the briefcase which Tony swung from his left hand.

'What the hell do you need a briefcase for?' he demanded, 'Why didn't you leave it in the hotel? This isn't a business visit, surely you -.'

'Ah, yes,' Nigel interrupted hurriedly, 'and how is your business, Tony? Still prospering are you?'

Tony's face hardened. 'I would be, but I was shafted by my partner, the bastard. Should have known not to trust a Jew. Bloody Yids'

He stopped again and stared around vacantly. 'Where's Viv? She is coming, isn't she?'

'She's walking ahead of us, old boy,' Nigel reassured him, 'and if you keep stopping we'll never catch up with her. Come on.'

They walked on. Nigel glanced at Jim, who was glowering, no doubt because of Tony's anti-semitic outburst. Dammit, the last thing he needed in this situation was for Jim to start venting his spleen. Best to steer clear of Tony's business interests.

'How's that delectable young lady you had in tow last time we saw you?'

'Who? What young lady?'

'You were with a blonde, Tony. Tracey, was it? She couldn't have been more than 25. We were green with envy, weren't we, Jim?'

'Not my type,' grunted Jim.

Tony's brow furrowed as though deep in concentration; then realisation evidently dawned. 'Oh, *her*. She was a bitch. She tried to shaft me as well. It's no big deal. Plenty more fish in the sea. Hey, it's really good to see you two again. Is that other guy coming?'

Nigel was beginning to feel the strain of keeping up his end of the conversation. He'd begun to have an inkling of what Tony's problem might be. Why wasn't Jim being more help? He was a social worker, after all; he ought to be used to situations like this, though distressed entrepreneurs probably weren't part of his caseload.

'What other guy's that, Tony?' he asked, trying to make his enquiry sound casual.

'You know, what's his name, the fellow with long hair and beads, he was a bit of a prat.'

'Jeeesus.' Nigel heard Jim's exasperated sotto voce blasphemy.

'He's here, old chap, you'll see him again in the next pub. Just don't expect long hair or beads.'

'What's his name?'

'Eric, Eric Jackson.'

'That's him. He used to fancy his chances with Viv, didn't he? What a wanker.'

'Here we are,' said Alan, turning into the open door of the Cittie of York.

Eric and Vivienne were taken by surprise; there'd been no indication that they were near a pub, no outside tables or drinkers, no overhanging sign, no hanging baskets. They followed Alan into what seemed to be a hotel lobby.

'This'll surprise you, I bet,' he said, ignoring the entrance to a bar to his left and hurrying straight ahead.

They entered a vast, high ceilinged room, light and airy but with no windows immediately visible. Eric stood and gaped.

'What an amazing place! Isn't it incredible, Viv?'

Vivienne assented. It was indeed spectacular. The room was rectangular: to the left the counter extended half-way down the long side fronting an empty space: there were no tables or chairs except at the far end. Looking up, the ceiling was vaulted, and huge oak vats occupied the wall above the bar counter. The source of light was revealed as a row of windows high on the right hand wall. The place was blessedly cool, and empty.

'How old's this place?' Eric asked.

Alan grinned, full of vicarious pride. He considered the pub to be the jewel in the crown of the day's itinerary, and his only regret was that it couldn't be saved till last. 'There's been a pub here since the 15th century, apparently, but how old do you think this building is, mate?'

Eric peered about him. His first impression was of Victoriana, but it was too uncluttered, no ornate mirrors, no knick-knackery. He had to concede that he had not the slightest idea.

'Well, it was rebuilt in 1924, though parts of it, especially downstairs, date from much earlier. My eldest son told me about it, but the first time I came here was in February.'

'Amazing,' said Eric, 'I'd like to have a close look round.'

Vivienne, though impressed by her first sight of the place, was not an enthusiast for architectural history, and she was more concerned that the uncluttered spaciousness provided no hiding place from Tony.

'Where are the private cubicles you mentioned, Alan?'

Alan grinned again. 'They're not immediately obvious, are they?'

He led them further into the room and indicated something akin to an old fashioned railway carriage with separate compartments extending down the right hand side opposite the bar. Each compartment contained a table and, Vivienne was quick to register, only four chairs.

'Get Tony in one of these,' said Alan, 'and he won't be visible from the bar; won't be heard, either, if we sit him by the inside wall. I'll get two more chairs from another booth.'

'No, we'll be too crushed.' Vivienne was emphatic. 'Let's split up. Jim, you sit with Alan and Tony, I'll go in another booth with Nigel and Eric.'

'OK by me,' said Eric, 'I'll get the drinks in. What d'you want, Al?'

'I think I'd better go on to fruit juice for a while.'

'Good idea,' said Vivienne, 'We'll do the same, won't we, Eric?'

'But I've only had a pint.'

'Plenty of time for beer later. You know what you're like if you drink in the afternoon.'

Eric moved towards the bar, just as Nigel, Jim and Tony entered. There was a flurry of indecision about who should buy drinks for whom and who should sit where, eventually resolved not entirely according to Vivienne's plan, for she found herself alone with Nigel in one booth while the other four occupied another. Tony had seemed rather subdued when he came in, perhaps overawed by his surroundings, but on his way into the booth stubbed his toe on the large triangular cast iron stove which stood in the way, prompting an outburst of cursing. He was hustled into the far corner of the booth. Eric examined the stove and asked Alan how, if it were ever lit, smoke was able to escape, as there seemed to be no flue.

Alan's explanation about under-floor piping, delivered standing by the stove, was audible to Nigel and Vivienne. They listened with ostentatious interest, each in fact groping for an opening conversational remark. When Alan joined the others, they were left facing each other in silence, like strangers in the train compartment that their surroundings so closely resembled.

Vivienne sipped her orange juice and set down her glass with unnecessary care.

'London's changed so much since I first came here,' she said brightly, 'When I was a girl and used to come up from Suffolk there were still men walking around in pinstripes and bowler hats.'

'Just wait till later in the afternoon,' Nigel eagerly seized on the topic. 'Tired middle-aged commuters taking a quick half before catching the train home are a thing of the past. The pubs will be full of young people hell bent on the pursuit of an evening of pleasure.'

'Not here, so close to the City, surely?'

'Oh yes, especially here. Swinging London isn't confined to the Kings Road or Soho. It's taken over the whole area contained by Ken's congestion charge zone.'

'Has it really?'

Nigel took a sip from his glass. He'd gone on to mineral water. He hesitated for a moment before replying.

'But it's not that long since you've been to London, surely? Don't you still see Belinda? Is she still living in Bayswater?'

Vivienne blushed slightly, and stared into her orange juice. 'I don't come as often as I used to. Yes, Belinda's still in Bayswater. She probably hasn't changed much. Single people tend not to, I find.'

'That's because they don't have to accommodate the whims of partners. Couples tend to take on their partners' characteristics.'

'Heaven forbid,' said Vivienne with feeling, still staring into her glass.

There was a burst of hilarity from the adjacent booth. Alan's guffaw and Eric's high-pitched giggle were unmistakable.

'Eric sounds happy enough,' observed Nigel.

'He ought to. He's been looking forward to this reunion for months.'

'Haven't you, then, Viv?'

She looked up and met his gaze.

'What do you think? Ambivalence wasn't the word for it.'

'Yes, it must be a bit isolating being one woman with a crowd of rowdy old men. I can quite understand why you didn't come to the last one in Leeds, though as it happened you wouldn't have been the only woman. Tony brought along a young bimbo.'

'Don't be so bloody ingenuous, Nigel.'

It was the first time she'd spoken his name. He chose to ignore the reproof.

'Are you all right, Viv? I mean in general, not just today.'

She stared across towards the bar.

'Am I all right? I'm a 61 year old woman with a materially comfortable life, daughters married off, no grandchildren, keeping the thoughts of advancing of old age at bay by cultivating my literary interests in the company of women of the same age in a similar situation. I share a house with a man who's in his own place most of the time. You don't have to live apart to be separated.'

'Viv, I – '

'Oh, don't get me wrong. I'm not unhappy. Not happy, either. It's just that sometimes I'd like to experience those wild swings of emotion that caused so much angst when I was a teenager. Raging hormones, they call it, don't they? Wish I had some hormones left to rage.'

She took a sip of orange juice. Nigel was uncomfortable with hormones and didn't know how to respond. To tell her that she was still a disconcertingly attractive woman, which she undoubtedly was, would have sounded trite and patronising. He was also uncertain, despite the reference to her teenage years, whether she was not in fact alluding to a more recent past, and whether she was inviting a similar admission from him: her previous reference to his ingenuousness seemed to indicate this. She had also responded to his earlier rather daring question about Belinda. But, ever cautious, he was wary of opening a conversational avenue along which she might not wish to be led. He decided to play safe.

'I think I can empathise. Life becomes a bit thin and bloodless at our age, doesn't it? Even when one engages in something that ought to elicit a fervent emotional reaction, it doesn't happen, not in the way it used to.'

'You mean things like music and art?'

'Well, yes, to an extent,' he said.

She did not ask him to elaborate and they sat in silence.

'And how are Ella and Imogen?' he heard himself say.

'Thriving, of course,' she replied, 'Aren't all professional young women these days? We don't see that much of them. They're closer to Eric than they are to me; I was never really the maternal type. We must be one of the few couples where the father speaks longer on the phone to his children than the mother. But what about you, Nigel? How's Melanie?'

'Melanie's okay.'

'How does she like Stow? She was a Londoner, wasn't she?'

'Yes. From Streatham.'

'She was a colleague, wasn't she? One of your fellow operatives, I suppose?'

Nigel had informed the Jacksons of his marriage after the event, on a Christmas card. Eric had made a congratulatory telephone call, but the receiver had not been passed to Vivienne. He was surprised that she was quizzing him now: was it politeness, or was she really interested?

'No, she wasn't an operative. She was a PA to one of the Section Heads.'

'A PA? Really?' Her voice registered the half-disguised surprise that was the reaction of all his professional friends on learning of his wife's former status. It annoyed him, even coming from Vivienne. Whatever else, he was not ashamed of his wife. He took another sip of mineral water.

'Melanie's a very intelligent woman and she was highly valued in the Service. Not everyone started life with our advantages, Viv.'

'Nigel, I wasn't implying – '

'She would have gone to University had she not had to support her widowed mother and younger sister. I got to know her very well after Glasnost.'

'Glasnost?'

He hesitated, until reassured by the guffaws coming from the neighbouring booth that his reply would not be overheard.

'Yes. All our duties were reappraised when it seemed the Cold War was ending. Far fewer assignments abroad. I found myself in HQ a lot more, and I worked quite closely with Melanie.'

He forbore to tell her that he'd been aware the Melanie had long had a dewy-eyed affection for him that verged on a schoolgirl crush. Though pretty in an understated way, she'd been shy and gauche, unable to respond in kind to the risqué comments of some of his more debauched colleagues. Immersed in his own affair, he'd continued to treat her with the kind consideration he always had.

'An office romance, then,' said Vivienne, not looking at him.

'I suppose you could call it that.'

In fact, for Nigel, it had all been rather prosaic. When his hopes for a future with his long term lover collapsed, his relationship with Melanie had taken on a strange role reversal. Though he never divulged the reason for his sadness, she offered a comfort that was almost motherly. Fearful of the prospect of an eternity of evenings alone in his Kensington flat, he'd asked her out to dinner, the start of a four-year liaison which culminated, to her joy and his bemusement, in their becoming engaged. He was comfortable with her, then. He'd enjoyed acting as her mentor while introducing her to the restaurants, theatres, art galleries and museums which had until then formed no part of her life. The educational gap between them had sometimes worried him, but she was bright, curious, and in his company had developed a confidence and joie-de-vivre that he found refreshing. He'd found that he'd come to love her, without actually being in love. He'd decided to settle for that. He didn't relish a life alone.

'What made you decide to move to Stow?' Vivienne seemed determined to continue the interrogation.

'Early retirement, for one thing. I'd had enough of London. Too many ghosts. I wanted to move back to the Dales, but it was too far from London for Melanie. Also, she didn't like ....' He tailed off, still uncertain about how much Vivienne wanted, or needed, to know.

'What didn't she like? Nigel, it's me you're talking to. I've given you some idea about how things are for me and Eric. Why won't you reciprocate?'

For the first time that day they made prolonged eye-contact. Nigel fought to extinguish the small candle of hope that had been flickering ever since the reunion was first mooted. After all, he'd asked after her welfare: why shouldn't she ask after his?

'She didn't care for the way my people were with her. You never met them, did you. Dad was ok. It was my bloody aunts and cousins, and some of my old school friends. Wharfedale's quite county, you know. Not easy for a girl from Streatham. She was patronised, made to feel she wasn't good enough for me.'

'Poor Melanie. But, surely, the Cotswolds are just as county? How did you persuade her to move to Stow?'

'Moreton-in-Marsh is only a few miles away. There's a rail connection from there to Paddington.'

'It must be a lovely place to live. And a great environment for a child to grow up in. Oh, Nigel, how remiss of me; I haven't asked about your son. Oscar, isn't it? He must be ten now?'

He'd been tensely anticipating the question just as one awaits the blast of air into the eye when the optician tests for glaucoma, and the jolt was no less severe for being expected. He then felt like a candidate woefully unprepared for an oral examination. He took a deep breath.

'There's something you've not been told about Oscar,' he said.

In the other booth the four men were engaged in the pastime beloved of those who shared a youthful past, reminding each other of the girls they used to fancy, debating which ones were lookers but who didn't oblige, which ones were goers, and whose party it was when Pam Lucas had started stripping off to *Let's Spend the Night*

Together and when old Malc Kennedy had thumped Dave Harness when he emerged from the bedroom with Carole Pearson who was a real raver despite being a third year sociologist. Tony came to life during these exchanges and claimed to have shagged most of the girls mentioned, at which point Alan reminded him that in the late 1960s chicks had been screwed, not shagged, though birds *had* been shagged in the 1950s and seemed thus to be again today. Eric, temporarily freed from uxorious restraint, asked them to recall the occasion when they'd first got stoned, wasn't it when Mike Phillips had scored down at the Three Coins blues club and they'd all had a drag on Woodhouse Moor? Alan and Tony couldn't remember the Three Coins, where was it? Eric said he thought it was near the Merrion Centre, and this reminded Alan of that new pub down there which they sometimes used to visit to ogle the chicks from the town, the General Wade was it called? Jim, who'd become increasingly quiet during these reminiscences, said that to hear them talk anyone would think all they ever did at University was to booze and chase women, and had they forgotten the political activism in which some of them had been engaged, the demos against the Vietnam war, and why was it that students these days seemed to have no political commitment whatsoever?

As the discussion turned to student politics and which demonstrations each had attended and how Jack Straw had made it to be President of the Union the year after they'd graduated, Tony relapsed into silence. He sat brooding in his corner of the booth, sniffing occasionally and fiddling with the catch on his briefcase before standing suddenly and announcing that he wanted a slash; where were the bogs? Having received directions from Alan he left, still clutching his briefcase.

'He seems to have calmed down a bit,' Eric observed.

'Don't bank on it,' said Jim, 'there were a lot of mood swings when we were walking here. Dunno what's wrong with him. Nigel kept jollying him along but I dunna have the patience for that.'

Alan was still focussed on the past. 'Hey, d'you realise Claire Short was a contemporary of ours at Leeds? Apparently she transferred from Keele after she'd had that illegitimate kid.'

'She kept a low profile, then,' said Jim, 'I don't remember her. She certainly wasn't active in Lab Soc.'

'For God's sake don't tell Tony,' said Eric, 'He'll claim to have shagged her.'

They all burst into male-bonded mirth and began a debate on how sexually active Tony had actually been, eventually reaching a consensus that, even with the aphrodisiac effect of his Mini, most of his claims had probably been bullshit. Fortunately the topic was exhausted when Tony reappeared. He stood at the entrance to the booth.

'My round,' he said, but then evidently had some difficulty in remembering what each ordered. Eric offered to assist him. As they both moved towards the bar Tony noticed Nigel and Vivienne, deep in conversation in their booth.

'Viv!' he shouted jubilantly, 'Let me get you a drink! What do you want?'

It took Vivienne three attempts to convince him that all she wanted an orange juice. Nigel, though not invited to place an order, asked for a mineral water.

The bearded young man behind the bar was of Mediterranean or possibly Middle Eastern origin, but his English was impeccable and his manners immaculate, despite being referred to as Gunga Din by Tony. Eric ordered the drinks and directed Tony to deliver the pints, while he took the orange juice and mineral water over to Nigel and Vivienne, receiving thanks from the former but no acknowledgement from his wife. She looked rather strained, he thought, but he knew better than to enquire after her welfare in the presence of a third party. He returned to his own booth.

'So you don't mind being served by Osama bin Laden?' said Tony.

'What d'you mean?'

'The wog behind the bar. Looks like a bloody Muslim to me. Thought they weren't supposed to have anything to do with booze.'

'Keep your voice down, Tony, for God's sake,' urged Alan.

'Why should I? Those bastards are getting everywhere. It's the same in Leeds. Chapeltown's overrun with 'em. When I were a lad it were the Yids, then they moved out when the blacks moved in; now it's the fuckin' Muslims. Soon it'll be the bloody East Europeans. It's not our country any more. I'm voting BNP next time.'

Jim, sitting opposite him, glowered and started to speak but was nudged in the ribs by Alan.

Eric intervened. 'How's your business, Tony? Prospering, are you?'

'Course I am. Why shouldn't I be? Forty years of hard graft, not like you bloody teachers. I've got a big deal coming up: stand to make a million.'

Jim again made to speak but Eric's response was immediate. 'I'm glad you're doing well, Tony, but I can assure you that teachers also have to work hard, and we don't get the rewards enjoyed by people like you.'

Alan envisaged the imminent collapse of the camaraderie that had seemed to be developing. 'Come on you two,' he urged, 'No more politics today. We've still got a lot of catching up to do.'

'Yes, you're right, Al,' said Eric, then, 'Tony, I've been meaning to ask you, how's your wife? Number three, isn't she?'

'What d'you mean? Are you taking the piss? How's *your* wife then?'

'Viv's fine. Look, I wasn't taking the piss, I honestly thought -'

'Viv? *Viv*? You married Viv?'

'Of course I did, Tony, why else would she be here?'

'But …. but she's with that other fella.'

Eric looked quizzically at Alan who hissed, 'He probably means Nigel. Let it go, mate.'

Thirty years in education had conditioned Eric never to let misconceptions go uncorrected.

'Viv's sitting with Nigel, yes, but it was me she married, I can assure you.'

Tony sat broodingly for a few moments, apparently digesting this information. Eric studied him, noticing that Vivienne had been right, he did look a bit seedy. His hair, though thick and greying only at the temples, was lank and greasy and the shoulders of his jacket were peppered with dandruff. He was chewing the inside of his cheek, but suddenly stopped and addressed Eric, very loudly.

'Do you still manage to give it to her? Bet you can't get it up. She's wasted on you, a looker like her. She always was. She always wanted a real man, not a wimp like you. You were a right bloody prat with yer bells and beads and joss sticks. I always thought you were a secret queer.'

'For God's sake, man —'

'Oh, that's got to you, hasn't it? Bet you *are* a queer, aren't you? Why don't you come out of the woodwork like all the other poofs and nancy-boys have since Blair came to power? This country's run by bloody homos: if I had my way –'

There was a crash. Jim's chair overturned as he leapt to his feet and grabbed Tony by the lapels.

'You *bastard*,' he shouted, 'you fuckin' racist homophobic fascist bastard. You were a shit when you were at university and you're a bigger shit today. Why don't you piss off back to Leeds? We don't want you here.'

Tony's arms flailed uselessly as he was violently shaken back and forth to the accompaniment of *bastard, bastard, bastard,* from Jim. Eric and Alan had risen from their seats but stood by impotently, aghast at the physical manifestation of aggression by their contemporaries. They assumed such behaviour was the prerogative of young men.

The barman had heard the crash and Jim's outburst. He emerged from behind the bar and began to walk hesitantly towards the source of the commotion: such occurrences were rare in the Cittie of York. He was saved from having to intervene: Nigel emerged from his booth and grabbed Jim's forearm.

'OK Jim, that'll do,' he said, but Jim maintained his grip on Tony's lapels. He suddenly released them with a shudder as Nigel applied forefinger pressure to nerve endings in his shoulders before moving deftly to position himself between the two protagonists. He took Tony firmly by the upper arm and manoeuvred him past Jim, then stood with him outside the booth.

'It's all right, young man,' he said to the barman, 'I'm sorry for the disturbance. I'll be removing this man from your premises in a few minutes. Come, Tony, I think you need to pay a visit to the toilet first – and bring your briefcase with you.'

Tony's face crumpled and he allowed himself to be led away. The barman returned to his post. Jim stood massaging his shoulders. Alan and Eric had resumed their seats: they were the epitome of despondency. The silence was tangible, and it prompted Vivienne to leave her booth, her expression an amalgam of worry and disgust.

'What was all that about? Where are Nigel and Tony? Eric, I really have had enough of this.'

'It was a bit of a disagreement between Jim and Tony,' said Alan, 'but it's over now. Nigel sorted it. He's taken Tony down to the gents, then I think he's going to get him out of here.'

'He ought to take the bastard and drop him in the Thames,' said Jim, 'Christ, I could murder a cig.'

'I don't blame you for wanting to have a go at him,' said Eric, 'Wish I'd had the guts to.' 'Why? said Vivienne, 'What's he been saying?'

'He was coming out with the most appalling bigotry, then he started having a go at me, accused me of being gay, for God's sake.

'What? Why? What else did he say?'

'Oh, it was all rubbish, Viv,' said Alan, 'There's something seriously wrong with him. His memory seems shot to pieces – he seemed to think that you and Nigel are married.'

Vivienne looked aghast. 'What the hell gave him that idea?'

'Calm down, Viv,' said Eric, 'it was probably just because you two were sitting together. Al's right: his memory seems a bit shaky.'

Their conversation was halted by the return of Nigel and Tony. Nigel was holding the briefcase in one hand and grasping Tony's arm firmly with the other. Tony seemed diminished, apathetic. He allowed himself to be steered to a chair and listlessly complied with Nigel's demand to sit there for a moment.

The group ignored him and looked at Nigel expectantly.

'He's not well, as you probably gathered. Certainly not well enough to continue this jaunt.'

An exhalation of relief escaped from Vivienne, and Alan couldn't contain a smile.

'What shall we do with him, then?' he asked.

'I'm getting a taxi to take him back to the hotel,' said Nigel, 'Once he's there and propped up in the bar he'll forget all about us. I'm going to go with him to make sure he gets there. I'll catch you lot up later.'

'But why do *you* have to take him?' Vivienne's voice verged on the shrill, 'Can't he look after himself?'

'No, Viv, I don't think he can.'

'Can't someone else take him?'

Nigel raised his eyebrows at her. 'I don't think Eric or Jim would be inclined to, would you, chaps? And this is Alan's day, not fair to ask him.'

'I'll come with you if you like, Nigel,' said Eric.

Vivienne's response to this was a horrified 'No!'

'That's decided, then,' said Nigel quietly, 'Keep your phone on, Al, so I know where to find you.' He turned to Tony. 'Come on then, old chap.'

Tony rose submissively and was led towards the exit, watched expressionlessly by the barman. Only Alan wished Tony goodbye, and he received no reply.

Chapter 9

THE CHESHIRE CHEESE, FLEET STREET

They gave Nigel a few moments to escort Tony away before emerging from the Cittie of York. The sky was a lowering purple and heavy with menace. Sheet lightning suddenly flickered behind the rooftops opposite to be followed by a basso profundo growl of thunder. Alan was relieved: the threat of rain meant that he could suggest they order a taxi. He didn't think he'd be able to make the walk to Fleet Street in the heat, and he was still shaky after the altercation between Jim and Tony. He felt no regret that Tony had been removed: there was little point in having the full complement of old friends if one of them continually disrupted proceedings to such an extent that it threatened the continued presence of others. Good old Nige: he could always be trusted to rise to occasions like these. He'd handled Jim very deftly as well, though perhaps Jim didn't see it that way: he looked ill-tempered and continued to massage his shoulders.

Alan hailed a passing cab and they piled in just as the first outsize drops of rain began to splatter on the pavement. He asked the driver to drop them at the Old Bank of England in Fleet Street, then sat back, waiting for the inevitable post-mortem on the events they'd just witnessed. It wasn't forthcoming: as they edged down Chancery Lane

Eric made reference to the rain and expressed the hope that it would clear the air, Jim grunted and stared at the passing scene, while Vivienne remained silent, a slight frown on her brow and her lips pursed. Alan inwardly cursed Tony for the pall he'd cast over the company.

As they turned into Fleet Street the rain suddenly became torrential, the street emptied of pedestrians and the driver, swearing at the ineffectual thrashing of his windscreen wipers, turned on his headlights. Evidently distracted, he drove past the Old Bank of England and; on hearing Alan's shout, came to a sudden halt some 50 yards further on.

'You've driven past it,' said Alan, 'can you reverse back?'

'No chance, mate, not in this downpour, I can't see a bleedin' thing. If you want dropping outside that pub I'll have to take you up Farringdon Street to Holborn Viaduct and come back down again. Course, you could always go to the Cheshire Cheese, it's just up there.' He indicated an alley by which the cab had stopped.

Alan didn't need telling; the Cheshire Cheese was next but one on his intended itinerary. Bugger: once again his plans had been disrupted. This time it was more worrying; with Jim's prejudices in mind he'd particularly wanted to visit the Old Bank of England before it began to fill with affluent City workers starting their weekend celebrations. But the silence of his closely confined companions militated against a continuation of the taxi ride, and the soaking they'd receive made a walk back to the Bank unthinkable. He was frozen by indecision.

Vivienne spoke, for the first time since leaving the Cittie of York. 'Oh, let's get in there, Alan; one pub's very much like another, surely?'

Alan winced at her artlessness, but was glad to have the decision made for him. He concurred, told his companions to make for the alley, and groped in his pocket for the fare.

The transaction completed, he joined Eric who was standing in the alley reading a sign on which was listed all the monarchs who had reigned during the pub's 250 year history. Jim and Vivienne had evidently already entered.

'Amazing!' Eric enthused, then, spotting another sign, 'Rebuilt in 1667! Oh, of course, after the Great Fire of London, I suppose. How long before that had it been a pub, then?'

'I dunno, mate; there's probably a tourist guide in the bar; let's get in there.' It was not that he was desperate for a drink, he just wanted to sit down.

They found Jim and Vivienne standing uncertainly in the semi-darkness of a space between a small room to the right in which sat a solitary elderly customer, and what appeared to be a restaurant to the left.

'Is Viv allowed to go in there?' said Jim, indicating an antique notice at the entrance to the small room which proclaimed 'Gentlemen Only Served in this Bar'.

Jim was so rarely given to wry observations that for a moment Alan thought he was being serious. Perhaps he was. Who knew what legislation-defying chauvinism might still exist in the pubs of Stoke-on-Trent?

'Just try stopping her,' said Eric, a remark which provoked a hostile stare from his wife. 'Another incredible place, Alan,' he added, peering into the dark panelled room which was dominated by a large open fireplace topped with a high mantle. 'Who's that?' he said, noticing the portrait of what looked like an eighteenth century gent hanging above it.

Alan, despite his desire to sit, decided to humour Eric's love of history. 'D'you fancy a quick tour round? There are lots more rooms, and there's no rush for a drink, is there? Is that okay, mate? he said to the young man behind the bar. He received a nod of assent.

'Yes, let's do that,' said Eric eagerly, 'Are you coming, Viv?'

'No. I'll stay in the Gentlemen Only room in the hope that one might eventually enter.'

'I'll stay with you,' said Jim, 'I've seen enough already. Any place that has to put sawdust on the floor in an attempt to be authentic inna worth exploring further, I reckon.' He indicated the sparse scattering of wood shavings that were dotted over the oak floorboards.

'Curmudgeonly old bugger,' said Alan as he led Eric away.

Eric was an enthusiastic companion on the tour: Alan was heartened by his delight and at his gratitude for being shown such a fascinating place. However, such was his interest in the fabric of the pub and its contents that he lingered rather too long in each room for Alan's comfort: it took ages to tear him away from the 7th edition of Dr Johnson's Dictionary in the Chop Room, even though it was housed in a glass case. At least down in the Cellar Bar Alan could take advantage of Eric's prolonged perusal of the room to visit the cramped toilet, listening to his exclamations of delight through the door as he stood at the urinal. Eventually they reached the Cheshire Bar, which, though bereft of customers, was overseen by a woman of indeterminate age, listlessly engaged re-arranging bottles of spirits.

'Let's have our drinks down here,' said Eric, 'I'd like to savour this room. I'll nip upstairs and get the other two. You get 'em in, Alan, I'll have a half of whatever's best.'

'It'll have to be Sam Smith's; it's all they serve,' said Alan, but Eric was already half-way up the stairs.

He returned a few minutes later, alone. Jim had already bought himself and Vivienne a drink and they were sitting side by side in the small bar. Vivienne said she was quite content to remain where she was, thank you very much, and there was no need for Eric to join them if he wished to remain downstairs. Eric said that he was sure she and Jim had much to talk about after all these years, and with some relief went back to join Alan. Viv could be an embarrassment when she was in one of her non-communicative moods, and he was content to let Jim take the strain for a while.

'They're going to stay upstairs,' he said to Alan, taking his seat at the rough-hewn table. A half-pint awaited him.

'Anti-social buggers,' said Alan, 'what's the matter with 'em?'

'I expect old Jim wants to pour out all his angst, just like he used to with Viv back in Leeds, don't you remember? She used to spend hours listening to him.'

'I don't think she'll find him so angst-ridden now, mate.'

'Why's that then?'

Alan started to respond, but appeared to think better of it, taking a swallow from his glass instead.

'So, you approve of my choice of pubs, then?' he asked.

'Oh yes, especially this one; congratulations, Al, you've done us proud.'

He gazed round the room: with its honey-coloured stone walls and flagged floor it had obviously once been the vaults, but he knew better than to quiz Alan further about the pub's history. Alan was singularly incurious about the past, and had no romantic notions about it. Eric loved to feel the past wash around him. He could imagine sitting here two centuries ago, the room full of Regency bucks and old bewigged denizens smoking clay pipes and being attended by busty serving wenches. Gone, all gone, even the smoke. Vivienne always accused him of lacking imagination, but were he to have attempted to explain he knew the response would have been at best uncomprehending, at worst scornful.

'Pity about Tony,' Alan said, 'Though I must say it's a relief to be rid of him. What d'you think's wrong with him?'

'No idea. You saw him more recently than I did; was he like that in '97?'

'No. He had a dolly-bird in tow. Was on his best behaviour, well, as good as he ever did behave; boasted a lot of course, and very right wing.'

'Al, be honest, when we were at University, did you actually *like* him?'

'Oh, he was all right, good entertainment value. I was never sure why he latched onto us lot, though, I mean, he wasn't really into the music, was he? Cars and women were more his scene.'

With that Eric had to be content. He should have known that Alan would never make disparaging remarks about others, even after the space of forty years. Easy-going Al. Not always the most exciting company, but always pleasant to have around, never moody, always saw the best in people, but, for a social animal, he'd seemed oddly uninterested in women. Of course, he'd been overweight, and his ginger hair had done him no favours. Looking at him now, as he sat sipping his beer, Eric suddenly became aware of his weight-loss. He hadn't noticed it before: that was Al's problem, one tended not to notice him when in the company of others. In fact, he realised, Alan had aged a lot: his face, when studied objectively from the point of view of a stranger rather than an old friend, was on the verge of that disintegration which, when complete, results in one becoming anonymous and unseen by anyone under 40.

Alan was still talking and he jerked himself into full attention.

'Sorry, what was that, Al?'

'Miles away, weren't you? I was saying that Nige handled Tony very well, don't you reckon? He's still got that public-schoolboy self assurance, and he looks bloody fit, doesn't he? Looks as though he works out every day.'

'He probably does. He used to in the flat, and that was in the days before we all became obsessed by our health. How's *your* health, Al?'

'OK,' said Alan shortly, then 'You and Nige always got on well, didn't you? How long was it you shared a flat?'

'Two years. Yeah, we hit it off well.'

They had, in fact co-existed well enough. There had been times when Eric had found himself envying Nigel's good looks, athleticism, intelligence and charm, but underlying all that was the shyness which saved him from the normal arrogant self-assurance of his class. And he'd been hopeless with girls – he'd been overawed by Viv at first, and even when he'd got to know her there had always been a strange, polite constraint between them.

Alan drained his glass. 'Viv still looks fantastic, mate,' he said, 'We all thought you were a lucky bugger back then, and you still are, to have a woman like that at your age.'

The implication behind Alan's remark was that Eric hadn't worn as well as his wife, and Eric was about to challenge this, semi-jokingly of course, when he realised he didn't wish the conversation to turn to marriage. A change of topic was called for.

'Enjoying your retirement are you, Al?'

'Too right. I'd had enough of all the bureaucracy. Have to watch the pennies, though. I don't have a headmaster's pension. How about you?'

'Well, I miss some of my old colleagues. Actually, what I miss most is the gossip, if I'm honest. But yes, I was glad to get out. I was finding the decline in standards distressing.'

'Standards of what? Teaching?'

'Well, partly that: some of my newer staff were distressingly uncultured, but it was the pupils mainly. Many of them arrived at 11 semi-literate, with no desire to learn, they disrupted classes, showed no respect whatsoever for authority, and if we tried to discipline them we were likely to be assaulted. It wasn't like that in our day, eh, Al? Of course we were lucky enough to be around when there was selection. I think the end of the 11 plus was a betrayal of the able working-class child: it robbed him of an escape route.'

Eric sat back on his seat, confident that Al, ever-compliant Al, would express agreement. It was not forthcoming.

'I think that's bollocks, Eric,' he said.

'What? Why?'

Alan proceeded to tell him. He accused Eric of seeing things through the rosy glow of his schooldays in affluent Henley and an early teaching career in equally well-heeled Warwickshire. He went on to say that in the Grammar School he attended pupils often ran riot, and that in the

121

1950s more than a third of grammar school pupils failed to get even three O-levels, and that in the Sec Mods things were many times worse because of the abysmal funding and the low expectations of working class kids. 'So don't give me all this crap about the 50s and 60s being a golden age for education, mate,' he concluded, adding 'Have you started reading the *Daily Mail* by any chance?'

Eric was stunned, not just by the vehemence of Alan's response but by the cogency of his argument. Al never used to have strong feelings about anything, or if he did he kept them well hidden. It must be all those years teaching in a bog-standard comprehensive in west London that had so embittered him. His barb about the *Daily Mail* had hit home, for Eric had a guilty secret. While he was comfortable with the *Guardian*'s stance on the occupation of Iraq, the environment, taxation, public spending, race and immigration, he privately abhorred the opinions expressed in the paper's Education Supplement, believing it to be little more than a mouthpiece for the unreconstructed leftists in the N.U.T. Eric didn't care for the N.U.T. He'd had one of its militants on his staff, and she'd made his life a misery.

'Fancy another half?' he said.

As he watched Eric waiting for service at the bar, Alan wondered what had possessed him to react so aggressively to his assertions. First he'd offended Nigel, now Eric. Was it he who'd changed, or his friends? Had he invested too much in the belief that people remained true to themselves, despite what life may throw at them? Or was he now upset by traits that would have been laughed away in one's salad days? Alan, though always a vague but unenthusiastic Labour supporter, had never been an ideologue, whereas at university Eric had espoused progressive politics and educational thinking with the same enthusiasm with which he'd adopted the trappings of psychedelia. Come to think of it, Eric had always been a sucker for the Next Big Thing, a dedicated follower of fashion; his eagerness to keep up with the latest trends had been gently mocked by those for whom enthusiasm of any kind was uncool. Perhaps his egalitarianism had long gone the way of his shoulder length hair. Best to keep off education, then: a pity, he'd assumed they'd have much to talk about, and it would have been interesting to have heard an ex-headmaster's perspective.

Eric returned with two half pints.

'Cheers, mate,' Alan said, 'Do you think we ought to go and join Viv and Jim?'

'No, not yet,' Eric resumed his seat quickly, 'I like it down here. We've still got lots to catch up on.'

Alan was grateful for Eric's evident wish to put their spat behind them. 'OK,' he said.

'So, what sort of music are you into these days, Al?' Eric asked, 'What do you think of all this modern rubbish?'

Alan sipped his beer. Strange, he'd been drinking for over four hours now, but it seemed to be having no effect at all.

'I still like the blues when it's performed live in a pub, but that's hard to find these days. I started getting into jazz when Miles brought out his 70s stuff, and I like it more and more. But not all modern stuff's rubbish, is it? Have you listened to Joss Stone, or Katy Melua, or Amy Winehouse?'

'Never heard of 'em,' said Eric dismissively.

'Are you serious? How can you *not* have heard of Amy Winehouse, the antics she gets up to?'

'As far as I'm concerned the music died in the mid 70s when Punk came out. It severed its connections with its roots and none of them wrote any intelligent lyrics. After that it was downhill all the way as far as I was concerned. I still get a kick out of the old stuff – Stones, Beatles, Kinks, Beach Boys, early Dylan – and it stands the test of time.'

Surely, Alan thought, Eric was being deliberately provocative, merely pretending to be a dinosaur like those old judges who asked what the Beatles were.

'But what about all the great stuff that came out in the 70s?' he entreated, 'The American bands like Little Feat, and JJ Cale, and the New Wave like Police, and Joe Jackson, even the early Dire Straits? And the Stones and Clapton were still bringing out some decent records, and I reckon Dylan's 70's albums were amongst his best. OK, there was a bit of a bare patch in the 80s with all this techno stuff and later on rap – I don't pretend to understand that – but weren't you heartened by Britpop? Oasis and Blur?'

'It all passed me by, Al. I was too busy building a career, I suppose. And Viv wasn't into it. She's quite a classical music buff now – goes to concerts in Birmingham with her literary friends. I quite like it myself – the tuneful bits, anyway.'

Alan took refuge in his beer and stared round the room. He supposed Eric could be said to have grown up, something that Sheila said, affectionately, that *he* ought to do. But blimey, maturing was one thing, becoming an old fossil was another. OK, it didn't do to become one of those ridiculous old men who pretended to be hip to youth culture – they were laughed at by those whom they sought to espouse – but at the chalk-face Alan had learned not to disparage the concerns of his charges. As a parent and grandparent he'd found there was much that could be learned from the younger generation if one took the trouble to listen to them.

'But what about your children?' he asked, 'Didn't you ever get into the stuff they liked when they were teenagers?'

'Oh, my girls were never tearaways,' said Eric, rather smugly, Alan thought, 'They went through a phase of being silly, but they soon grew up. By the time their GCSEs approached they buckled down to work. And as for today's teenagers, well, they're aliens as far as I'm concerned, a race apart. They're impenetrable and unapproachable.'

Well, yes, to an extent they were, Alan supposed. But with their wild enthusiasms and outlandish fashions and gravity-defying hairstyles and arcane speech patterns they evoked in him the time when he and his friends had similarly adopted any craze that would be incomprehensible to their elders. The kids, Alan believed, were all right. They inhabited a world which he'd lost and couldn't recapture, and he took care not to resent them for that. And the very fact of their being alien made them unthreatening, except en-masse, of course, but hadn't it always been thus? Weren't the crowds of Hoodies just the end of a long line that stretched back through the Skins and the Mods and the Rockers, back to the Teds? As individuals, in small groups, teenagers were usually inoffensive enough, unlike some of their elders. It was, thought Alan, the young adults, those in their late 20s and 30s, Thatcher's children, who posed the greatest threat to one's well-being, for they seemed to know exactly where they were going and to have no compunction in doing down anyone who stood in their way.

'Things haven't really changed for the better since we last met, have they?' said Eric.

'How do you mean?' Alan wasn't sure he wanted to hear this.

'Remember how we thought we were going to change the world? All the optimism, peace and love? It didn't work out, did it? The 60s destroyed the old world and promised a new one which never happened.'

'Well, it's not been all bad, mate. The end of the Cold War for a start — we always had nuclear Armageddon hanging over us, didn't we? At least my grandchildren don't have to live with that. And we're a lot more tolerant, aren't we? Think what it used to be like for blacks and gays, and …. oh, people like single mothers, and think of all the educational opportunities young people have now, and all the modern technology like email and mobile phones, and….' He tailed off.

Eric straightened in his chair, and Alan braced himself for an erudite rebuttal of his statements. He remembered that there'd had been something of the didactic in Eric even when a student, however much he'd tried to disguise it under the veneer of youthful insouciance.

'But Al,' he said, 'at least mutually assured destruction meant that the Cold War was always unlikely to turn hot; your grandchildren face a far more uncertain future, what with Islamist terrorism and global warming. But I wasn't really thinking about international events; it's what's happened in *this* country since the 60s that's been so distressing. In our pursuit of a more egalitarian society —'

'Christ, I don't reckon Thatcher and her crowd tried to pursue that,' Alan interrupted, aware as he spoke that he was to an extent contradicting his original assertion.

Eric sipped at his beer, stroked his beard, then slipped into head-teacher mode.

'I wasn't thinking about economic equality. I'm talking about the loss of civility in our society, the lack of respect for others, the growth of impatience, hastened, incidentally, by your precious mobile phones and the internet. Look, we grew up to believe that a concern for others was the pillar of our progressive politics, but all that seems to have disappeared. Everyone seems to think they have the right to behave exactly as they wish. If you challenge bad behaviour you're treated with blank amazement at best, outright hostility at worse. There aren't any social norms any longer, are there? Civility used to be an expression of social solidarity; now it's seen as some sort of quaint out-dated middle-class affectation – '

'But – '

'Hang on, Al. What's happened is that our culture has been proletarianised. Politicians pretending to be football enthusiasts, so-called quality newspapers pandering to vacuous celebrities, and as for television! Quiz shows, reality shows, soaps: even news broadcasts and documentaries have been dumbed down to the extent where they're painful to watch if you have a modicum of intelligence or education. Don't get me wrong, I don't want to return to an age of deference, but we've become a country of semi-educated, vulgar, mawkishly sentimental, pleasure-seeking yobs.'

He took a swallow from his glass and set it down assertively on the table, then folded his arms in an 'I rest my case' gesture.

'You might have a point,' said Alan, though even as he'd listened he thought Eric was guilty of gross over-generalisation. But if you were articulate and confident you could get away with it. Alan had always found it difficult to articulate his beliefs, perhaps, he sometimes thought, because he was so often unsure what his beliefs really were. Not so much recently, though, for he too had begun to feel an impotent rage over the way things were going. But his perspective, living as he did on a teacher's pension in Ealing, was very different to that of Eric. The inequalities that still existed, which indeed seemed to have worsened recently, were all too evident in London, where conspicuous displays of wealth existed side-by-side with an impoverished underclass. But it wasn't the obscenely rich that angered Alan: it was the comfortable so-called middle-classes with their 4x4s and second homes in the country and their holidays abroad and their private health schemes and children at independent schools, those people who railed against taxation and loss of freedom, those whom the right-wing press called 'Middle England' but who wouldn't survive a month on the national average income, let alone on Alan's pension, of which he was now supposed to be ashamed because it was public sector and index-linked. Perhaps Jim's right, he thought, perhaps the whole system needs demolishing. The trouble was, he had little faith in Jim's vision of what would replace it.

'Come on, Eric,' he said, 'Let's go up and join the others.'

In the upstairs bar, Jim had been finding it hard to connect. Vivienne seemed distant, distracted, not at all the briskly cheerful girl he remembered. He started by asking her what she thought was wrong with Tony, but she remained silent, looking through him while slowly shaking her head. Notwithstanding the annoyance he still felt following his manhandling by Nigel, he gave magnanimous praise for the way he'd dealt with Tony, and commented on Nigel's obvious fitness and ability to look after himself. To this she gave not even a non-verbal response, but stared over his shoulder, seeming to find interest in the activities of the lad behind the bar.

He had to shake her out of this. He was never comfortable exchanging confidences, but it was something women seemed to like, and Viv had always been an understanding companion during his dark nights of the soul back in Leeds. He'd always been grateful to her for that; perhaps it was time to tell her; it might at least provoke a response. And this was the time to do it, without the presence of the others and before she could be distracted by the inevitable influx of late-afternoon customers.

'I never had the chance to thank you,' he said, touching her hand briefly across the table.

'What?' She started, flinched almost, evidently somewhere else.

'I said, I never had a chance to thank you.'

'For what? What are you talking about, Jim?'

'For the way you helped me, back in Leeds.'

'Helped you?'

'Yes, the way you used to sit and talk to me when I was depressed. I must have been a pain in the arse, duck; but you were so patient. It was depression, real depression, I wanna just feeling down. It was like a bloody great wall between me and everyone else. Only you took the trouble to get through it. You were a life saver.'

Vivienne shuffled in her seat and made patterns on her glass with her index finger.

'Well, I'm glad I was of assistance.'

Christ, what a cold response, thought Jim. What's the matter with her? Buggered if I'm going to let it go at that.

'It was more than just assistance, wasn't it? You spent hours just sitting with me, talking to me about anything, and listening when I managed to respond. You just listened,

Viv; that was all I wanted. God knows what old Eric must have thought, the time you used to spend with me. Did he mind?'

'What?'

'Eric: did he mind you spending time with me?'

'Eric? Oh, no. No, he didn't mind.'

'Understanding bloke, your Eric. Not many men would have let his girl spend ages alone with another feller, especially a girl like you.'

'What do you mean, a girl like me?'

'Someone as attractive as you, Viv. Everyone fancied you, you know.'

She snorted and looked displeased. What was wrong with *that* remark, Jim wondered?

'Any road, it was good of you. Pity I had to wait 40 years to thank you. I had me speech ready to give you on that last night, but never had a chance to deliver it.'

'Last night?'

'Yes, the last night in Leeds, you know, the pub-crawl.'

'Oh, that.' Her eyes left him and focused again on the young man behind the bar.

'Hardly got a chance to talk to you all that evening. First Eric gets pissed out of brains, then bloody Tony starts coming on strong to you. You were in a strange mood that evening, Viv.'

'I don't remember. It was a lifetime ago. D'you think it's time we joined Eric and Alan downstairs? We're being a bit anti-social.'

Jim had always regarded Viv's voice as posh when they were at University, but he now noticed that it had become even more cut-glass. He felt a slight twinge of dislike – that sort of accent seemed designed to put poor oiks like himself in his place. Bugger the woman; she wasn't going to get away with it.

'No, hang on, Viv; I'm surprised you dunna remember, 'cos it was the only time I'd ever seen you, well, sort of flirting with Tony. It was only later I realised that it was probably the best way of coping with him. He really thought he'd made it – God, the look on his face when you left us in the chippies! I thought he was gunna cry for a minute. Then he said he was gunna puke, so he left us, he said he was -'

'As I said, I don't remember that evening.'

'Bloody hell Viv, you can't have forgotten how Eric got pissed and had to be helped home by Nigel? I bet he got in the neck from you next day, didn't he? Anyway, I anna finished; Tony said he was gunna drive back to Roundhay, but he didn't, cos I saw him early the next morning, he was –'

Vivienne exploded. 'For God's sake, Jim, can't you give it a rest?'

Her eyes blazed. Jim had never heard her so strident.

'Fuck, what's the matter with you, Viv?'

'What is it about you men?' Her voice was suddenly Thatcheresque, several tones lower; she spoke slowly and deliberately, clearly enunciating every syllable. 'You're all obsessed with re-living the past. It's how we are *now* that's important. I'm interested in how your life is *now*, not how you were or what you did or thought 40 years ago. It would be nice to think that you had a similar interest in me.'

Jim raised his hands, a gesture of surrender. Bloody hell, she was a formidable woman.

'OK, duck, sorry. You're right. Look, I'm empty. Fancy another?'

She half rose. 'Don't you think it would be best if we joined Eric and Alan?'

'No, give it a few minutes, Viv, please; there's something I want to tell you.'

'If it's about Leeds I'm not interested.'

'No, it's about me, and about the present.'

She sat down.

'All right. But no drink for me, thanks.'

During their exchange four men had entered, exclaiming about the bloody weather and examining their expensive jackets for signs of rain damage. They just beat Jim to the bar, for which he was not ungrateful: it would give him time to marshal his thoughts. If there was one person in whom he might confide about his present circumstances then it was Viv, and she seemed to be inviting such confidences. As he waited for the four men to be served, he debated how to introduce the topic of his partner.

Should he tell Viv the whole story, perhaps? About how his initial dislike for his new colleague had been tempered by Nicky's undoubted attractiveness and seeming loneliness? Stoke pubs were not places to drink alone, and the night-clubs of Hanley and Newcastle-under-Lyme were uninviting for anyone over 30 even when accompanied by a partner, something that Nicky, surprisingly, appeared not to have. He'd mentioned that the Wheatsheaf provided good live music, mainly blues, and that it was worth visiting if Nicky liked that sort of thing, and that he'd be going along that evening if Nicky cared to tag along. At the Wheatsheaf, his suspicions about his colleagues' true nature had been confirmed. It had taken three years for them finally to set up house together. Jim was at long last free of a lifetime of fruitless self-denial about his predilections, even though he'd insisted that as far as their colleagues and his mothers and brothers were concerned they were merely two bachelors sharing accommodation.

Jim was not a demonstrative man, and found it hard to express his love for Nicky. But he cherished him for the way he'd rescued him from the grinding pressure of having to appear straight, no, to try and *be* straight, a pressure which had led him to enter two doomed relationships with women, the failure of which had served to exacerbate the troughs of depression to which he'd become increasingly prone. He'd come to accept that he'd have to live his life alone, and had rationalised his situation by telling himself that it would stand him in good stead, it being a dress rehearsal for the ultimate solitude of old age. In a rare outpouring of emotion he'd told Nicky how he'd dreaded getting old. 'But now,' he'd added, 'I've got you.' this being the nearest he'd ever come to articulating his devotion.

No, there was no need to tell Viv all this. It would sound like an attempt at self-justification, and Nicky, born at the time of the Wolfenden Report and living his life in times when it was possible, even de rigueur, to celebrate his predilections, kept telling him there was no need to justify himself. He'd just come out with a bald statement of the fact. She'd tell Eric, of course, and then it would get to the other two, but at least Tony was out of the picture. Not that it mattered what that bastard thought.

Tony. Suddenly, all thoughts of Nicky were driven from his mind as that half-forgotten incident of forty years ago flooded back into his mind. *Tony*: that last evening in Leeds; Tony leaving Sweaty Betty's soon after Viv's departure; Tony in Clarendon Road at five o'clock the following morning; Clarendon Road, on which stood the Henry Price student flats; the Henry Price, where Viv had lived. *No*, surely not? He dismissed the idea. But – she'd been flirting with him all evening. A picture came to him of the two of them in the Original Oak, Viv, flushed, seemingly uncaring that her mini had ridden up to expose her pants; Tony's hand on her knee. *Christ*.

'Yes, sir?' The barman addressed him. The four new customers were taking their drinks to one of the lower rooms.

'A pint, please.'

As his beer was poured he glanced over at Vivienne. A mature, smart, attractive, self-possessed woman, but today so edgy in Tony's presence. If what he had begun to suspect was indeed true, why did it concern her so much after all these years? Had it developed into more than a one-night stand? Had she ever told Eric?

Suddenly, to confide in Viv that he was gay was of no consequence. It would be like telling a stranger. Her opinion, once so important to him, mattered less. He did not condemn her (though why, of all people, did it have to be Tony?), it was just that she was not who he thought she was. It was akin, he imagined, to accidentally discovering that one was adopted: one's acquired parents would still be loved for all the care that they'd bestowed, but one would never quite forgive them their economy with the truth.

He carried over his pint and sat down. Vivienne favoured him with a slight smile.

'Sorry I was a bit abrupt, Jim,' she said, 'It's just that –'

'Oh, never mind about that. I've got summat to tell you.'

'So you said. It sounds intriguing.'

He took a swallow from his pint. Might as well come right out with it.

'I'm gay.'

He hadn't known what reaction to expect: the silence yes, but not the burst of laughter that followed. It was the first time she'd laughed that day, he realised.

'What's so bloody funny?'

'You are, Jim. Did you really think I didn't know?'

He stared at her.

'You know? How could you possibly? I only came out eight years ago.'

She reached across the table and rested her hand on his.

'Jim, I realised you were probably gay when we were at University, even though you might not have acknowledged it yourself.'

'But how? I wasn't bloody limp-wristed, we Stokies aren't camp. I even took a few girls out from time to time.'

'I'm almost ashamed to tell you how I knew. It reeks of conceit.'

'Go on.'

'I was attractive. When you're attractive you come to expect what we used to call vibes, sexual vibes I mean, from men. You never gave off any, even when I was alone with you and holding your hand.'

She was still holding his hand now, he realised, as evidently did she, for she squeezed it briefly before releasing it.

'Well, bugger me,' he said.

'Sorry Jim, can't help you there.'

He guffawed, and she joined in.

'Are you happy, Jim?'

'Yes. I've got a partner. His name's Nicky.'

'I'm glad. He's obviously doing you a lot of good.'

'Does it show that much, duck?'

'Don't fish for compliments, Jim! Hairstyle, clean clothes, capped teeth, no ciggies?'

'Aye, well. I took a bit of persuading.'

He had. He had only slowly succumbed to Nicky's patient campaign to undergo refurbishment. First to go had been the lank, thinning, collar length hair which Nicky mocked as verging on a Bobby Charlton comb-over, to be replaced by the crop which Jim had to acknowledge took years from him. Then new shirts and jeans had made an entry, even chinos, once he'd been persuaded that to wear them didn't constitute a counter-revolutionary act. His teeth, however had been the object of a two-year war of attrition, Jim only being persuaded to attend to them when an abscess resulted in a long-overdue visit to the dentist who said that years of neglect and smoking had resulted in his incisors being beyond restoration and that capping was the only solution. He'd agreed to this when it was explained that because the procedure would not be undertaken for purely cosmetic reasons it would be available under the NHS. Thus he was equipped with a gleaming set of gnashers, a wonderful incentive, Nicky said, for him to stop smoking. For all his dental makeover, he could not break the habit of covering his mouth when he laughed, and laughing was something he'd begun to do more often.

'I'm really happy for you, Jim.'

'Thanks, duck.' A thought occurred to him. 'Viv, did you tell Eric you thought I was gay?'

'No. It was only a strong suspicion anyway. I don't talk of old times with Eric.'

I bet you don't, he thought. Poor old Eric.

'Have you just got a pint in?' said Alan as he entered the room, Eric following behind, 'Sup up, it's time we moved on to the next one. God knows what's happened to Nigel.'

Chapter 10

Tavistock Square

'You can damned well pay the fare,' Nigel said.

He leapt from the taxi into the rain. It was easing slightly, but, linen jacket in mind, he ran to the cover of the entrance to the Tavistock Hotel. Turning, he could see no evidence that Tony was complying with the order; he was slumped forward in the back seat, apparently fumbling with something on the floor.

That bloody briefcase, Nigel thought. He composed his face into its habitual expression of calm detachment before abandoning his shelter and running back to the taxi.

'Tony, just pick up your case and get into the hotel. I'll pay. Wait for me in the foyer.' His voice, though quiet, was steely, determined and not to be disobeyed. Tony scrambled out and stumbled towards the hotel, while Nigel fumbled with his wallet and then received appreciative thanks from the driver for an unnecessarily large tip.

'Right, Tony,' said Nigel, when he'd joined him, standing by the reception desk, 'First things first. You owe me £20.'

The expected protest did not materialise; the cash was proffered meekly. God, what a pathetic figure he is, thought Nigel, yet what damage he had done: such are the consequences of all those inadequates who are unaware of their own inadequacies.

'Do you have your room key?'

'Key?'

'Swipe card, Tony, the thing you use to unlock your room.'

'Oh. Yes, I think so.' He grovelled in his back pockets and produced it, somewhat bent.

'OK. What's your room number?'

'Forgotten. It's on the card, isn't it?'

Suppressing a sigh, Nigel turned and sought the advice of the receptionist. Though she'd been watching Tony and eavesdropping on the conversation, her face as she divulged the room number had all the stereotypical inscrutability of her race.

'Right, come on then, I'll make sure you get to your room.'

'Why? I don't want to go to sleep, I want a drink. Lots of nice things to see down here.' He leered at the receptionist. 'I always fancied a bit of chink.'

Nigel resisted the almost overwhelming urge to slap him hard round the face, and instead grasped him firmly by the upper arm and led him towards the lift.

'Haven't you caused enough trouble for one day? If you carry on the way you've been behaving you'll end up in serious trouble, and I won't be around to rescue you. So I suggest you stay in your room, have a sleep, or watch TV. You might find a porn channel; no doubt that would be to your taste.'

'Where are you going, then?' Tony asked as the lift doors closed. Christ, he stank. Not just of booze, but of stale body-odour and unwashed underclothes.

'I'm going to rejoin the others, of course.

'Well, I might catch up with you later, then.'

'Possibly,' said Nigel, secure in the knowledge that Tony had no idea of the itinerary and that any phone call from him would remain unanswered.

They walked along the carpeted windowless corridor, lined with identical doors, a scene with which Nigel was familiar from his times in countless hotels in every major city in Europe. Only Tony's sniffs broke the muffled silence.

'Here you are, room 431,' said Nigel. Tony fumbled with the swipe card; Nigel grabbed it, used it expertly and pushed Tony into the room.

'Right, Tony. I might see you later this evening when we get back, but don't bank on it. Look after yourself, if you know the meaning of the phrase.'

He turned and left the room without looking back and hurried along the corridor. He decided against waiting for the lift – Tony might appear again – and made for the stairs, leaping down the four flights two steps at a time with an agility that belied his years. The physical activity was cathartic. He entered the foyer, apologised profusely to the receptionist for the behaviour of his companion, received a dazzling smile in return, and emerged onto the front steps of the hotel, where he stood, looking out across Tavistock Square.

The rain had stopped, but the sky still threatened. Traffic swished along the wet road in surges dictated by the traffic lights at the junction with Woburn Place. A few pedestrians had tentatively emerged, the tourists amongst them distinguished by waterproofs and umbrellas. The freshness that the rain had provided when the storm broke was already dissipating as the standing water began to vaporise in the heat.

He cursed Tony under his breath, using all the foul expletives and blasphemies that he was renowned for never using, even in all-male company. It was as he'd expected: Tony's briefcase, when he'd opened it in the pub toilet, contained a large bottle of vodka wrapped in a Tesco's bag. Nigel had met alcoholics before, knew all the traits, all the dissembling and self-deception, the brash self-confidence vying with maudlin self-pity, the lapses of memory. But Tony was revealed as doubly dependent, on the vodka and on the white powder which filled a polythene bag stashed in a separate pocket of the briefcase. A twinge of liberal conscience prompted Nigel to wonder, for one short second, what adversity had prompted Tony's descent into degradation. Even at university there had always been a lack of ease about him half hidden under the bluster. But he deserved no pity; he'd had all the advantages, he was flawed and was reaping the harvest of a lifetime of selfish excess.

He felt a sudden urge for a drink himself, a proper one, and time alone to digest the enormity of what Tony had told him in the taxi. He needed to collect his thoughts, to compose himself, to become the usual blasé, unruffled Nigel before he could face the others. He wasn't sure that he could do it, and for a moment was tempted to go straight to Paddington and speed back to Gloucestershire, but there was no comfort to be had there. And he mustn't spoil the day further for poor old Alan for whom this reunion obviously had particular importance.

The pubs in the Euston area didn't appeal, so decided to walk to the nearby Hilton; the anonymity and quiet of a hotel bar in the late afternoon would suit his mood and meet his need for reflection. He crossed the road and began to walk through Tavistock Square. The plane trees were still dripping from the downpour, the benches were empty of their usual tattered casualties, and it was strangely hushed apart from the wash of traffic noise seeping through the shrubbery. His thoughts were interrupted by the wail of a fire engine as it sped from its base on the Euston Road, reminding him that he was but yards from the scene of carnage outside the headquarters of the BMA. It had been his intention sometime on this visit to pay homage to the site, but his public concerns had been superseded by private agonies.

He left the square and entered Upper Woburn Place. As he approached the hotel he remembered that it was the Hilton in which Eric and Vivienne were booked: might they return prematurely? Viv had several times that day threatened to do so, but then that had been while Tony was present. God, no wonder she'd been on edge. No, they'd probably stick with the group, and in the unlikely event of their returning he doubted that they'd visit the bar.

He pushed through the revolving doors and was seized by the unwelcome recollection of helping a drunken Eric through similar doors at the *Hyde Park* in Leeds forty years before. If only Eric had stayed sober on that evening – but then he remembered that Tony had laced Eric's beer. The bastard! Had he planned the whole affair?

He entered the bar. It was a spacious room; a scattering of business types occupied the easy chairs grouped around the large low tables. Sky 24 hour News broadcasted silently from a large TV attached to a wall. He ordered a double gin and tonic and carried it to a table in the corner where he had an uninterrupted view of all the occupants of the room. He downed half the glass in one gulp, the sharpness of the drink a welcome contrast to the blandness of the carefully-paced half pints he'd been consuming all day.

It didn't calm him, rather it had the effect of reviving the shock and outrage that he'd felt in the taxi when Tony had revealed his secret.

At first he'd not taken him seriously. Alcoholics live in a Walter Mitty world, and in any case Tony had been making wild claims and accusations from the moment Nigel had discovered the contents of the briefcase. But he'd been insistent, and his long-term memory seemed to have been functioning again, for his account of the events of that Leeds evening matched Nigel's almost exactly, right up to that point when he'd left Sweaty Betty's.

Over the years Nigel had rarely given that evening much thought; too much had intervened in the years since. He remembered it had been something of a disaster, given that much of his time had been spent ministering to the drunken Eric. He recalled that Vivienne had been uncharacteristically coquettish after Eric's departure, and that Jim had been more than usually morose, but little more. A blip had occurred on his radar when, earlier this afternoon, Jim had revealed that he'd seen Tony in Clarendon Road at dawn the following morning, but he'd thrust from his mind the potentially alarming dawn juxtaposition of Tony and the Henry Price flats as being too improbable to consider. But now Tony had provided a triumphant, blow by blow expose, had revealed his knowledge of something that he should not have known, and in doing so had destroyed the one certainty that Nigel had clung to through all the vicissitudes of his life.

Trust. *Never trust anyone.* The maxim had been drilled into Nigel throughout his training. He'd learned to examine strangers carefully, to assess them, evaluate them, and to apply the same scrutiny to his colleagues, friends and lovers. But Nigel had had but one real lover, and for her he'd made an exception, though he'd been aware that there must have been others who had carried out the assessment of the risk she might pose for him and for the service. When he married Melanie and retired to the Cotswolds he believed he'd left behind the days of suspicion. Now, shattered by what he had learned, his former view of the world had reasserted itself. Never trust anyone, not even lovers.

How could she? Vivienne, with Tony? The man who represented everything that he, and he'd thought she, despised; brashness, arrogance, rapaciousness? Nigel loathed sexual adventurers, but he'd come to learn that many didn't. In the louche and perfidious world in which he'd worked he found that there was indulgence towards the predator. What Nigel had been raised to believe, that gentility and selflessness are universally admired and wickedness abhorred, he'd since learned to be wrong. Selfishness can be attractive: people feel at ease with low moral standards, they are discomforted by those with scruples. But Vivienne? Surely not. He couldn't believe it. But the evidence was compelling . Nausea swept over him.

He gazed round the bar. Even in his distress he found himself once more checking the faces, postures and clothes of those present, ever watchful for the out-of-place, the nervous, the overly alert. Only one couple stood out from the anonymity of business suits and holiday casuals: they were sitting side by side in the far corner, holding hands, intent on each other. He observed them closely; they were much older than they'd seemed at first glance, about his own age. Their apparent youthfulness stemmed from their body language: they had not the slightly bored acceptance of each other's company that characterises so many mature couples in public places, they were alive to each other, laughter alternating with tender glances. They were in love; no, more than that, they were lovers. Envy swept through him, compounding the nausea. The reunion could not, now, signal the start of the future of which he had once dreamed. And he knew that there was no future with Melanie.

At first, all had been well, in Stow. He loved living in the place, not just the barn conversion, but the town with its antique shops and book stores and traditional pubs and fine eating places. An amiable man, he'd soon begun to make friends with the locals, before social isolation had been forced on them. Now, he realised that Melanie had from the start been uncomfortable with their new acquaintances, and they with her. Educational differences could sometimes be overcome, but in rural Gloucestershire it was class that was the issue, and Melanie was not just working class, but urban working class.

Then came Oscar. Nigel's first reaction to the diagnosis had been inconsolable grief, followed by a terrible anger that had never really left him. A first-born son represents the continuation of the line, a passing on of the name. His own father had been similarly devastated, and the distaste of some of his other relatives was such that, on the one occasion that Oscar had been taken to Yorkshire, they could not bring themselves even to see the child. Nigel suspected that they blamed Melanie for tainting the Templeton line with her faulty lower-class genes. Sometimes, in his less rational moments, he caught himself thinking the same. As Oscar became more demanding, taking all Melanie's attention, he took refuge in frantic DIY and gardening and long walks alone: in the evenings he shut himself in his study, reading. He'd long ago abandoned surfing the net for possible cures. He could not even bear to accompany his wife into Stow shopping, unable to handle the stares of the ghoulish or the expressions of sympathy and support for the compassionate when they tried to communicate with an infant whose only response was to gurgle and grunt. It became even worse when the infant grew into a child and the means of perambulation became a wheelchair, a nightmarish Heath-Robinson contraption in which he was confined by a plethora of straps, splints and supports.

Melanie had begun to complain of isolation, stuck out in the barn with no contact, even visual, with other people. It was, she said, bad enough in the summer, but the winters were intolerable. The barn stood at 600 feet: driving rain and bitter winds accompanied the long black evenings unpunctuated by a single light. When the twice-daily journey to deliver and collect Oscar from the special school in Cheltenham began to weary her, she began to voice her desire to move into the town. Although nothing had yet been said, both were aware that she and Oscar would soon make the move without him.

And now the hoped-for solace of the reunion had been taken from him by that bastard. The faint hope that he'd not even dared articulate to himself had been dashed. A hideous image of an isolated old age bore down on him – alone in a room with a gas fire and a book or the TV his only company. Even worse would be the summer evenings when he'd be taunted by the balmy twilights of his youth and haunted by what might have been.

He jerked to his feet, spilling his gin over the table top. He mustn't sit, brooding. He must join the others, and do his thinking while on the move. He always thought best when active. Action would calm his inner seething. He felt as in a dream, the sort of nightmare where morbid curiosity combines with despair, where horror looms with a dreadful inevitability.

He left the hotel and pulled out his mobile. It seemed though hours had passed. Which pub would they be in now? How should he behave when he rejoined them? He knew how to keep his feelings hidden, and could if need be act as though nothing had happened. But how would he respond if Vivienne wished to pick up the thread of the conversation they'd begun in the Cittie of York? And what about Eric? Did he know?

Did it really matter? It was 40 years ago, a minor drunken youthful misdemeanour should have no significance for him today. Eric had probably known, and their marriage had survived, hadn't it? Oh yes, that bloody marriage had survived.

He hailed a passing taxi. He'd phone as soon as he'd got in it.

Chapter 11

THE OLD BANK OF ENGLAND, FLEET STREET

'It's stopped raining,' said Alan.

It had, but the sky was still lowering. The pavements were crowded, the afternoon hiatus was over, offices had disgorged their occupants who, despite the heat, were walking purposefully, intent on whatever the evening had in store.

'This lot are bound for the suburbs, I suppose,' said Jim.

'Not yet they ain't,' said Alan, 'This is London, mate, they'll be heading for the boozers. It's an old London tradition, drinking before getting the train home. But most of this lot'll carry on all evening, especially the young ones; a lot of 'em live in all the flats that have gone up in Docklands.'

'Where are we headed, then?' said Eric.

'Just a few yards up the road, the place where the taxi should have dropped us. Be prepared for a surprise.' He led the way, Jim hard on his heels, followed by Eric who was solicitously enquiring after his wife's welfare.

'Fuckin' hell,' said Jim as Alan turned to mount the wide steps outside a stately Italianate building, 'Is this a pub? Looks more like a bloody bank.'

'It was once, that's why it's called the Old Bank of England, you pillock. Come on, and when we're in put aside your Stokey prejudices, for God's sake.'

He pushed through the doors. They were instantly assailed by a wall of loud chatter and uproarious laughter: the place was filling up.

'What d'you reckon to this, then?' asked Alan, a question which evidently assumed an appreciative response. It was not immediately forthcoming: his companions stood gazing about them, taken aback by the vast space, columns soaring to a high, ornate plaster ceiling from which were suspended three outsize brass chandeliers.

'Bloody hell, Al.' Eric was the first to react. 'You can certainly pick 'em. It's fantastic, isn't it Viv?'

Vivienne concurred, with reasonable enthusiasm.

'What's its history, Al?' said Eric, 'How long has it been a pub? When was it built?'

'Well, it was – '

'Never mind that now,' Jim interrupted, 'Let's grab a seat while we can.'

They hurriedly occupied a table near the entrance: it afforded them a view down the length of the room. The walls were hung with large oil paintings, the windows were framed by heavy curtains of gold and black. All the furniture was solid, the wooden tables polished to a dull sheen. The middle of the room was dominated by a rectangular island bar with high bookcase-like shelving in its centre, housing arrays of bottles and glasses. Customers, many of them female, were clustered round the bar waiting for service.

Jim shuffled in his seat. 'Why are all these buggers dressed up to the nines?' he complained.

'Because they've just come from work. We're in the City, Jim, and near the Inns of Court; most of this lot'll be professionals. Thirty years ago all the pubs here would have been full of men and all wearing pinstripes, except for the journalists of course, before they decamped to Canary Wharf, but this wasn't a pub then. For God's sake relax, mate.'

'It's marvellous, but totally bizarre,' enthused Eric, 'Nothing like this in Leamington, eh, Viv?'

'Probably not,' said Vivienne, 'but we don't go to pubs to find out, do we?'

'I'll get 'em in,' said Alan, 'What are you all having?'

The ordering process was interrupted by a text alert on his phone. He read it, and tapped out a reply.

'Nige is in a taxi, 'he said, 'he should be here in about ten minutes. Right, let's have your orders again.'

Vivienne rose hurriedly. 'Not for me at the moment, Alan. I need the loo; where is it?'

'They're upstairs.' He pointed to a flight of carpeted stairs leading to a long balcony which ran the length of the room. 'At the end of the balcony.'

She hurried away. Alan took the orders and made his way towards the bar.

'Looks like we're going to have a bloody long wait,' said Jim.

'It doesn't bother me,' said Eric, 'there's so much of interest to look at in here.'

They stared round the room. The clientele all had a sheen of youthful prosperity, but were not as formally dressed as first impressions had indicated. Most of the men had dispensed with jackets and ties, but wore striped or patterned shirts, some untucked, and suit trousers. Many of the women were similarly trousered, but with sleeveless blouses and, in a few cases, tight, low cut tee-shirts. Those wearing skirts were bare-legged. Some wore flip-flops, others high heels. They were all in high spirits.

'D'you realise we're the oldest people in here?' said Eric.

'What's new? It's the same everywhere.'

Eric hoped that Viv wouldn't be long, or that Alan would be served quickly, or that Nigel would arrive. Jim could be hard work to be alone with, he thought, remembering the many times in Leeds when his responses to attempts at conversation were restricted to 'yes', 'no' and 'maybe'. Despite Jim's sarcastic references to his home counties upbringing, Eric had never disliked him; rather he'd been in awe of him for the strength of his convictions and his impeccable working class credentials. When Vivienne had opined that his moodiness should be regarded as an affliction rather than merely a disagreeable character trait, Eric had made clumsy attempts to be sympathetic, to little avail. Even when Jim was relatively up-beat, entertaining them with his blues guitar, he was never given to exchanges of confidences, and had never shown any curiosity about the private concerns of his friends.

'So how are you, then, Jim?' he asked.

'I'm all right.' The reply was emphatic. In fact, thought Eric, he *did* look all right. The closely cropped hair suited him. He was heavily lined, and looked his age, but healthily so. Glancing at him, he was surprised to see that he was being stared at appraisingly. Jim never used to engage in eye contact.

'You and Viv are all right?'

'Us? Yes, thriving.'

'Good.' The stare was maintained. Eric began to feel slightly uncomfortable.

'Got summut to tell you. I've already told Viv, so you'd know soon enough.'

Christ, thought Eric, what's coming? Is he married, or bankrupt, or terminally ill perhaps?

'What's that then, Jim?'

'I'm gay. I'm living with a fella.'

Eric's surprise overwhelmed him. It was not just the nature of what had been revealed, but the very fact of its revelation. He looked at Jim, then around the room, then at Jim again. He had not the slightest idea how to respond. Jim continued to stare at him.

'Say summat for God's sake.'

'I don't know what to say, Jim.'

'Don't you like queers then? Is that it?'

'Good God no, I've got no strong feelings either way … I mean, well, best of luck to you Jim; I'm glad you're ….. you're settled.'

Jim laughed. 'Well, that's a novel way of putting it. At least you don't have Tony's homophobia.'

Eric didn't consider himself homophobic in the slightest. He'd come across a few gays in his career; there'd been one on his staff. How people lived their lives was their own concern. He didn't have a problem with the physical act, for it was beyond his comprehension and remained private. It was the growing tendency for public expressions of masculine affection that he found disturbing – there was a couple in Leamington who held hands while walking down the Parade, and once he'd seen them exchange kisses, causing him to turn away in embarrassment. And the domestic side of gay love he found bizarre in the extreme – two men choosing bed linen, having breakfast in bed together, making joint visits to parents. The image came of Jim cosying up to his partner on the settee while they watched TV, or discussed recipes – Jim, of all people!

'I can assure you I have no problems with …. with the way you are,' – Jim snorted at this – 'It's just that I had no idea; I mean, when we were students …..'

'Oh, I'd hardly admitted it to myself, back then. Your Viv had an idea though: perceptive woman, your Viv.'

'Viv knew? She never told me.' As soon as the words were out, Eric regretted them. In a successful marriage there were no secrets.

'Well, it was a long time ago. Anyway, talking of our student days, I've always wanted to ask you summat.'

'What's that, then?

'That last pub crawl we had; you know, when you got pissed out of you brains, and Nige had to carry you back to the flat.'

'What about it?'

'How much do you remember about it? I never got to see you afterwards, except the time I came to your cottage, and Viv didn't seem to want to talk about Leeds then.'

Eric found this new Jim, the conversationalist, the one enquiring about others memories, a little disconcerting. But at least his question gave an opportunity to talk about something other than his sexual orientation.

'I don't remember a lot, nothing after being in the Hyde Park. I don't know what happened, really. Reckon I must have been sickening for something before we started drinking. Why do you ask?'

'Oh, just curious. I suppose Viv told you about what happened after you left?'

'What d'you mean? You just carried on up the Headingley Lane pubs, didn't you? Then you lot went to Sweats and she went back to her flat.'

'That's right. I bet Viv gave you a hard time the next day, eh? She never did like blokes getting pissed.'

'No, she was very reasonable about it, actually.'

'*Was* she, now?'

'Yes. What's all this about, Jim?' Eric felt the first flickering of annoyance at the interrogation.

'Nothing, nothing. Just re-living old times. You and Viv are all right, I suppose?'

'What do you mean by that?'

'Just fascinated by long marriages; they're a rarity these days. And Viv was a cracking bird, even a queer could see that. She still is. I bet you've had to fight off a few predators, eh?'

Eric stood up.

'I'm going to help Alan carry the drinks. Make sure our seats aren't grabbed.'

Emerging from the ladies, Vivienne wasn't ready to join the others. Although Jim's revelation had served to distract her from the griping apprehension from which she'd been suffering, the relief was but temporary, and it had returned with renewed vigour when Alan announced Nigel's imminent return. She could do with a brandy, but to have asked for one would only have drawn attention to her malaise and provoked expressions of husbandly concern from Eric. She couldn't cope with that. Whenever she was on edge Eric's well-meaning ministrations had the effect of driving her to near screaming pitch.

Walking on to the balcony she noticed an unoccupied table at the far end: it had only two chairs against it, the others having evidently been purloined by members of an adjacent all-girl party. She hurried towards the table and sat. Her position afforded a bird's-eye view of the crowd below: she spotted Alan and Eric waiting to be served at the bar and Jim sitting alone, no doubt impatient for his drink. She found that when she sat back in her chair she was invisible to most of those below, but she still had a view of the pub doors. Thus seated, she would have advance warning of Nigel's entrance, and time to compose herself before joining them all. She might even have sight of Nigel's expression, perhaps some indication of his state of mind, though probably not: she knew that in public he always ensured that his features were composed.

'Is this chair taken?' She was addressed by a young woman dressed in black trousers and a matching low-cut shirt: she had long straight burnished auburn hair with blonde streaks, and she was impeccably made up. When Vivienne confirmed that it was not, the young woman grabbed it and carried it to the adjacent table where she was greeted effusively by her friends.

Vivienne, notwithstanding her anxieties, found herself observing and listening to the young women. In fact, on close observation, some of them were not in the first flush of youth – the oldest was perhaps in her early forties, with the taut, expressionless features of one who had her first encounter with botox. Their style of dress was eclectic, the one common factor being that they all displayed amounts of breast varying from a discreet hint of cleavage to a brazen display of voluptuousness. All had sleek, shiny hair and complexions that spoke of careful maintenance. Objectively, Vivienne could appreciate their physical attractiveness. She was careful with her own appearance, made the best of her remaining assets, and was philosophical about those that

154

had diminished. But, looking at the young women, she felt a twinge of regret that she couldn't flaunt the amount of bare flesh which they did with such seeming insouciance. Not that she would ever have done so, but it would be nice to have the option. For a moment she felt as she did when her daughters paid their rare visits, slightly faded.

They were drinking heartily, with far less discretion than the way her generation had been raised to believe was seemly, apart from those ardent feminists who'd taken pride in downing pints. They seemed to be on white wine or cocktails. They spoke loudly, in accents that were not quite BBC, interrupting each other, talking over each other. She picked up on one thread of their conversation: it concerned various male colleagues; their attitudes to them were dismissive, verging occasionally towards contempt. It belied the sexiness of their appearance. They would no doubt claim that they dressed to assert themselves, not to attract men. Vivienne was aware of the phenomenon of Girl Power, and had dismissed it as unworthy of the serious feminism of her contemporaries in the 1970s, but these girls evidently had pride in their gender, a pride made manifest by the choice of clothes which shouted 'This is me! Take it or leave it!'

A burst of raucous laughter followed a monologue from one of the younger women which had been liberally laced with four-letter words. They seemed not to need charm; they probably saw it as false, manipulative. They made no enquires regarding each other's welfare and they were totally engaged with the present moment and the immediate future. How old did you have to be, thought Vivienne, before one's friends started to say 'How are you?' or 'Do you remember the time when?'

155

Another woman joined the party: she stood greeting her friends, then noticed Vivienne sitting alone. She turned to her.

'Are you staying long?' she said.

Vivienne started. 'Not much longer. Why?'

'Well, I noticed you haven't got a drink, so I thought maybe you'd be leaving soon. Like, we're in for a long session, and I'd like your chair if you've finished with it.'

There was no 'Please', no 'Would you mind', Vivienne noted. It probably wasn't deliberate insolence, just a demonstration of the modern patois from which expressions of manners were absent. For some reason she felt less confident than she might have had the remark been made by a young man. She had to force herself to say that she would only be a few moments, if she, the woman, wouldn't mind standing for a little while more.

'Whatever,' was the response to that, and the young woman turned to her friends. Vivienne overheard her say that the old bitch didn't wasn't going to leave yet. This shook her: the remark wasn't intended for her to hear, but the fact that it had been made flew in the face of her assumptions about female solidarity. Eric always maintained that manners had declined, impatience had grown, and 'old' was used as a term of abuse. Certainly some of the young now seemed to resent the old with a vehemence that was frightening. She remembered Imogen's peroration during her visit last Christmas –'Your fucking generation had it made, mum: free education, full employment, affordable houses, jobs for life, and now dad's got a nice fat final-salary index-linked pension. Don't you *dare* criticise us! *We're* not having it so easy.'

Was it ever thus, she wondered? There had always been a generation clash, certainly since the the 50s, but was it ever as overt, as in-your-face? Were I and my friends so aggressive to strangers of our parents' age, she wondered? She thought back – no, surely our youth revolution had been a gentle affair? Our parents' attitudes and lifestyles had been mildly derided, and things they did seemed cold and stilted, but there was no hatred, and by the time we reached our thirties a rapprochement had been achieved. We certainly didn't envy them, whereas today's thirty-somethings obviously resent the trappings of comfort that our generation have taken such pains to acquire. And they are so supremely confident, regardless of their abilities! Do they have any self doubt? Do they ever experience guilt?

Despite herself, Vivienne found herself envying them. The folk-memory was wrong: the late 60s had not been liberating for women. Girls were expected to be sweetly submissive, to sit quietly rolling joints for their men, to provide food when the munchies set in, to provide the free love which their partners demanded. The pill had liberated men, not women, for it had freed them from responsibility. Not that Vivienne had ever been the archetypal hippie chick, she was far too assertive for that, but neither had she participated in the burgeoning hedonism of the times. It was partly guilt, of course, she'd still had a lingering adherence to the mores of her upbringing; that, and partly that Eric had been so reasonable, so undemanding. Then, by the time she was the age of these young women, she was married, bringing up a family, regretting that she'd never cast her net wider on the waters of experience when she'd had the chance.

But her envy was not just for the life they had before them, it was visceral, for she was observing them from across the chasm of the menopause. Vivienne had not found the change the liberating experience that Germaine Greer had claimed it could be. It wasn't just the hot flushes, the clumsiness, the growing obsession with health fads, the flawed complexion, the creped neckline, the disappearing breasts. She could have coped with all that, had her libido petered out along with her periods. But it hadn't; she was still a sexual and sensual being. The playground of the body wasn't just the provenance of the under-50s. Her capacity for pleasure and enjoyment was undiminished – if anything it had deepened. But it was hypothetical, for opportunities no longer came along, at least, not those that her innate fastidiousness would allow her to grasp. Watching these young women she remembered, with sad clarity, what it was like to be new.

The woman who'd spoken to her was standing by her companions, still complaining loudly about her need for a seat and glancing at Vivienne. Her friends expressed sympathy. Vivienne's envy of them was subsumed by a growing contempt for their slang-ridden ungrammatical mode of expression. For heaven's sake, these were professional women, yet seemingly unable to string a sentence together correctly. Again, she had to concede that Eric might be right: these, he would say, are the products of the education system post 1975, with no grounding in grammar, with little basic history or geography or foreign languages, in fact no bloody general knowledge at all. He would say they'd been propelled into their chosen professions by rigorous grounding in vocational studies at one of the newer universities where they'd been trained to memorise and regurgitate facts but not to think, analyse, synthesise, nor even read outside the narrow confines of the syllabus. They were now on the career ladder, motivated by money, conspicuous consumers, aware of their rights and affronted by any attempts to restrict their individual freedom to do whatever they liked regardless of the effect on others. Did they, she wondered, have a thought for their collective future? Were they concerned about environmental degradation, global warming, the erosion of the welfare state and civil liberties? Listening to them, it seemed to Vivienne that they had no such concerns. She never encountered women like these in the library, nor amongst the members of her reading group. She felt a wave of familiar disquiet: despite all her efforts to keep in touch, the world was moving on, the torch had passed to a new generation that she didn't understand. She'd experienced this unease when the youthful Tony Blair had first been elected. To see policemen as boys was bad enough, but politicians should be older, wiser. It was why she'd found John Major so comforting – until she realised that he was of her generation.

Enough of this. She stood up and tapped the shoulder of the standing woman.

'Here,' she said, 'Judging by the speed at which you're consuming your wine I think you might have need of this chair before too long. I'm so sorry to have kept you waiting.'

The woman stared at her, her face registering blank amazement.

'Right,' she said eventually.

Vivienne smiled at her sweetly.

'And a pleasant evening to you,' she said, and walked away along the balcony. Pausing at the top of the stairs she saw Nigel's blonde head amongst the throng by the door. She hurried down in order to reach the table before he did.

'I've got you one in,' said Alan as Nigel took his seat. 'You've sorted Tony out, then?'

'Well, I've delivered him to the hotel, but he's got problems way beyond my ability to solve. This is some place, Al.'

'Haven't you been here before, then?'

'It was in the process of refurbishment about the time I left London. I've heard about it, of course, and –'

'What did you mean about Tony's problems?' Vivienne interrupted.

'Oh, he's not a well man. I can remember this place when it actually was a – '

'What do you mean, not a well man?' It was Jim's turn to interrupt.

Nigel sipped his half of Fullers.

'It would appear that he's an alcoholic,' he said.

'Christ!' said Jim.

'Bloody hell!' said Alan, 'Are you sure?'

'How did you find that out?' asked Eric, 'Did he admit it?'

'He didn't have to. His briefcase contained a bottle of vodka, half empty. Hence his lapses of memory. Look, I really would like to forget about him for the rest of the evening. He's caused enough disruption for one day. Where are we headed after this, Al?'

Alan was only too ready to turn the conversation away from Tony. 'Well,' he said, 'I thought we might take a break from boozing for a while. We can stroll up to St Pauls, then across the Millennium Bridge and head for Borough. There are two more pubs there I'd like you to see. Then we can decide where we're going to eat.'

'Sounds good to me,' said Nigel, 'Are you up to the walk though, Al? It's still damned hot.'

'Of course I am. Christ, Nigel, you're like a mother hen.'

In fact he was feeling much better. Tony's removal from the scene, topped by the revelation that he also was a sick man, had acted as a schadenfreud-induced tonic.

'That's an excellent plan,' said Eric, 'We've never seen the Millennium Bridge, have we, Viv?'

Vivienne had been sitting deep in thought throughout the exchange. She started.

'So Tony's memory's been affected, has it?' she said, to groans from Alan and Jim, 'Has he forgotten about … well, is it like dementia, can he remember the distant past but not what happened yesterday?'

For the first time since entering, Nigel looked at her, and retained her gaze.

'Not quite like dementia. His memory comes and goes. There are some things in the distant past he appears to remember very clearly, in very great detail.'

Vivienne, whose arm had been resting on the table, jerked suddenly and knocked over Jim's glass. Beer splattered over the surface and began to drip on the floor. A foursome standing close to them took prompt evasive action and one of their number made a remark, intended to be overheard, concerning senile delinquency.

'I'm sorry, Jim,' she said, 'I'll go and get you another.'

Jim said she wasn't to worry, he'd get it.

'No, I'll go,' she said, 'I haven't got a drink myself.'

'I'll come and help you,' said Nigel.

'Viv seems a bit strung out', said Jim, 'What's bothering her?

'Yeah, I noticed that,' said Alan, 'Didn't she really want to come on this jaunt?'

161

'She's all right,' said Eric shortly.

'She doesn't seem to like talking about Leeds,' said Alan, 'I always thought she enjoyed herself there, I mean, she was –'

'So, Jim,' said Eric, 'What sort of job do you reckon Gordon Brown will make of things?'

'I'm not holding out any hopes,' said Jim gloomily, 'Despite all the hype he's just as big a free-marketeer as fuckin' Blair. Look at this lot –' he gestured at the youthful drinkers around them – 'Christ, ten years of a Labour government and look at them – all on bloody great bonuses just for shuffling money around. Mark my words, the whole edifice will come crumbling down soon, and it won't be soon enough for me.'

'Still forecasting the collapse of capitalism, are you?'

'Course I am. The gap between rich and poor has widened, hasn't it? And the NHS is being sold off, planning laws are being loosened, training's being farmed out to private industry, trades unions shat on, illegal wars. I dunno why I'm surprised. This is what always happens with Social Democrats in power.'

'Come on, Jim, back in Harold Wilson's time you used to rant about the Prices and Incomes policy. You said it curtailed free collective bargaining. You can't have it both ways, either you have a free market or a planned economy.'

'That's a dichotomy you get when you try to manage capitalism'. Jim's features had become animated. 'It's just one example of the contradictions inherent in the system. A prices and incomes policy would be valid as part of a truly planned economy. In fact it'd be an essential step on the road to true socialism, and I'll tell you something else –'

'Oh God, spare us the Marxism, mate,' said Alan, 'It was the bloody Marxists in the unions who landed us in the shit in the 1970s, and we all know what that led to, don't we? Bleedin' Margaret Thatcher, and we haven't recovered from her yet.'

'If Wilson had had the guts to introduce a socialist programme then there wouldn't have been the need for union action.' Jim's voice was raised: those standing close to their table stopped talking and eyed him suspiciously. 'His government was a fuckin' disaster.'

'Easy to say in retrospect,' said Alan, 'but there's one thing Wilson did that we should all be grateful for; he kept us out of the Vietnam War, didn't he? If he hadn't managed that, all of us could have ended up in body bags in the Mekong Delta.'

'You're right, Al,' said Eric, 'and that government introduced some much needed social reforms, like the abolition of hanging, easier divorces, easier abortion, relaxation of theatre censorship –'

'Just bloody libertarianism,' snorted Jim, 'bloody Roy Jenkins, right-wing pillock.'

'The most progressive Home Secretary of the last century,' asserted Eric, 'and of course, there was the decriminalisation of homosexuality.'

He looked meaningfully at Jim, who scowled. He emptied his glass.

'I don't remember any of you lot being very enthusiastic about it at the time,' he said, 'All you lot were interested in was pop ephemera and trendy films.'

'But there were some bloody good films,' said Alan. He'd noticed the looks being directed towards them by the surrounding drinkers and decided it was time to steer Jim away from the class struggle. 'Remember *Billy Liar*? And

Darling? And *Alfie*? Why do they never show any of those on the box? All you get are endless repeats of *Four Weddings and a Funeral* and *The Full Monty*.

'Would the fact that the Julie Christie was in two of those have anything to do with your fond memories?' asked Eric.

'Well, she was an ace-looking girl, wasn't she? Even you must admit to that, eh Jim?'

Jim looked at Alan sharply before remembering that he was not yet party to his secret.

'Aye, yes, she was a looker,' he conceded, 'Anyone fancy another?'

'Viv's getting you one Jim, had you forgotten?

Nigel and Vivienne stood shoulder to shoulder at the bar, staring fixedly ahead, forced into physical contact by the crush around them, but miles apart. They'd not spoken since leaving the table. Both had questions burning to be asked; each dreaded the answer the other might give, neither dared break the silence that cocooned them in the midst of the shouting, laughing throng. Of all the possible permutations of events that could have happened, this, thought Vivienne, had to be the worse. If anyone had said that this long awaited reunion would destroy all his cherished memories, thought Nigel, then he would have laughed in his face. Though neither of them knew it, both were struck simultaneously by the same thought – that they were embarrassed, and that though quarrels can be made up, forgotten, embarrassment, unless lanced by explanations, always remained in the memory.

'Yes?' A barman directed the question at Nigel.

Vivienne chose to answer. 'A pint of bitter and a double brandy, please.'

It provided some sort of opening, thought Nigel. 'I've never known you drink spirits,' he said, turning to face her.

She continued to stare ahead.

'Shall we talk, Viv?'

'Should we? To what end?'

'Come on, Viv, we've got about another three hours in each others company. Do we then part with everything left unsaid? We'll probably never see each other again'

The barman presented the drinks. Vivienne gulped at her brandy.

'All right. But how? We can't leave the others.'

'We can detach ourselves on the walk over the bridge; if necessary lose them for a while.'

She took another sip of brandy.

'I thought maybe you might have access to a safe house nearby,' she said.

The remark was made without a smile, but the flash of her old acid humour, and her reference to his past gave him a flicker of hope that something could be salvaged.

'We'd better get back to the others,' he said, 'Old Jim'll be getting edgy without a pint in his hand.'

Chapter 12

The dome of St Paul's glowed orange against the black cloud to its east, highlighted by the re-emergent sun that had begun its slow summer descent towards the rooftops of the West End. This view of the cathedral, framed by the buildings along Fleet Street, never ceased to move Alan. Unchanging against the backdrop of the new office towers of the City, it produced in him a welling of pride in being a Londoner. He could never see it without thinking of the photograph of the dome standing amidst the smoke of the blitz. The phrase 'a symbol of defiance' had become hackneyed through overuse, but it had resonance for Alan, who'd been raised on the stories told by his mother of the camaraderie of the East Enders, of the nights spent in the tube stations, and of the part played by his father who, injured at Dunkirk, had spent the remainder of his war as a firewatcher. He had never known his dad. His parents survived a near miss from a V2 rocket and had been patiently awaiting a brighter future when, just after Alan's birth, his father had been carried off by emphysema in the bleak snow-bound tightly-rationed winter of 1947.

Eric and Jim were walking alongside him, and he was about to tell them his thoughts, but decided against it. London pride had been handed down to him, but not

166

to them. Eric's family's only real wartime hardship in Henley had been to have an evacuee boarded on them. As for Jim – well, if there had been air raids on Stoke, he'd never spoken of them. Nigel and Vivienne, walking several yards behind, would be even less likely to empathise: the Yorkshire Dales and Bury-St-Edmunds were as far removed from the cockney experience as it was possible to be.

Lost to the conversation between his companions, and thinking of his father, Alan was overtaken by nostalgia for a past he'd never known, the war, the 1930s, big bands, crooners. It was almost as though he remembered it, life in England 'before the war', that phrase with which his mother's generation had seemed to begin all their reminiscences. Perhaps it was the result of his childhood: when not playing with his friends in the bomb-sites that still remained in Woolwich well into the 1950s, he'd spent hours listening to his mother's old 78s on her wind-up gramophone. God, he could smell it now, the brass and felt, hear the hiss as the needle hit the record, feel his fingers fiddling with the spares kept in the hidden tray at the side of the machine. That gramophone had accompanied him on his journey into adolescence, when his mother's Fred Astaire and Al Bowlly records had been cast aside in favour of the Everly Brothers and Buddy Holly, finally to be discarded when the arrival of 45s necessitated the purchase of a Dansette.

His mother, and his childhood, had been much in his thoughts in recent months.

'Do you think much about the 1940s?' he blurted out.

Eric and Jim ceased their conversation.

'Bloody hell,' said Jim, 'We were only four when they ended; what are you on about?' He hiccupped.

Alan stopped. The pavements were almost empty, permitting stationary discourse. The others stopped as well.

'I suppose I mean our childhoods,' he said.

'Not a lot,' said Jim, 'Why, do you?'

'Yeah, increasingly. Things that have gone, mainly.'

'Interesting, Al,' said Eric, 'What sort of things?'

'Oh, you know, things like Brylcream, and Meccano, and Spangles – remember them? And 78 records, and Sturmley-Archer gears on yer bike.'

'That's right!' said Eric eagerly, 'Remember Fry's Five Boys chocolate bars? And packets of five fags –'

'Yeah, Park Drive, weren't they?'

'I thought they were Player's Weights. And The Eagle comic – did you used to listen to Dan Dare on Radio Luxembourg –'

'Yes! Remember 'Keynsham', spelt K E Y N S H A M? – who was that fellow?'

'Horace Batchelor, and his fool-proof method of winning the pools.' Jim joined the reminiscence. 'Don't forget the bad things, though.'

'Trust you, you miserable old sod,' said Alan, 'What bad things?'

'The cane at school for a start, and darned socks, and the nit-nurse, and no heating, and one bath a week, if that – Christ we must have all stank.'

'What are you three in earnest conversation about?' said Nigel: he and Vivienne had caught them up.

'Al's been reminding us about the things that are no more,' said Eric, 'things from our childhood.'

'You'd be enjoying that sort of conversation then, wouldn't you?' said Vivienne.

Alan glanced at her. Blimey, she always did have a waspish side, but old Eric seemed to be really getting it in the neck today. Alan had always found Viv rather intimidating when at University; and he didn't feel up to having a heart-to-heart with her today, not like Jim had obviously had with her in the Cheshire Cheese. It now seemed to be Nige's turn, though looking at them they didn't have the demeanour of a couple who'd been interrupted in the middle of a tête-à-tête. In fact, Nige looked a bit downcast, and he hadn't been his usual urbane self since he'd rejoined the party in the Old Bank of England. Neither had he done what he was wont to do when discord threatened the party – he made no emollient remark to pre-empt the potential for bickering between husband and wife.

Alan decided to continue with his theme.

'We never used to talk about our childhoods when we were at university,' he said.

'Of course we didn't,' said Eric. 'It wouldn't have been cool, would it?'

'Look, let's get on, shall we?' Nigel intervened. 'We've a way to go before we cross the river.'

They crossed Farringdon Street and began the ascent of Ludgate Hill. Eric noticed that once again Nigel and Vivienne had fallen behind. At least it left him free to resume the conversation without wifely disparagement.

'What about hymns and prayers and passages from the bible?' he said.

'What are you on about now?' said Jim.

'I bet if I started singing a hymn you'd both be able to join in. And with prayers, and bible readings. And come to that, bits of poetry – *I wandered lonely as a cloud* – go on, Al, what's the next line?'

Alan obliged, somewhat breathlessly.

'What's your point?' asked Jim.

'We're probably the last generation to have a received culture in common. My kids might know a bit of that stuff, but their kids won't. It wasn't just things we learned at school, either. We all used to listen to the same radio and watch the same TV programmes, didn't we? Two Way Family Favourites and the Billy Cotton Band Show on Sundays, Hancock's Half Hour, The Goons, Sunday Night at the London Palladium –'

'Dinna have a TV in our house,' grunted Jim, 'not till the 60s anyway, when me mum heard about Coronation Street.'

Eric ignored him.

'The whole family used to sit round the TV and watch the same programmes,' he warmed to his theme, 'and talk about them the next day at school, and at work I reckon. It was a common culture, we all shared the same experiences. Even my mum and dad used to watch 6.5 Special and Top of the Pops with me, though they weren't too keen on *Oh Boy* – Cliff Richard was far too racy for them. But you see what I mean? When did things start to fragment?'

'It's all bloody ephemera, what you're talking about,' said Jim. 'I'm more concerned about real issues. If it's the so called fragmentation of society you're getting at, then it always was fractured. Thatcher made it worse of course, and since then ….'

Eric shut out Jim's all-too familiar monologue, delivered, he noticed, in words that had begun to be slurred. He was mentally developing his own thesis. When did it all start to break up, and why? How did we get to the state we're in now, a plethora of discordant and conflicting sub-cultures, people shut in their little boxes, zappers in hand, flitting between scores of indifferent TV channels, kids doing the same in their bedrooms when they weren't texting or being seduced in internet chat-rooms? And those same kids, owing allegiance to separate tribes – what happened to adolescent solidarity, when we were all dressed alike, were all turned on by the same bands? When was it that there became too much choice? When did Englishness cease to be? And what made it happen? Affluence, mobility and multiculturalism amongst other things, he supposed. Nobody stayed in one place any more – his was the first generation to move away from home in any numbers – had things begun to change even then?

Why were the events of his youth so well defined? He could remember exactly where he was, whom he was with, how he felt, when nuclear oblivion threatened over Cuba, when Kennedy and Churchill died, when *Sergeant Pepper* was released, when the Soviets invaded Czechoslovakia, when the small step was taken for man and a giant leap for mankind. But the decades since had passed in a haze: he was alive to it all that happened at the time, of course, the Winter of Discontent, the Falklands War, the poll tax riots, the fall of the Berlin wall, but all these events prompted no personal flashbulb memories, evoked no personal history, with the exception of 9/11 of course. Sometimes he felt as though a great chasm had opened up between what and where he was now, and who and where he had once been. The previous week he'd been looking through his old photograph albums: there'd been a snap he'd taken of Henley High Street when he was seventeen or so – it had the appearance of a bygone age, few cars, old-fashioned shop frontages, old men in flat caps and old women in headscarves, young mothers pushing ornate prams. It was more akin to the 1930s than to today. Yet it was the start of the sixties – though of course there was yet to be the Chatterley trial and the release of the Beatles' first LP.

It would be good to get Nigel's perspective on this. He was conscious that half the day had gone and he'd yet to have a proper conversation with his old flat-mate. He turned, ready to address him – (beside him Jim had lapsed into silence) – and noticed that Alan had fallen behind and seemed to be making heavy weather of the slight incline. Nigel and Vivienne had caught him up.

'Hang on, Jim, let's wait for the others,' he said, 'Looks like old Al's flaking again.'

'Are you all right, old chap?' Nigel was asking.

'Yeah.' Alan was gasping for breath. 'It's just this bloody heat and this bloody hill.'

'Have you developed asthma in your old age, Al?' Eric's question was genuine: his deputy head had developed the affliction in his late fifties and had to take early retirement. However, as was so often the case, his expression of concern was misconstrued, for Alan's response was to tell him not to take the piss.

'Can you make it up to the cathedral?' asked Nigel, 'You can have a sit-down on the steps, have a rest.'

'Of course I can,' said Alan, waving away Nigel's proffered arm.

The party walked slowly into the small piazza in front of the cathedral. Suddenly, workaday London was left behind; the piazza and the steps leading to the entrance were thronged with crowds distinguished by their generational, ethnic, linguistic and sartorial diversity. Alan found a space on the lowest step and sat down with a gasp of relief. Nigel, Eric and Vivienne clustered round him, uncertain what to do next.

Jim was staring around.

'It's the first time I've ever been here,' he said.

His admission diverted Eric's attention from Alan.

'You must be joking.'

'No, why should I? Never had any reason to come to London.'

'But, St Paul's, for God's sake! I thought everyone had been here, if only once.'

'Well, I 'anna.'

'Bloody hell. Hear that, Nige? Jim's never been here before.'

'Well, one does tend to avoid the tourist-traps,' said Nigel. 'I've not been here for –oh, must be twenty years'. He glanced at Vivienne. There was a flicker of acknowledgement before she looked away.

'That means you won't have seen Paternoster Square since its make-over,' said Eric. 'Hey, why don't we go and have a look while Al gets his breath back? Is that ok by you, Al?'

Alan nodded.

'I'll stay with him,' said Vivienne. Turning towards Eric, she hissed, 'He's as white as a sheet, don't you notice *anything*? We can't leave him alone. You three go if you want, but don't be too long.'

'Are you sure, Viv?' said Nigel.

'Yes.'

As the three left, Nigel giving her a backward glance and the hint of a wave, Vivienne turned to Alan, still seated, still panting slightly.

'Right, Al,' she said, 'What are we going to do with you?'

Nigel's head was full of the conversation that he and Vivienne had yet to have, but as they entered Paternoster Square surprise at its transformation took him aback, giving temporary relief from the incessant re-running of the scenario of forty years before. When he was last here the Square had been hideous, a monument to 1960s architectural brutalism. Now it was lighter, more open, the central piazza on a human scale, the surrounding buildings an eclectic mix of office blocks of varying heights and styles, built in a mixture of Portland stone, granite, marble, slate and brick, set off by the reconstructed Temple Bar and the narrow Corinthian column topped by an urn covered in gold leaf. It was a hotchpotch, but somehow it worked. And it was alive with people.

'What do you reckon, then?' asked Eric.

'It's certainly an improvement on what it was before,' Nigel replied, 'and I like the way it's brought to life by all the retail outlets. Somehow it's comforting to see shops like Boots; they save the place from being a mere heritage site. Though,' he added, 'I can't see what city workers would want with Black's Outdoor Leisure.'

'Especially those bastards in there,' said Jim, pointing to the Stock Exchange. 'How long's that been here?'

'It moved from Threadneedle Street a few years ago,' began Eric, but Jim suddenly had more pressing needs to attend to.

'Christ, I'm aching for a slash,' he said, 'I bet the bloody developers didn't think about public bogs, did they?'

'They probably had no idea that visitors would have consumed six pints in as many hours,' Nigel retorted,

'You're best bet is to try one of the shops – look, there's a Starbucks. You might have to buy a coffee first, though.'

'Bugger that,' said Jim, and hurried away.

'He's certainly sinking them, isn't he?' said Nigel.

'Yes. Look, Nige, before Al got queasy we were talking about childhood memories, and I got to thinking about when it was that society changed – you know, when it was that everything seemed to fragment, no sense of community, no common culture, everyone doing their own thing, d'you know what I mean? It wasn't like that in the 60s, was it? When do you think it all started to go pear-shaped?'

Nigel was relieved that Eric wished to talk in abstractions. Not that he should be surprised; in their flat, when students, Eric had always insisted in trying out his woolly sociological theories after an evening in the Original Oak. It was one of the things that Nigel had always found rather irritating about him, not that he ever let on. Eric had about him a boyish enthusiasm which verged on naivety, and it still seemed to be with him. He was obviously obsessed with the 1960s, one of those sad cases who had never moved on. He wondered how Eric had managed to make it to be a head-teacher – presumably enthusiasm helped when in front of an interview panel, but he imagined he must have been subject to barely-disguised mockery from his pupils, and probably also from his staff.

He was not in the mood to humour him.

'On the contrary, I think that many of society's present ills had their origin in the 60s.'

'How do you make that out? It was a wonderful decade.'

'It had its moments, I grant you. But wasn't it then that our obsession with celebrity and fashion and shopping began? Think about it, Eric: Harold Wilson snuggling up to the Beatles, colour supplements full of the doings of models and footballers and photographers? Not very different to Blair inviting Liam Gallagher to Downing Street, and all the rubbish in *Hello* magazine. Swap George Best with David Beckham: what's the difference? The only difference is that we were young and gullible enough to take it all in. Some of us have grown up since then.'

Eric looked crestfallen. Nigel decided to reign back.

'I agree that the 60s started it all, and we were lucky enough to be in at the start. But ever since then that decade has been constantly re-cycled for each new generation, each one of which thinks it's as unique as ours did. However, I do sense that an entirely new culture, if you can call it that, is emerging, and one that we can't understand.'

'What's that, then?'

'It's based on disposability. Look at all these people snapping away with their digital cameras – how many of them will download the results onto a computer, let alone get them printed? In our day we'd have taken a few shots and carefully stuck the prints into an album. I bet you still look at the photos we took when we were at Leeds, don't you?'

Eric acknowledged that he did.

'Well, this lot take so many images that they cease to be significant: they might look at them once on their cameras, then delete them without a thought. And emails – how many of them are printed out? They're read and instantly disposed of. I still have letters written by my father and grandfather, and they're a marvellous record of their times. God help future historical researchers, say I.

The same with music. I wonder how long the kids'll keep all the stuff they download on their iPods, or whatever they call 'em? Imagine having a music collection without record sleeves to cherish!'

'You're right,' said Eric. 'I've still got all the original Beatles and Stones LPs; mind you a lot of the sleeves are a bit tattered and beer stained.'

'I bet you've got them displayed on a wall, eh? In your study, perhaps?'

'No,' Eric said sorrowfully, 'Viv said they looked tacky.'

I know she did, thought Nigel. Poor old Eric, he was still a bit wet. At university it had taken about six months for Nigel to become aware of it, fascinated as he'd first been by his flat-mate's apparent savoir-faire and his immersion in the movements and trends of the day. But he'd gradually come to realise that Eric was a dilettante, a follower not a leader, accepted with benign amusement by the more avant-garde in the University union. Eric's puppyish enthusiasm for every new rock band, every new fad, every new hairstyle, had begun to grate – his adoption of a flowered tunic, skin-tight velvet trousers and a headband Nigel had regarded as risible in the extreme. Though nothing had ever been said, both had become aware that by their final year Nigel had become the dominant personality to whom Eric deferred. But there was nothing really to dislike about Eric, and Nigel had refrained from ever challenging him, with the result that their time together passed amicably enough. But now, together briefly alone for the first time in forty years, Nigel found he couldn't connect with Eric's regressive excitations.

He resorted to commenting on the architecture, and was relieved when Jim re-appeared, looking more comfortable.

'We'd better get back to Alan and Viv,' he said.

Alan was still slumped on the cathedral steps. Vivienne was perched beside him.

'How're you feeling, Al?' asked Nigel.

'Better now. Sorry to be such a drag.'

'He's not up to walking all the way to the next pub, though, are you Al?' said Vivienne, in a tone that brooked no dissent. 'Look, we've decided that it would be best for him to take a taxi across to Borough.'

She stood up and brushed down her dress.

'Are you sure he's up to carrying on?' Eric muttered to her, 'Might it be best if he went back to the hotel for a rest?'

'No. This tour means a lot to him, can't you see that? Only two more pubs to go. But someone had better go with him in the taxi – not Nigel, he's already had to cope with Tony. You go with him, Eric. Nigel knows where we're heading for, don't you, Nigel?'

She looked at Nigel meaningfully.

'Well, why don't we all go by taxi?' said Eric.

'No, I want to walk over the Millennium Bridge: Nigel can lead us.'

'But I want to see the bridge as well –'

'Oh, don't be so selfish, Eric. You can come back and see it tomorrow. We've plenty of time before our train. Anyway, it might be best if Jim went with you in the taxi, just in case Al has another turn.'

'I wish you buggers wouldn't talk as though I wasn't here,' Alan said plaintively.

'What do you think, Jim?' asked Nigel.

'Suits me. I'm getting a bit knackered myself. Could do with another pint, as well.'

'That's settled, then.' Vivienne was emphatic. 'We'll see you in the – what's the name of the pub, Al?'

'The Market Porter. Have you been there, Nige?'

'Know it well, old boy.'

'Come on, then, you old sod,' said Jim, pulling Alan to his feet.

Nigel and Vivienne watched as the three walked slowly back to the top of Ludgate Hill. They didn't speak until they were safely in a taxi and it had driven off.

Nigel turned to Vivienne. 'Is that serendipity or what?'

'Opportunity-seizing combined with assertiveness on my part,' she said. 'You used to say it was what made me exciting to be with.'

In the taxi, Eric was quiet. He was angry. Over the years he'd resigned himself to Vivienne's disparaging remarks, but these were usually made in private. Today, though, she had no compunction about demeaning him in front of his friends. What had got into her? Ever since Tony had left the party she'd been tense and brittle. He was regretting having cajoled her into attending in the first place: an all-male gathering would have been much more relaxed. He was beginning to feel relieved that the two of them were booked into the Hilton – perhaps he could persuade her to retire early, leaving him free to enjoy a last drink or two with the others at the Tavistock. Not that Alan would be up to it, though.

He looked at Alan. His colour had returned, but there were still beads of sweat on his brow. Jim was quizzing him about the next pub – would it be a real boozer, not a pretentious yuppie bar like the last? Alan assured him that it would – things were different south of the river.

That was certainly the case. Despite his anger, Eric registered the change as soon as they crossed Southwark Bridge. The taxi dropped them in Borough High Street and into a different world. It was a mess: many of the shops were unoccupied and boarded up, the pavements were uneven where they were not broken, dubious-looking alleyways led off the road which was cluttered with traffic lights, yellow lines and hastily constructed pedestrian refuges, the whole dismal scene monitored by dozens of security cameras festooned over the street furniture. The few pedestrians were ill-clad, their faces either pinched or bloated. The all-pervasive odour of stale fried onions was trapped in the sultry air.

'Bloody hell, Al,' he said, 'What have you brought us to?'

'You're going to see a bit of Dickensian London; it's through here.' He indicated an art deco entrance bearing the legend 'Borough Market'.

'Are you up to walking it?'

'Yeah. It's only a few yards. We go through the market; you won't see any traders though. You have to be up early to catch them.'

He led them under the Victorian-style arched roof and they wandered between the shuttered market stalls. Eric said that he'd heard of the place, wasn't it the haunt of celebrity cooks? Alan confirmed that Jamie Oliver and Nigella Lawson were known to have purchased produce here, to which Jim responded that he bet they didn't do their own fuckin' shopping. Alan said the place that been under threat from redevelopment because of the upgrading of the Thameslink line, but that it had been saved, he thought.

'Why do you think it's worth saving?' demanded Jim, 'It's only a bloody market'.

'It's part of old London. Heritage and all that.'

Alan's response was spirited, an indication that he was feeling better, Eric thought. He wished *he* did: he was still smarting from the effects of Vivienne's vindictiveness and was wondering whether he dare challenge her about it when she and Nigel arrived. Probably best to wait till they were alone; he didn't want to risk further humiliation.

'Here we are, then,' said Alan as they emerged from the market. They were confronted with a homely looking pub, bedecked with hanging baskets.

'Christ, what's that smell?' said Jim.

'It's coming from Neil's Yard,' said Alan, 'Pity it's closed. They have a marvellous selection of cheeses. It's well worth a look inside.'

'Bugger that, I need a pint. It's my round – come on.'

'Hang on a sec, Jim. Do either of you recognise this place?'

'Why should I? Never been here before. It's just a tatty old street.'

'It's marvellously Dickensian,' said Eric, 'but why should we recognise it?'

'*Bridget Jones' Diary*,' said Alan. 'A scene from it was filmed here – the fight between Colin Firth and Hugh Grant, d'you remember?'

'Oh, right,' said Eric, 'Now if it was dark I might have –'

'For Christ's sake. let's get in the pub.' Jim was already heading for the door.

The Market Porter was almost empty. Jim looked around suspiciously, but was evidently mollified by the wooden floor, the sturdy unpretentious tables and the array of pint glasses on a shelf suspended from the ceiling over the bar. There was a large selection of beers, and a conspicuous lack of air conditioning.

'What d'you recommend?' he asked.

'Harvey's is as good as any,' said Alan, 'but I've had my fill. Mineral water for me, please.'

'And an orange juice for me,' added Eric, taking a seat.

Muttering about being accompanied by big girls' blouses, Jim made his way to the bar, returning to the table with the order and taking a defiant swig of his beer before sitting down. Eric observed with some amusement his demonstration of machismo, and observed that he would have thought big girls' blouses would have been to Jim's taste. It was an ill-advised remark; Jim glowered at him, and launched an attack.

'You never could take your ale, could you, Jackson? Not even at Leeds. Remember the state he got into on that last pub crawl, Al? Drunk as a fart after two pints, incapable after four.'

'Yeah, I'll never forget it,' said Al, 'Don't know who was the more pissed off, Viv or Nigel.'

'Tony was chuffed though, wasn't he? Made a great play for Viv once Eric here was out of the way, didn't he?'

'Yes, I vaguely remember that.'

'Old Viv seemed to quite enjoy it, didn't she? Reckon old Tony thought he was going to get his end away.' He took another swig, belched and grinned maliciously. 'Perhaps he did.'

'What are you on about, Jim?' said Alan, 'Viv left us when we went to Sweats, remember?'

'Yeah, she did. But Tony left soon after, didn't he? Wonder where he went to?'

Eric suddenly felt a wave of dislike for Jim. He'd forgotten about the occasional outbursts of malice that came from him in their student days. Eric had been in thrall to him then, but, given what he now knew, wasn't prepared to tolerate these ridiculous innuendos. What rubbish the bastard was spouting.

'I'm surprised you noticed what Viv did that night, after all, it wouldn't have been women you had your eye on, would it? He had other interests, you see, Al, but we didn't know about it at the time.'

Alan looked puzzled. Jim scowled, put down his glass with studied deliberation and leaned across the table, his face inches from Eric's.

'You always were a naïve wanker,' he sneered, 'What was Tony doing in Clarendon Road at five o'clock the next morning? And don't fuckin' come the wise-arse with me.'

'What the hell are you on about?'

'I saw him there.' Jim's voice was triumphant. 'I was out on one of me early morning strolls. I reckon he'd spent the night in the Henry Price.'

Eric laughed. His amusement was genuine. The fellow must be unhinged; he was certainly drunk. Tony with Viv! The prospect was farcical. He said as much.

'I know what I saw.'

'You're talking bullshit, Myatt.'

Even as he said it, a vague feeling of unease came over Eric. Then he forced himself to be rational – no, it was nonsense. Jim was obviously riled at his allusion to his homosexuality, and was just lashing out. If Tony had tried

183

one of his come-ons, Viv would have put him down like she always had. And she would have told him, Eric, about it. She always did

All this sniping was unfair on poor old Al, whose gaze was swivelling between him and Jim like a tennis spectator. Eric had no wish to continue this spat – probably best if he put some distance between him and Jim; he could do with some air anyway, it was stifling in this pub. He took two swallows of orange juice and stood up.

'I fancy a bit of fresh air,' he said. 'Thought I might walk back to the Millennium Bridge; I really want to see it – and I'll probably meet Nigel and Viv. It's easy to get to from here, is it, Al?'

'No problem. Just head along Stoney Street, through the Clink and follow your nose to the river. Can't miss it. Then follow the path west. But why break up the party?'

'I'll be back soon, Al.'

He left.

'What was all that about?' Alan asked Jim, 'What did he mean about you having other interests?'

It's good to be by myself for a while, Eric told himself. He'd forgotten how claustrophobic close contact with a large group could be. It was years since he'd been thus confined, not since his time in teaching, and even then he'd had the luxury of the headmaster's office to which he could escape. Since his retirement and the departure of the girls he'd led a rather solitary existence: Vivienne's days were spent at the library and many of her evenings with her literary friends. At first he'd enjoyed the freedom to potter alone about the house, to indulge his fancies, but after a while it began to pall, and sometimes he was haunted by bleak visions of what life would be were he ever to be widowed, for he had no close friends. Those morbid thoughts came to him most often when he woke, wanting to piss, at 2 am in the mornings.

Throughout his adult life he'd often experienced these dark nights of the soul. His self-esteem was at its lowest when the rest of the world slept. He'd worried about his effectiveness as a head teacher – in his guts he knew he lacked charisma, that diligence and enthusiasm were not in themselves enough for inspirational leadership. He'd suspected that his staff found him risible. There was, he knew, a rather silly man hidden by the carapace of mature professionalism from under which he'd faced the world. Now that shell had been removed. He'd hoped that today he'd find comfort in the company of those similarly freed from the trappings of office, but the day was being disappointing. He seemed unable to connect; his friends weren't responding in the way he'd expected, in the way he remembered they once had. It was understandable that Jim should be different, for he now inhabited a world beyond Eric's comprehension. But Nigel – there was a distance there, a reserve, coupled with a tendency to challenge the assumptions that Eric remembered the two of them once had shared. And Alan – even he seemed to be less cheery, more inclined to disagree; but perhaps this was due to the bug he seemed to have caught. As for Tony – well, Eric had written him off hours ago.

Distracted by his thoughts, he found he'd paid insufficient attention to Alan's directions, and found himself outside a large pub with outside seating overlooking the river. Alan hadn't mentioned a pub, had he? He'd said to make for the river – well, here he was, but there didn't seem to be a path going west alongside it. Had he gone wrong? He retraced his steps until he got back to the covered alley that housed the Clink museum – yes, he'd come through here, had mentally noted the origin of the term 'clink', so where had he gone wrong? He looked across the Thames, noticing for the first time the Gherkin amongst the more angular blocks on the opposite bank. London had become an exciting city to be in, he realised, and its river frontage compared favourably with those of Paris or Rome, cities with which, he was ashamed to realise, he was the more familiar. All those bloody school trips.

The tables outside the pub were filling up. He glanced at his watch; 7.30, the start of the long London Friday night. Looking at the youngsters sitting chatting and laughing, he supposed many of them would still be carousing well into the small hours and would think nothing of it. It occurred to him that in Leeds, back in the 60s, the pubs shut at 10.30, then it was usually fish and chips back at the flat. Apart from the occasional party, were they really the wild times that he thought he remembered?

He shook himself. At this rate he wouldn't make the Millennium Bridge in time to meet Nigel and Viv crossing it. He approached the nearest table, and diffidently asked one of the young men sitting there the way.

'Dunno, mate, sorry,' was the response, 'Never walk that way; come here by car, don't I?'

'Oh, I know,' said one of the females in the party, 'Like, you go down there – ' (she pointed away from the river) '- and under the road bridge, then there's a path takes you there.'

Despite her sentence ending with the rising inflexion that Eric so disliked, he thanked her profusely.

'No problem,' she said, and smiled at him.

Cheered by the affability of the contact and the smile of an attractive young woman, Eric followed her directions, and soon found himself by the river again, passing the Globe theatre. A crowd of teenagers were emerging from it noisily, a school party, he supposed, though they seemed to be unsupervised and spread over the pathway, the girls yelping and giggling, the boys guffawing, shoving each other, shouting insults. Suddenly they burst into song, clapping to the rhythm, before just as suddenly breaking into a run and heading off towards what Eric could now see was the footbridge. He envied them. Who wouldn't give all he had to be that age again, just for a few hours to be bright-eyed, loose-limbed, nimble-fingered, fleet of foot, and to feel immortal? Better still, to live in those days when everything was possible, but to know what you have since learned; to combine the wisdom of maturity with the vigour of a 17 year-old.

He reached the base of the bridge, mounted the steps and stood gazing along the length of the gleaming silver walkway towards the dome of St Paul's on the other side. The view was spoilt slightly by the mass of people on the bridge, solid phalanxes walking in both directions. Few seemed to be pausing to take in the scene.

He set off towards the north bank. Surely Nigel and Viv must be nearly over this side by now? Perhaps he'd missed them when he'd lost his way. Well, he'd walk to the middle and if he hadn't met them by then he'd turn back. The thought had barely left his consciousness when there was a break in the crowd ahead of him, and he saw them. They weren't walking. He saw what they were doing. He was rooted in shock, paralysed in disbelief. He could do nothing except wait for them to turn and see him.

Chapter 13

MILLENNIUM BRIDGE

They walked along the south side of St Paul's, unspeaking, not looking at each other, suddenly shy in each other's company; two elderly adolescents on a first date.

How do we start this? thought Nigel. It was he who said they must talk, but now he didn't know how to begin. The direct question would of course be ungentlemanly. He risked a glance at Vivienne; she was staring ahead, her features an unreadable mask. Was she waiting for him, was she dreading the question, afraid of giving the answer? Did he really wish to hear it? And when it was given, and if it was what he feared, what of afterwards? Could he retain his composure? Would he be able to tolerate the company of the others? Would he not rather slink away to mourn alone?

They turned to cross Carter Lane. Automatically, he reached to cup her elbow in his hand. Did he detect a flinch? She'd always been appreciative of his manners, unlike some women who'd mocked his courtesies as an affectation. It was in fact the converse: such behaviour had been instilled into him from the time he took his first steps. When accompanying a lady he would no more have walked on the inside of the pavement, or pushed ahead of her through a door, than he would have struck her, or sworn at her.

He let go her arm on reaching the other side. The memorial to the Blitz fire-fighters confronted them, smoke-blackened figures grasping a hosepipe that pointed towards the cathedral. They stopped and read the inscription on the plinth. It provided a conversational opening.

'Old Al's dad was a fire-fighter in the war,' Nigel said.

'Was he? I never knew that. Al never spoke much about his background, not to me anyway.'

'Strange, even though we weren't born during it, the war was very much part of our childhood, wasn't it? It was all our parents seemed to talk about. Then of course there were all the films in the 50s, remember *The Dam Busters*? And *Reach for the Sky*?'

'They were boys' films, Nigel. I was taken to see *Oklahoma!* and *Genevieve*.'

'So you did.' Nigel recalled that they'd had this cinematic conversation before, and the circumstances in which they'd had it. He looked at her: she evidently remembered the occasion, for she was blushing slightly.

'Of course, the war's history to our children's generation,' he said.

'And ancient history to our grandchildren,' she replied, then, 'Oh Nigel, I'm sorry, how tactless of me.'

'What d'you mean?'

''Going on about grandchildren when you ..... when .... Look, Nigel, you never did get to talk properly about Oscar; bloody Tony's antics interrupted you. I never really got the chance to say how sorry I am.'

Nigel seized the moment. 'Viv, we're not here to talk about Oscar. I'm more interested in what you appropriately called Tony's antics.'

For the first time since the others had left them, she looked directly into his eyes.

'I can't talk properly while we're walking,' she said, 'Is there anywhere where we can sit?'

They walked to the pedestrianised area which served as a promenade leading to the Millennium Bridge. Across the river the chimneys of the Tate Modern were lit up by the sun, now low on the western horizon, but Nigel had no eyes for the scene: his mind was already focussed on another urban setting in a previous decade. Despite the crowds milling around the bridge approach, they managed to find a vacant bench and sat. About six inches separated them.

'I suppose Tony said something about that last evening in Leeds?' she said, staring ahead.

'He said a great deal. But Tony's an alcoholic. Alcoholics are notorious liars and have poor memories.'

'So I suppose you want *me* to tell you what happened?'

'If you have something to tell me then, yes. Is it something I really want to know?'

'I can't answer that question, Nigel.'

'You'd better just give me your account, then.'

*   *   *

In her room in the Henry Price, Vivienne was waiting for Eric to collect her. The nasal voice of Ray Davies leaked through the thin walls from the adjacent room which was occupied by Jennifer, a second-year Geographer whose company she'd learned to avoid. Not that she had any objections to Geographers per se, but this one was a rather desperate loner who tried to compensate for her unfortunate looks and total absence of personality by a ferocious promiscuity and an enthusiastic adherence to all that was new in the world of fashion and music.

Her latest enthusiasm was for The Kinks, hence her constant re-playing of *Waterloo Sunset*. Vivienne quite liked The Kinks, their music was evocative of the London she didn't know but could imagine, and they retained a comforting cosy Englishness about them, a welcome relief from the Beatles who seemed recently to have gone rather peculiar. However, to admit this to Jennifer would provoke unwelcome invitations to girlish intimacy, and it was bad enough having to share a shower and toilet with her. The Henry Price building, erected three years previously, was the first recognition by the University authorities that students were no longer attracted to conventional halls of residence with their refectories and wardens, and it provided instead private bed-sitting rooms grouped round communal self-catering kitchens. However, resources had evidently not stretched to allow each room to have en-suite facilities: the compromise was one toilet and shower between, literally between, two rooms, each occupant having a key to lock the door from the inside when engaged in ablutionary activities. Vivienne was always careful to do so, but Jennifer rarely did, even on the occasions when she was sharing the facility with a young man, resulting, for Vivienne, in one highly embarrassing occurrence which Jennifer seemed to find arousing. Vivienne had begun to suspect that Jennifer's predilections were eclectic, and she took pains to keep her at arm's length.

She examined herself in the mirror. She was wearing a new mini dress, the shortest she had ever purchased. She wasn't sure that she could safely sit down in it, especially in the Packhorse and the Eldon, both pubs being the haunt of Engineering students whose raucous appreciation of exposed female flesh she found distasteful. It was too warm to wear tights, which would at least have provided a measure of security. Although proud of her body and conscious of her attractions she was still to an extent the captive of an upbringing which held that girls should not only be modest, but be seen to be.

Why was she dolled up anyway, she wondered? It was only a pub-crawl after all, okay, the last one of her undergraduate years, but hardly the rave-up to end all rave-ups. She was painfully aware that they'd not been invited to any of the parties that she knew were being held tonight, at least not those thrown by the cream of the University Union. In fact that was not quite true – *she'd* been invited, but it had been made clear that the invitation did not extend to Eric, nor, by association, to Nigel, Alan, Tony or Jim. She knew only to well the reason why, for she had come to see her friends as the in-crowd saw them: Eric, secretly mocked for his desperate attempts to be with-it; Nigel, viewed with some suspicion for his haute-bourgeois origins; Tony, too aggressive when drunk; Jim, too depressive when sober, and Alan, too bloody nice, no wit, no irony. They had made it only to the fringes of the elite. Though long suspecting this, it had been confirmed one afternoon when she and Alan had been queuing for coffee in the MJ lounge, wondering whether to join the Union president and his acolytes who were lounging at a nearby table. Eric, Nigel and Tony had entered, and she overheard a remark from one of those seated – 'Oh Christ, here come the Second Division.' She'd glanced at Alan who'd grinned at her ruefully. 'Never mind, Viv,' he'd said, 'It could have been Division Three North', a remark she did not fully understand but which followed by 'Better not tell Eric, eh? He'd be mortified', an observation that showed a degree of perception on

Alan's part which had surprised her. The incident served to deepen the gnawing feeling of dissatisfaction with the way she'd spent her time over the past three years – always in Eric's company.

She glanced at her watch and felt the familiar shaft of annoyance at Eric's habitual lateness. She wished Margaret were still resident in the room now occupied by Jennifer, but she had graduated in Law the previous year. Margaret had been her confidante and mentor, an attractive blonde from Doncaster who combined a fearsome intellect with an earthy enjoyment of her own sexuality. One evening, over a bottle of cheap red wine and to the accompaniment of *Rubber Soul*, she'd articulated Vivienne's problem with devastating directness – 'Men see you as unapproachable, you know. You're not aware of the signals you give out, are you? It's because you're so preoccupied trying to resolve your inner contradictions.' She was right, of course. Now Vivienne felt she was hurtling towards a future with Eric that she wasn't certain she wanted, but she was unsure what sort of alternative would be welcome.

What signals am I giving out tonight she wondered? Well, her clothes gave out a very definite message. And who knows what the evening might bring? They might run into some other members of the Entertainments Committee in one of the pubs, might be after all invited to a party. But she knew she was reconciled to the familiar scene – Eric trying to combine concern for her wellbeing with attempts to be cool, Jim sunk in gloom and requiring counselling, Nigel being gentlemanly in that rather aloof way of his, Alan affable but slightly boring as ever, and Tony being outrageously suggestive. Tony was far too aware of his own swarthy attractiveness. He was one of the few men whose features were enhanced by a moustache, moustaches having suddenly become fashionable.

A hammering at the door signalled Eric's arrival. She let him in and chided him for his lateness before urging him to remove that silly headband; they were going on a pub-crawl, not to a love-in. Sheepishly he complied, and she hurried him out of the building and along Clarendon Road.

The Eldon and the Packhorse were much as she'd anticipated, heaving with students and locals, standing room only, air blue with smoke, beer spilled on the floor, singing in the side rooms, shouted conversations by the bar. In the latter pub she found herself trapped in the snug doorway alongside Alan and Jim, and was only dimly aware of an altercation at the bar between Eric and Tony, before being apprised of the cause of the contention by Nigel coming over and soliciting the support of Al and Jim for a visit to the Brikkies. She didn't share Eric's affection for the Brikkies: the attentions of aged drunken Irishmen were even less welcome than those of undergraduate Engineers. There was one dirty old specimen who'd once thrust his hand up her skirt when she was on her way to the toilet whilst muttering that if she dressed like a whore then bejesus she should expect to be treated like one. She'd dared not protest: students were allowed in the pub on sufferance, and in any case she would have been more embarrassed by Eric's impotent expressions of disapprobation than she had been by the assault itself.

So she was sympathetic to Tony's desire to go straight to the Hyde Park, but they were in a minority. It was in the Brikkies that Eric began to behave stupidly: why he hadn't learned to pace himself she didn't know, she'd told him often enough. After their hurried exit she berated him again, loudly, and noticed that Tony was listening and grinning at her: when she glowered at him he responded with a wink which she found oddly conspiratorial.

When Eric collapsed in the Hyde Park her anger and embarrassment were such that the slight puzzlement she felt about such inebriation resulting from the consumption of so few pints was banished by an overpowering desire to be rid of him for the evening. Once Nigel had helped him out through the revolving doors, she turned to her remaining companions.

'Well, I'm not going to let Eric's stupidity stop me enjoying myself,' she said.

'But d'you think he's okay?' asked Alan, 'He hasn't had that much to drink. Perhaps he's not well.'

'If he's not well then Nigel can tuck him up.' She took a swig of her cider.

'Right on, Viv!' Tony raised his glass to her. 'Make the most of your freedom, love'.

He extracted a Players No. 6 from the packet on the table, flipped it into his mouth expertly and lit it. Vivienne suddenly felt an overwhelming desire for nicotine: she and Eric had managed to give up smoking the previous year, but unlike Eric she'd never managed to overcome the cravings, and getting through Finals without the crutch had been torture. She'd been tempted to have secret drags in Eric's absence, but he would have been bound to have smelled it on her, or in her room; his senses were annoyingly acute.

She succumbed. What the hell.

'Give me one of those, please, Tony.'

'Hey, you *are* up for a good time, aren't you?'

He looked at her, gave her the second wink of the evening, offered her one from the packet. As he lit it for her he muttered 'What else can I tempt you with tonight?'

She glanced at Alan and Jim, but they were turned away watching the antics of a crowd of revellers in full flower-power regalia who'd just entered and were clustered round the bar. She gave Tony a cool appraising stare, grateful for the opportunity that the manipulation of a cigarette gave for making a considered response. He stared back, smiling engagingly. He had incredibly white teeth. There was no denying that he was attractive. He was a womaniser, of course. She didn't like him very much, but the dichotomy was in itself erotic. She found herself comparing him with Eric – and with the others, for that matter. She felt a disquieting stirring within her.

'You can tempt me with another cider when we get to the *Oak*' she said.

'I was hoping I could offer you more than that.'

'Who knows? You might be lucky. I might feel like a gin and tonic.'

'Wow! Far out!' was his sarcastic response to that.

Walking up Headingley Lane to the Original Oak, she took care to accompany Jim, partly out of guilt for not having paid him the attention that he always felt was his due, partly to distance herself from Tony while she tried to resolve the ambivalence in her feelings for him. She found herself straining to hear the conversation he was having with Alan as they walked a few paces behind, but it was drowned by the roar of traffic. Eventually she resigned herself to giving her full attention to Jim, who was complaining about having to visit the Oak, it was too full of poseurs for his taste. She made empathetic noises, but in fact she rather liked the pub: the rowdier elements were confined to the downstairs bars, leaving the spacious Oak Room upstairs with its low tables and hassock-like Biba stools free for occupation by blasé postgraduates and the offspring of those more affluent Headingley residents who had yet to be displaced by the steady advance of the student population along the Otley Road. When she'd first visited the place with Eric back in their first year there'd still been a men-only room, full of elderly gents dressed in heavy tweed suits, who'd greeted her appearance at the door with 'Hey up! Woman!' resulting in her hasty departure. Eric had been intrigued and had revisited the room with Nigel: they'd later reported delightedly that the conversation had seemed to comprise only breathy exhalations of 'Eeeh', 'Aye,' and 'Now then!' The single-sex bar had since been swept away to accommodate faster-drinking students, the elderly denizens being displaced to who knows where.

They found a vacant table in the Oak Room, and Tony hurried to the bar, returning a few minutes later with two pints of draught Double Diamond, a Tetley's bitter, and a gin and tonic.

'Here you are then, Viv,' he smirked, 'Your luck's in – or is it me that's lucky?'

She looked at him levelly and sipped her drink – bloody hell it was strong, he must have made it a double. It was in her mind to challenge him, but then thought – come on, Viv, she told herself, it's my last student evening, relax, let it all hang out for once, where's the harm? She asked him for another ciggie.

Tony swivelled on his stool so he was facing her, leaned towards her and began to talk. He spoke rubbish of course, but it was amusing rubbish – he was quite witty in a heavy-handed sort of way. She found herself laughing, responding to his nonsense with nonsense of her own. A gin-induced feeling of euphoria swept over her. She was being chatted up. She'd almost forgotten what it was like, how to play the game: the half-hearted attempts of others to thus engage her had always been stifled by Eric's ever-vigilant presence. Jim and Alan, talking desultorily, were a thousand miles away on the other side of the table. Tony's nonsense began to get more risqué: she knew he was testing her, seeing how far he could push back the boundaries; for her part she felt relaxed about discovering how far he dare push. She gulped at her gin, Tony cracked a joke about one of the less attractive girls on the Union Executive, she laughed uproariously, throwing her head back and her legs out, no longer caring that the combination of low stool and short skirt was attracting the attention of those at the surrounding tables. Her knee grazed against Tony's: he reached out and touched it, confidently. Something stirred again within her. She knew what it was. She was feeling randy. Truth be told, she quite often felt randy, but was rarely tipsy enough to admit it to herself, let alone to Eric.

She looked up and saw Nigel standing at the bar. She'd forgotten all about him. He was staring at her: his face, usually so composed, registered shock. Did she really care what he thought? She considered the question. No, it wasn't important. He was a fanciable man, but so bloody straight, in his own way just as buttoned up as Eric. The two flatmates suited each other. It was entirely appropriate that Nigel should have looked after Eric tonight – he'd probably been far more solicitous towards him than she would have been.

Nigel carried his drink over to them. He was asked half-hearted questions as to Eric's welfare. She found herself resenting his presence, for Nigel took pains to ensure everyone was included in the conversation, which became general, even Jim making the odd contribution. It was hard to resume the one-to-one banter that she and Tony had been enjoying. They had to content themselves with meaningful glances.

At Jim's insistence they swallowed their drinks quickly and made their way across the road to the Skyrack, a pub much more to Jim's taste, though he was scathing about Dutton's ale. It was standing room only in all the small lounges. Tony deftly organised the arrangements so that he was crushed next to her by the bar, and she felt his hand surreptitiously stoking her lower back, creeping slowly and in circling movements to the top of her buttocks. She found her eyes closing as she sank into an erotic haze, then quickly pulled herself together and hissed in his ear 'No, not now, not here!' before ostentatiously showing attention to the conversation being conducted by Nigel, Jim and Alan.

'No, not now, not here!' The ambiguity of those five words would come to haunt her down the years. Even at the time she wasn't sure what she'd meant to convey, part of her hoping that Tony would understand it as an absolute negative. But he didn't, for as they left the Skyrack on their way to the last pub of the evening he muttered 'Later, then,' and the part of her that hoped he'd understood 'not here' to mean 'somewhere else' caused her not to challenge his assumption. At least it had the effect of cooling his public expressions of ardour, and it was a rather subdued quintet that had the final drink in the Woodman before catching the bus back down Headingley Lane.

She'd doubted, as soon as it was proposed, that she could face fish and chips, but nevertheless accompanied the others to the door of Sweaty Betty's, still uncertain about how she wanted the evening to end. There, however, the smell of stale cooking oil and the rowdy crowd within produced a sudden longing for the fragrance and peace of her room. She bade them a hasty farewell, and walked back to the Henry Price, relief and disappointment battling within her.

Back in her room she undressed, and in bra and pants rinsed her face and cleaned her teeth before donning her rather tatty dressing gown. She debated whether to have a final coffee in the communal kitchen, to chat to her corridor-mates when they eventually returned from the various parties to which most had been bound. But many of them would be accompanied by men, and she couldn't face mixed company now, not when the couples would be in that febrile state which spoke of the imminence of delayed copulation. There was nothing else to do but go to bed, she supposed. Perhaps she'd have a cup of tea. Tea was her shameful secret, to be consumed only in the privacy of her room, for it had parental, even old-maidish connotations, and the ritual of its preparation would be mocked by the Nescafe swiggers that comprised most of those along her corridor.

She sat on her bed, trying not to think of the evening, of the opportunity missed, or of her lucky escape: she could still not decide what it was. Eric came to her mind: she felt a renewed spasm of anger not just at his drunken stupidity but at his long-standing lack of ardour which, whilst comforting at the start of their relationship, had come to cause her increasing frustration and discontent and which, she told herself indignantly, was responsible for her behaviour this evening. She would have to speak to Eric. They were both bound for Birmingham, he to take a Certificate in Education, she to join a course in Librarianship, with the intention of eventually marrying when he obtained his first job. If this evening had done nothing else, it had convinced her that they must consummate their relationship before she committed herself to a life with him. Oh, be honest, Viv, she said to herself, we must have a fuck before I die of frustration and go off the rails completely. She coloured, for she had never before even thought in Anglo-Saxon.

Raised voices, guffaws and giggles, at first heard faintly in the depths of the stairwell, rose in a crescendo as the perpetrators entered the communal kitchen and began clattering about with crockery. A drunken male voice began to sing 'Let's Spend the Night Together', his mates providing the 'Da-da-da-da dat-dat-da-dah-da' accompaniment. The Stones they were not, but the females in the party seemed appreciative, for they whooped with evident delight. A profound depression settled over Vivienne.

There was a banging on her door. They'd probably run out of sugar again. The attempt to organise a system of communal purchasing had long broken down, but Vivienne could always be relied on. Resentment at her corridor-mates' assumptions mingled with her depression, but she grabbed her bag of Tate & Lyle and opened the door. Tony pushed in and slammed the door behind him.

'How did you get in?' Her voice hovered uncertainly between indignation and curiosity: the outside doors were locked against non-residents after 11pm.

'Waited till that lot came in, sneaked in behind 'em. Didn't know they were from your corridor.'

'I was just about to go to bed. What do you want?' God, what an inane question.

'You know what I want, Viv. You want it too, don't you?'

He lunged towards her. She sidestepped, pulling her dressing gown tightly round her.

'Wait!' Another ambiguous statement. Why hadn't she just said 'No'?

'Wassa matter, Viv? Christ, this is our last chance.'

He advanced towards her again. She moved behind a chair.

'Are the others still at Sweats? Do they know you've come here?'

'Course not. Told 'em I felt sick. Said I was driving home.'

'Tony, I'm sorry, I've been silly, leading you on. It's just that –'

'Don't say that, Viv.'

He reached out, grabbed her hand, tugged her from behind the chair. She could smell his aftershave over the odour of beer and cigs. He was the only one of the group to wear aftershave: she'd noticed it before and had found it pleasing. He put his hands on her shoulders, pulled her towards him, kissed her gently on the forehead. It was strangely unerotic.

'You're wasted on Eric, you know that, don't you?'

She didn't want to talk about Eric. She didn't want to talk about her discontents. She didn't want to talk at all. She wanted comfort, release. She put her arms round his waist. They stood in a chaste embrace for what seemed like minutes. He placed his cheek against hers. She could smell his sweat – it wasn't unpleasant, it was exciting. The stirrings within her began again. She tentatively pressed her loins against his; he responded, then lowered his hands, began gently to caress her buttocks.

She pulled away.

'Tony, I'm no good at this bit. Please, would you let me get into bed first?'

'Sure, Viv.' His voice was thick. 'I need the toilet anyway. Where is it?'

'Through there. Make sure you lock the door on the other side, and be quiet, please.'

He looked at her quizzically but nodded before turning away.

Hurriedly she turned off the light, removed her dressing gown, bra and pants, thrust them under the bed and got into it, pulling the sheet up to her chin. This was it, then. Vivienne Pearson, graduate, about to lose her virginity at the age of 21 to a man she didn't really like. Perhaps it was the best way, to be deflowered by one with whom there was no emotional involvement, one with whom there need be no post-coital embarrassment, one whom she would never see again. Despite her excitement and apprehension, there was also a strange detachment, almost an out-of-body sensation. She could see herself laying there, naked under the sheet, waiting for the titles to stop rolling and for the film to begin. She was even considering the end of the performance – *post coitum omne animal triste est* – would this be the case for her?

She seemed to have been waiting a long time. What was he up to in there? At last the toilet flushed; the door opened; he stumbled as he crossed the room. He climbed in beside her: she felt the shock, for the first time, of feeling naked male flesh pressed against her. He was breathing heavily. They exchanged their first kiss – there was too much tongue for Vivienne's taste. He placed a hand on her breast, then suddenly stopped and turned onto his back.

'What's the matter?' She was alarmed: had she been doing something wrong?

'Feel sick.'

'What?'

'I said I feel sick, for Christ's sake!'

He jerked into a sitting position, then staggered across the room, barging into a chair before he made it to the bathroom, where he vomited copiously and loudly into the toilet. He hadn't shut the door. Vivienne, instantly totally sober, pulled the sheet over her head. Disgusting! Disgusting! What had she been thinking of? What was she doing? How could she have put herself in this sordid situation?

Eventually he emerged. Pre-emptive action was called for.

'I think you'd better leave, please.'

'What? I can't, Viv, I'm in no state to drive.' He groaned and suppressed a belch. 'Can't I stay here till I feel better?'

The thought of sharing a room with him made her feel nauseous, but the variety of alternative scenarios that presented themselves were the more unwelcome: he might create a disturbance when leaving the building, he might crash the car, he might – oh God – he might walk across Woodhouse Moor and ask Eric and Nigel if he could stay at their place.

'Look, if you must stay you'll have to sleep in the chair. And you must leave as soon as it gets light.'

'But it's cold.'

'You'd better sleep in your clothes, then.'

'OK then. Sorry about this, Viv, I wanted –'

'I don't want to talk about it. Goodnight, Tony.'

She lay listening to him scrambling into his clothes, muttering under his breath, fidgeting around in the chair in an ostentatious attempt to find a comfortable position, before snoring announced that he had. She reconciled herself to a sleepless night but sank into oblivion almost immediately.

She was jerked awake by someone trying to clamber into her bed – what the hell? Then, instant recall.

'No! No! Get out!'

'Oh, c'mon, Viv.'

His foul early-morning breath wafted over her. The early morning light seeping through the flimsy curtain revealed crumpled features, rheumy eyes and a strong growth of black bristles. She was alert enough to feel relief that he'd not removed his clothes.

'Get *off* me. Get *off*!' She drummed her fists against his chest, suddenly conscious that she was naked under the sheet. He grabbed her hands and pinned them back against the pillow. She was seized with a fury and loathing that she'd never felt before, and spat in his face. He recoiled, releasing her hands, and she dragged her nails down his cheek.

'Fuck!' He bellowed the expletive and jumped away, then stood looking over her, blood already beginning to seep from the scratches. He'd dragged the sheet from her as he jumped, exposing the crimson birthmark that extended in a crescent from her navel to her hip. His face contorted into a gargoyle of hatred and contempt.

'You bitch. You fucking bitch. You know what you are? You're a fucking prick-teaser. You're an uptight, tight-arsed cow.'

Vivienne, shaking, pulled the sheet over her. With a supreme effort she managed to control her voice. 'Just go.'

'Oh, I'll go all right. I wonder what your little Eric will say when I tell him how you were giving me the come-on once he was out of the way?'

'That would be stupid, wouldn't it? How would you explain the scratches on your cheek? I'd make sure they all know you got those when you were trying to rape me.'

Her voice had faltered a little, but his lack of immediate response gave her first a chink of hope, then a measure of confidence.

'You wouldn't dare,' he said eventually.

'Just try me.'

'Eric's welcome to you, and to your bloody birthmark' was his final remark as he turned to the door.

*   *   *

Nigel had stared fixedly ahead of him as she told her story, oblivious to the crowds that passed in front of them. When she finished he continued to look ahead.

'So that was it, then?' he said eventually.

'Yes. That was it.'

'So it didn't happen?'

'Not what you've obviously thinking, no. What did Tony tell you?'

'It was incoherent. But he'd obviously seen a lot of you. You know, your birthmark.'

She gasped.

He turned to face her.

'So why did you never tell me? God, Viv, you had years when you could have. I thought we told each other everything.'

'I was ashamed, Nigel, can't you see that?'

'But you never ….. never actually……'

'Screwed, you mean?' He winced at her use of the word. 'No, we didn't, but ….'

'But you wanted to?'

'At times during the evening, yes, I did.'

He stood up. 'Come on, let's go. The others'll be wondering where we've got to.'

They set off over the bridge, forced into close proximity by the press of the crowds around them. Nigel was vaguely conscious of the backdrop – the viscous river, Tower Bridge to their left, the Tate Modern chimney stack ahead, the setting sun to their right – but his inner cinema took precedence, a constant re-running of the scene of Viv in her room with Tony, her carnal desires only dampened by the drunken ineptitude of her would-be seducer. Vivienne was silent beside him. Was there anything left to say?

A clattering ahead of them heralded the arrival of a group of shouting, singing teenagers. They ran towards them, rejoicing in their youth. One of them gave a casual 'Sorry' as he barged into Vivienne, before running off to join his mates. Vivienne winced and rubbed her shoulder.

'Are you hurt?' Nigel asked, 'Bloody louts.'

'Just youthful exuberance. The lad apologised.'

They set off again.

'Nigel, please try and understand. I was drunk. I was still a virgin after three years at university. You know what Eric was like, is like. I just felt I needed….. oh, God, I needed to ….'

'Yes?'

Abruptly she stopped walking and faced him.

'Why are you making this so bloody difficult? It was forty years ago, we were kids, it was of no importance, so much has happened since.'

Please, thought Nigel, let her not come out with all the clichés – young and foolish, water under the bridge, the past is a foreign country, of no significance in the great scheme of things – all the trite remarks with which the elderly comfort themselves, thus to fend off the desperation of having to live knowing that little of any personal significance will ever happen again, apart from bereavement and death. *There are times when I look back when I'm haunted by my youth* – who was it who'd sung that?

'You realise,' she added, 'it would never have happened if you'd told me how you felt.'

'Would it have made any difference? I was just as green as Eric when it came to sex. I couldn't have helped you in your hour of need.'

'That's not what I meant and you know it. If you'd just given a hint of your feelings it would have…….. oh, I don't know …. It would have opened up possibilities.'

'But Viv, I've explained so many times; Eric was my flatmate, you and he were practically engaged. You know my upbringing. How *could* I have told you?'

'Bloody, bloody Tony,' was her response to the question to which she had no answer.

'Yes, bloody Tony.' He paused for a moment, then, 'It all goes to show that the parable of the tortoise and the hare is wrong. When it comes to sex, the hare wins every time.'

'But it didn't, did it? Tony didn't cross the finishing line. You won the race eventually.'

'Apart from the small matter of your marriage in between, of course. Eric had already done several laps before I caught up. God, why are we talking in these ghastly metaphors?'

'But what I had with you was way beyond anything I have with Eric, you know that.'

Nigel reached out and grasped her by the shoulders. 'But you didn't leave him, did you? When it came to the crunch the bloody meek inherited the earth.'

As he said it he was aware that it was the first time that he'd spoken disparagingly to her about Eric.

Her face crumpled. 'I know. I bloody know. Do you think I haven't spent the last ten years regretting it? And now it's too late. You've got Melanie – and Oscar.'

To his horror, or was it relief? tears began to fill her eyes. He pulled her to him – a comforting embrace, that's how it started, until her cheek brushed against his and he kissed her forehead and she lifted her face to him, and then ten years fell away and the crowds around him evaporated, and it was only after they'd ended the kiss that they smiled and turned, to see, a few yards away, Eric, motionless, expressionless, watching them.

'Eric!' said Nigel, 'Viv's a bit upset.'

Eric remained still, his mouth slightly open.

'She's upset about Tony's behaviour, and I –'

'What the hell's going on?'

'I told you, Viv's a bit –'

'I saw you. I've been watching you. You *bastard*.'

He ran towards Nigel, arms flailing. Nigel grabbed his arms with ease, and held on to them. He could cope with physical expressions of anger, but there was part of him that wanted to let Eric hit him.

'Eric, listen, you've got this all wrong.'

'Bollocks!' Still in Nigel's grasp, Eric turned his face to Vivienne. 'You bitch! You slag!'

Some of the strollers had stopped and were watching the scene with interest, the younger ones with evident relish. 'Slap an ASBO on the old buggers!' a wag shouted.

'Eric, calm down. We can talk about this. I'm going to let you go now. Don't make a fool of yourself.'

Slowly he released his grip. Eric stood, looking first at Nigel, then at Vivienne, and then released a stream of foul-mouthed invective. A cheer came from the circle of young men who'd gathered round them. Nigel decided to let the flow run its course, but it went on and on, the repetition of the swearwords doing little to reduce their potency.

Vivienne had been still and silent throughout, but she suddenly turned on Eric.

'I've had enough! Why did you make me come? I'm not putting up with any more. I'm going.'

She turned to face the north bank.

'Where are you going, Viv?' said Nigel 'Back to the hotel?'

'I'm not spending the night with him. I'm going to Belinda's'

'Belinda's? Can you make it to Bayswater?'

'Of course I can. Just leave me alone.'

She set out, breaking into a near run, pushing through the crowds in her haste to distance herself from them. Nigel and Eric watched until she was hidden by the throng. The circle round them began to disperse.

'Best to give her some time to herself. She'll probably get a taxi from St Pauls,' said Nigel.

Eric was staring fixedly at him.

'How do you know Belinda?' he said eventually, 'How do you know she lives in Bayswater? What the fuck's been going on?'

Nigel was aghast. He'd broken a cardinal rule of his training – never divulge unnecessary information. There was no alternative but to confess; not to everything, only tell the minimum, but make that minimum the truth.

'I'll tell you, Eric. Let's walk. The others will be waiting.'

'The others? Fuck the others! D'you really expect me to carry on with this farce?'

'Yes, I do,' said Nigel firmly. 'We mustn't spoil it for poor old Alan.'

'For Christ's sake! Bugger Alan!'

'Haven't you realised Alan's very ill? He's set so much store by today. There's only one more pub. After that I'll talk to you, maybe back at the hotel. That's my condition, Eric: if you want to know what's been happening you'll have to pretend all's well just for another hour or so, for Al's sake. Come on.'

He led an agitated Eric back towards the south bank.

Chapter 14

Bayswater: Belinda

Belinda, glass of Rioja in hand, stood staring out of the open sash window down at the broad tree-lined street, which had that strange luminosity that comes with a fine summer dusk after an interval of rain. It was spoiled by the litter of parked cars, but still pleasing: the large stuccoed early-Victorian terraces exuded an air of gentility, though behind the elegant façades they'd all long been divided into flats like hers. She knew she was lucky to live here: the area, within easy reach of the West End and the City, managed to combine prosperity with cosmopolitanism, a consequence perhaps of the plethora of expensive hotels. The American, Greek and Brazilian communities, already well established when she'd first moved in over thirty years before, had later been joined by wealthy Arabs, but at least, she thought, there were no Asians or East Europeans, and the former Hallfield council estate had been in private ownership since Maggie Thatcher's sell-off in the 1980s.

Her father had provided a generous deposit for the flat when, after graduating, she'd insisted that advancement in her chosen career of journalism required that she live close to the hub of events. The area was then a bit raffish ('Some of these places look like knocking-shops' her father had grunted in a vain attempt to persuade her to live in a more sedate suburb), but when you're 21 raffishness is exciting, inviting, especially to one with Belinda's proclivities. Her career advancement and growing affluence had accompanied the march of new money along the streets of Victorian London, with the result that she'd never felt the need to move. Indeed, the flat itself had become something of a hub in those days when she was at the centre of things, surrounded by colleagues who'd become friends and sometimes lovers, and the friends of colleagues who'd become *her* friends, and sometimes lovers.

She swallowed her wine and fought against the temptation to pour herself another. She ought to eat first, but there was nothing in the kitchen cupboards that tempted her. She was in any case battling with her weight: always voluptuous, her figure had deteriorated markedly since her retirement. Deprived of the adrenaline of work and of the incentive to slim provided by the receding possibilities for seduction, she was finding to her horror that she was on the verge of assuming the ample proportions that had so plagued her mother.

The slight feeling of depression that dogged most of her days was suddenly edged with panic at the prospect of another evening alone. She was advancing towards the telephone with the notion of phoning someone, anyone, when it rang. She jumped. For an instant, hope triumphed over experience, but she told herself it was probably someone trying to sell insurance, or a recorded message informing her that she'd won a prize, the claiming of which would require a phone call costing more than the digital camera or weekend away for two that she'd been assigned.

The number on the digital read-out was unfamiliar, but she pressed the connect button nevertheless.

'Hi,' she said, a form of salutation she'd adopted when surrounded by younger colleagues.

'Belinda?' The voice was unfamiliar, rather breathless.

'Speaking.'

'It's me, Vivienne.'

Seconds passed while Belinda absorbed the information.

'Fucking hell,' she said eventually.

As she put down the phone, her first thought was of the untidiness of the flat. It was a tip. It always seemed to be, these days, despite its spaciousness. Therein lay the problem, perhaps: a smaller living space would have dictated neater habits, but she'd never been thus constrained, and any detritus left over from evening excesses had always been spirited away by her daily cleaner. Retirement and loss of income however had forced her to dispense with her treasure's services.

At all costs she must hide the effect of her reduced circumstances from Viv, who had always been neat and tidy and presumably still was. Oh my God, she'd need a bed making up. And would she be wanting to eat? Belinda hadn't thought to ask. She hoped not, for all she had in was instant meals and a few packets and tins. She hadn't yet adjusted to not dining out. Sometimes she still did, but increasingly rarely. Although Queensway and Westbourne Grove offered an array of bistros, gastro-pubs and echoing, brightly lit modern restaurants, these were not places of comfort for sixty-one year olds, especially when alone, and she usually was alone. Something else she must keep from Viv.

Spare bedroom first, then. It needed dusting. She found bedding, and grappled to insert the duvet in its cover, remembering too late that it was easier if the cover was first turned inside out, and then remembering she should in any case have dusted and hoovered the room before even starting on the bed. Panic resurfaced – perhaps she should have started with the living room or kitchen? And oh Christ, the bathroom – Viv was at her fastidious worst when it came to calls of nature and personal hygiene.

She grabbed the Dyson from the box room and push-pulled the machine over the bedroom floor, then used the tools to suck up the dust on the window sill and skirting boards. It wouldn't look too bad so long as Viv used only the bedside light. She dragged the Dyson into the living room; no, first dust the surfaces; no, first *clear* the surfaces. They were covered with old newspapers and glossy magazines, mostly the latter. She must hide them away, along with the overflowing ashtray, not let Viv know what rubbish she was reading these days nor that she'd taken up smoking again after twenty years of abstinence. Even the minimalist décor was passé, and the shine had long worn off the furniture. The bare floorboards were in need of restorative action.

How long had she got? Viv had been on the Millennium Bridge when she'd phoned. Twenty minutes in a taxi perhaps? She gathered up the magazines, threw them in the box room, returned to sift through the newspapers, consigned the copies of the *Daily Mail* to the paper recycling-bin in the kitchen, went back to the living room, put last Sunday's unread *Observer* on the coffee table, returned again to the kitchen to find a duster, whisked it over the surfaces, plugged in the Dyson, then stopped. Why was she bothering? It wasn't as if Viv was a close friend any longer. It was five years since she'd seen her. Viv had come to London on a shopping expedition, they'd met for coffee in Oxford Street, but found they had little to say to each other. Every friendship has its breaking point and such a moment had arrived, for Belinda had realised that Viv had no further use for her.

She turned on the Dyson and trundled it round the room. What had prompted Viv's request for a bed for the night? Belinda had asked why, but no explanation had been given, she hadn't even said why she was in London. In fact she'd sounded distressed, and had turned off her phone when Belinda's questions became more insistent.

She manoeuvred the machine on automatic pilot. It was most unlike Viv to display emotion of any kind. She'd always been self-contained, from the moment she'd first met her at grammar school, but they'd become friends of a sort in the fourth form, drawn together by their burgeoning appreciation of literature and drama. Belinda was the cleverer, but less studious, the more eager to explore the exciting world that, even in East Anglia, had begun to explode outside the confines of the single-sex establishment in which they spent their days. Urged by Belinda to get more with it, Viv had eventually confided that her parents were strict Methodists who would not countenance any deviation from the paths of righteousness. She'd professed to find the constraints irksome but it was evident that she shared her parents' faith, for she continued to attend chapel every Sunday even when she'd reached the 6th form.

Belinda's father had been a solicitor and her mother a doctor: comfortably off, they held progressive political and social opinions, and allowed her a freedom that was the envy of her peers. She'd availed herself of this to the full, paying scant attention to her 'A' level studies and losing her virginity to a lad from the boy's Grammar School after a joint 6th form hop, but nevertheless had retained a grudging respect for Viv, for her quiet self-confidence, her willingness to challenge her teachers, for her quick wit and her waspish observations about the foibles of their classmates. She'd also noticed, on the bus home from school, the glances that Viv had begun to attract from boys notwithstanding her unfashionable hairstyle and mode of dress: even in the 6th form she'd clung to ankle socks and had worn her school skirt at knee level, none of which could however disguise her wonderful legs, her slim lithe body, her pertly attractive features and the gloss of her dark-auburn hair. Belinda, whose curvaceous figure would have better suited the couture of the 1950s, had suppressed the first glimmerings of envy by reminding herself that Viv offered no competition, that she seemed to want no further contact with boys beyond the few chaste foursomes in which, unknown to her parents, she'd participated at Belinda's urging, and had felt a guilty waft of schadenfreude on hearing one of the boys subsequently refer to her friend as an ice-maiden. Remorse quickly followed when it occurred to her that Viv's modesty might well result from the birthmark, insouciantly displayed in the communal showers when she was eleven, but the source of acute embarrassment with the onset of puberty.

Belatedly, Belinda had engaged in hasty revision and equipped herself with sufficiently good grades to go to Bristol University where she'd spent three years of joyful hedonism, occasionally studying for her degree in English. Viv, with better grades, went off to Leeds, a university to which Belinda, having a vision of the city as a dour industrial backwater, privately thought her friend was better suited. They continued to meet during the vacations. It was during the Christmas holidays of their second year that Belinda was taken aback by Viv's appearance in the coffee bar, transformed into a ravishing Carnaby Street-clad dolly-bird, wearing all the gear with a panache to which Belinda could only aspire. Challenged to explain her metamorphosis, Viv had admitted to having acquired a boy-friend who was into modern styles, and that anyway, everyone was dressing like this now, weren't they? Belinda had expressed delight and asked whether the boy-friend was good in bed, but the question provoked a pursing of the lips and a change of subject: evidently some facets of Viv's personality had remained unaffected by the mores of the times.

The following summer, Viv brought Eric down to Suffolk to meet her parents and Belinda had been introduced to him one lunchtime in their usual coffee bar. She was not impressed. Beneath the studiedly fashionable gear – blue fitted shirt with tab collar, check hipster trousers with the obligatory white belt, black pvc mac – and the collar-length hair, he was a bit of a prat. He'd spoken using all the idioms of the time, pronounced all the opinions expected of undergraduates in the mid 1960s, demonstrated an encyclopaedic knowledge of blues music, but he was *uncool*. He was over-attentive to Viv, and spoke to Belinda in the manner of one seeking to impress by his savoir-faire. Above all, although reasonably good-looking, he was unsexy, almost asexual. When he announced his intention to become a teacher and Viv mentioned she was thinking of librarianship, Belinda, who already had her sights set on TV journalism, was torn between on the one hand mounting a rescue campaign to save Viv from a lifetime of boring mediocrity, and on the other accepting that the two were ideally suited. The fact that Eric had evidently been welcomed as a suitor by Viv's parents inclined her to the latter.

She'd met Viv a few times more during subsequent vacations and she was always accompanied by Eric, for whom Belinda's disdain deepened into contempt when he abandoned his mod image in favour of flowered shirts, flared trousers and hair over the ears. Belinda had eagerly grasped all the opportunities provided by the new freedoms, but secretly scorned their fey trappings. How could a woman of Viv's intelligence be attracted to such a shallow dilettante? She'd observed her friend closely, and on occasions thought she detected signs of impatience with his puppyish enthusiasms, but these were evidently suppressed, for the two had remained together for their post-graduate courses in Birmingham, where, to Belinda's incomprehension, they continued to occupy separate living quarters.

By that time Belinda was living in Bayswater and on the bottom rung of her career at the BBC. It was only a backroom job researching items for the local TV news programme, but she was assiduously networking, acquiring a slick metropolitan polish and a stable of admirers carefully selected for their value to her advancement. Immersed in the whirl of her new life, she'd relegated Viv and Eric to the recesses of her consciousness, and had been taken aback, the following year, to receive an invitation to their wedding. The ceremony and its aftermath, held in Bury St Edmunds and characterised by the sort of sobriety to be expected of any event organised by Viv's parents, had convinced her that this really was the end of their friendship, for Viv, on the one occasion when they'd managed to exchange a few words, had spoken of little but Eric's teaching post, the job she hoped to get in the County Library, and the lovely little cottage that they'd managed to buy in Warwickshire.

The telephone rang. Again she felt a surge of hopeful expectancy, only to be dashed on remembering that she was now no longer free to accept any invitation that might be forthcoming. There followed a twitch of irritation directed towards Viv.

'Hi,' she said.

'Belinda, it's Vivienne again.'

'Oh. Aren't you coming after all?'

'Yes, if you're sure it's ok. I'll be later than I thought. I've had to go back to the hotel to get my things; I'd forgotten I'd need them. I'm on my way now.'

'Hotel? Where? Are you in London alone?'

'No, I'm with Eric, well, not just him. With some of our old university friends. But I need to get away from them for a while.'

'University friends?' Belinda was suddenly alert to a variety of possibilities.

'Yes. It's a reunion. Forty years since we graduated.'

'Viv?'

'What?'

'Would Nigel be one of the friends by any chance?'

A hesitation, then, 'Yes, but there's a crowd of us and –'

'What's happened, Viv?'

'Nothing, really. Just feel I need a bit of space. I'll be with you soon. 'Bye.'

Belinda replaced the receiver thoughtfully. There must be more to it than that, she reckoned. In the earlier telephone conversation Viv had sounded distinctly agitated. Perhaps when she arrived she'd be more forthcoming, though it was always hard to penetrate her reserve. Viv had never been one for girly chats, not even when she was in the throes of her personal awakening back in the 80s.

At least, she thought, I've got a bit more time to prepare for her arrival. She entered the kitchen; it was reasonably free of clutter, the result of it rarely being used for serious cooking, but there was a patina of grime over the work-surfaces and the tiles needed re-grouting. In fact the whole room could do with a make-over, something she'd been on the verge of doing ten years ago, just before her career started to go into free-fall. What the hell, Viv needn't see the kitchen – if necessary she'd take her breakfast in bed.

There was time to take a shower and tart herself up a bit – no, clean up the bathroom before self-titivation. She felt mildly irritated that she should have to shower at this hour rather than indulging in the long soak that she always enjoyed just before retiring. Her solitude had begun to encourage such daily rituals. Adherence to them helped keep at bay the nagging awareness of the silence of her own company, helped prevent her mind from constantly re-living the events of her plentiful past.

She peered at herself in the bathroom mirror, always a mistake because the lighting was unforgiving. There was no denying that heavy make-up failed to disguise, and might even serve to emphasise, the fact that she was on the threshold of being elderly. Not blessed with good bone structure, hers had been the sort of fair-skinned pale-eyed plump prettiness that did not wear well. She lifted her jaw and patted its soft underside: how old had her mother been when she became undeniably possessed of a double chin? At least she'd inherited her blonde hair which was relatively easy to maintain with artful colouring and streaking, though close examination revealed that her roots needed attention. She wondered if Viv was now resorting to such artifice: when she'd last seen her, five years before, her auburn hair had been flecked with grey.

She turned her back on the mirror to undress. Those once outstanding features which had so enthralled her lovers were now a weighty encumbrance. Hurriedly, she stepped into the shower, turned it on, and gratefully abandoned her introspection in favour of conjecture as to the reason for Viv's leaving the re-union.

Nigel. It had to be something to do with Nigel. Belinda had a vague recollection of him at Viv's wedding – conventionally handsome, well built, somewhat over-gentlemanly for the time – but he'd made sufficient an impression for her to half-recognise him in the bar that lunchtime, back in the late 70s, when he made his re-appearance. She'd been having a meal with Viv, their first meeting since her marriage. She'd assumed they'd never meet again: apart from the exchange of Christmas cards with their one-line messages they'd had no contact since the wedding, Viv being immersed in child-rearing in her rural hideaway and Belinda living life to the full flitting between men, bars and restaurants and on the verge of a career breakthrough that might bring her in front of the TV camera. But Viv had phoned, said the kids were now of an age where Eric could be trusted to look after them, that she rather fancied a weekend break in London, and could they meet up? Belinda had agreed, rather reluctantly, assuming they would have little in common. So it had proved to be: Viv seemed provincial, mumsy and rather depressed, though in retrospect Belinda realised this may have been the result of her flaunting her flat, clothes and lifestyle.

Belinda had taken her to a pub for lunch despite Viv having shown signs of alarm on being informed that it was in Soho. They had finished eating and were groping for conversation when Belinda, peering rather desperately round the bar in the hope of seeing one of her colleagues, noticed a tall, fair man sitting alone at a corner table who was staring at them fixedly. There was something familiar about him. As he was not unprepossessing, Belinda treated him to one of the ambiguous half-smiles that she reserved for chance encounters. He'd immediately risen and walked over to their table, a chastened Belinda realising that his eyes were fixed on Viv.

'Viv!' he'd said, 'What are you doing here?'

Viv's eyes widened and she rose.

'Nigel! It can't be!'

They'd stood staring at each other with inane grins on their faces.

'Oh, Nigel, you remember Belinda?'

'Of course. How are you, Belinda?'

He'd shaken her hand formally. There'd been no physical contact with Viv, but their eyes had remained locked on each other. Belinda had seized on the opportunity for escape, saying she was sure they had lots to talk about, and that she in any case had things to do, and she'd see Viv back at the flat later, was that ok?

In the flat that evening Viv had seemed distant, pensive, though occasionally a smile flickered over her features, and she said she was quite happy to spend the evening by herself in the flat if Belinda wanted to go out with her friends. Belinda had made a show of objecting, but was relieved to be spared the duty of taking Viv along to the party to which she'd been invited, suspecting that she'd be out of her depth there. When she'd returned in the early hours Viv had gone to bed, and over the hurried breakfast that they'd shared before Viv caught her train back to Warwickshire Belinda had no chance to quiz her.

Only four weeks later she had received another phone call from Viv – would she mind putting her up for the night again the following Saturday? No, there was no need to feed her or entertain her, she'd be making her own arrangements, all she needed was a bed, was that ok? Belinda had assented, curiosity vying with resentment.

'What are you up to, then?' she'd asked when Viv arrived, 'Not meeting Nigel by any chance?'

She'd coloured.

'He's asked me to a matinee, *Les Miserables*. I don't often get the chance to –'

'Didn't the invitation extend to Eric?'

'Eric's not interested in the theatre. Are you going out this afternoon?'

'No, as it happens. Why?'

Her colour had deepened.

'Well, if …. Well, you see, I had to give Eric your phone number. If by any chance he should call…'

'Vivienne Jackson, are you about to be a naughty girl?'

'No! Of course not. It's just … well, I'd just rather he didn't know I was with Nigel. Nigel was his flatmate at University, you see. He'd be upset, feel left out.'

'I get it, darling. You're going shopping then, aren't you? Then no doubt we'll be going out together this evening.'

'Thanks, Belinda.'

With that she'd taken her case to the bedroom, emerging ten minutes later in a classically simple dress which enhanced her still-wonderful figure, then departing with a cheerful 'Bye!' and leaving behind a whiff of musky perfume.

It hadn't happened that weekend, Belinda was sure, for the following morning Viv had chatted cheerfully about the theatre performance and, with no evident embarrassment or shame, about Eric and the promoted post he'd just secured. Perhaps it was all platonic: knowing Viv as she did, it probably was. But the incident had spoken volumes about her marriage.

Two months elapsed before Viv had made contact again, with the same request for a bed, the same admission that she was having an afternoon meeting with Nigel, the same gratitude for Belinda's suggestion for an alibi in the event that Eric should phone. That weekend had evidently been the start of the affair: Viv had returned in the evening with the sated, lazy-eyed demeanour of a woman who'd spent the afternoon in bed. Quizzed by Belinda, she'd admitted, with enviable sang-froid, to what had happened, but had refused to give details, and had clammed up when asked about the state of her marriage.

'Is this going to go on, though?' Belinda had persisted.

'Yes, I rather think it is,' was the cautious reply, then, 'Is it ok by you if I stay with you occasionally? It won't be very frequently.'

'Well, yes, I suppose so, but won't you be spending the nights with Nigel?'

'Not possible. I need to be at your place in case Eric phones.'

Thus was established the pattern for the next ten years. Viv's visits to London had been irregular and infrequent, depending as they had been on Eric's willingness to look after the children coinciding with Nigel's availability. Viv had never been very forthcoming about Nigel's job – he was a sort of senior civil servant, she'd said – but Belinda had found it hard to reconcile what she presumed to be the regular habits of a Whitehall mandarin with the hurried last minute arrangements that Viv had to make in order to be with him. Belinda had found herself acting as a go-between in these assignations, taking phone calls from Nigel and then transmitting the messages on to Warwickshire. The weekends of their trysts had developed a regular ritual – Viv hurrying away soon after her arrival for her afternoon in Nigel's flat while Belinda remained in the flat to fend off the phone calls from Eric that never materialised (a duty which she gratefully relinquished on purchasing an answering machine), Belinda leaving for her evening carousals about the time that Viv returned, then Viv's speedy departure the following day, sometimes before Belinda had returned from whatever bed she'd shared the night before.

Only rarely had they had time together to talk. Although Viv had become far more relaxed, more cheerful, than she had ever been, a curtain came down whenever Belinda had introduced the subject of her affair and where it might be leading. Belinda hadn't really cared: she had her own liaisons to manage, and they'd begun to require more careful management than had been the case when she was the new kid at the Beeb.

There had been one occasion when Viv had opened up. To Belinda's horror there had come a Saturday night when she was without a date, without a party, without even a hen-gathering, and she'd reconciled herself to an evening in with her friend, taking care that there was an adequate supply of wine to oil the conversational wheels. Viv had returned from her afternoon at Nigel's flat looking even more replete than usual, and for once had not stopped drinking after her customary single glass of wine. Belinda had chattered about her job, her hopes for the future, the men in her life, the excitement of juggling affairs, and gradually Viv had begun to question her, to comment, then to offer snippets of information about her own affair, eventually hinting, albeit in her usual bowdlerised fashion, that she'd experienced a sexual awakening, not as a result of Nigel's expertise, but through a belated mutual exploration of a sensuality that neither had previously experienced. Bloody hell, Belinda had thought, no wonder she's so desperate for these weekends.

Looking back, that evening had been a watershed for both of them. Belinda, with an insight born of experience, noticed that as the years progressed, Viv's affair, though as intense as ever, had lost some of the joy of that first glad morning. She knew there comes a point in every illicit relationship when each partner privately begins to worry about the future, about where things are leading, about the commitment of the other. Viv had begun to return to the flat looking hunted, and had confided that Nigel was making hints that the infrequent weekend meetings were no longer enough for him. But by then Belinda had her own worries: her career had stalled. New brooms were sweeping through the BBC, the talk was a leaner, fitter organisation, of the out-sourcing of some facets of production. Worse, she was having to face the fact that her face was middle-aged, no longer able to compete with the new intake of brash young women, and that her dreams of programme presentation were over. She'd therefore been disinclined to waste her sympathy on Viv, she needed it all for herself. Her supply of escorts had begun to dry up.

She emerged from the shower, patted herself dry, put on a bathrobe and set about attempting to clean the bathroom. She had time only for a superficial makeover; the limescale on the taps, showerhead and vanitary unit, testimony to the departure of her cleaner, would have to remain. The toilet needed drastic attention: grimacing, she set to work with Harpic, brush and disinfectant, shame that she'd allowed things to slide so far accompanied by depression engendered by the awareness that the decline in her standards resulted from the lack of visitors whom she needed to impress. She'd always had sluttish tendencies: it had been easy to fight them when she moved in smart circles; there was little incentive to do so now. The other day she'd caught herself using the toilet with the door wide open, something that her once-ladylike grandmother had been prone to do in her final days of senile solitude, and she'd been gripped by a frisson of fear at what the future might hold. Her work, which had merged imperceptibly into her social life, had defined her. Now that it had gone, now that she had no deadlines, no assignments, no plans and no colleagues, she had lost her identity, and was at the mercy of her own company.

The bathroom as presentable as it would ever be, she returned to the living room, putting off the decision that faced her concerning what she should wear. Nothing seemed to fit her any more. She hoped to God that Viv might at last be showing some signs of deterioration, a spreading of the hips perhaps, or at least a thickening of the waist? Life was unfair: when she last saw her, Viv's figure had showed no signs of the ravages that by rights should have been inflicted by two pregnancies and the strains of childrearing, whereas she, Belinda, childless, had already begun to expand and droop southwards.

There is no pleasure so guilt-ridden as witnessing the misfortune of a friend. She remembered that evening, ten years before, when an almost-tearful Viv had returned to the flat to announce that Nigel and she would no longer be meeting. Belinda was lachrymose herself, having been informed the previous day that her services would no longer be required in the news team, but that in recognition of her past contribution a post would be made available in one of the independent production companies, in a research capacity. It had been a relief to attend to the woes of another, a comfort that Viv's life might henceforth be even less fulfilling than her own.

'But why is it over?' she'd asked, 'What's changed?'

'He wants me to leave Eric.'

'Why now?'

'He says the children are old enough to cope with it. He says if I don't leave now I never will.'

'Why don't you, then?'

'I'm too old to uproot. And I can't do it to Eric. He's not been a bad husband.'

'Well, why can't you just carry on the way you have been?'

'Nigel won't. He says it's not enough. He says he wants to spend ……he wants to be with me all the time.'

'It's a bit sudden, isn't it? Hasn't he given you time to think about it?'

'I've had six months to think about it. I agreed to give him my answer today.'

'And you won't meet again? Seems a bit over the top.'

'Nigel says if I don't join him then he's got to sort out what to do with the rest of his life.'

'Have you considered the possibility that he might have someone else in his sights?'

'No! *No!* Of course he hasn't! He's a gentleman. You don't mix much with gentlemen, do you? Not everyone hops from bed to bed, even these days.'

Viv's emphatic assertion and the implied criticism of Belinda's lifestyle had prompted the nearest the two had ever come to having a full-blown row. Belinda was affronted by the ingratitude shown for her years of hospitality and discretion, and had told Viv as much. Viv had responded by pointing out that Belinda was unqualified to comment on the lives of those who had family and marital responsibilities. The two had then retreated to their separate bedrooms and the following morning Viv had departed before Belinda emerged. Thereafter there had been no contact beyond polite messages on Christmas cards, until the occasion of their meeting five years previously when there had been a degree of polite rapprochement. Nigel had not been mentioned.

It was getting dark. She pulled the blinds and turned on the lamps, grateful for the kindly light, and was turning towards her bedroom, steeling herself for the task of choosing what to wear, when the door buzzer sounded. Viv already? At least her bathrobe was new. She went to the intercom.

'Viv?'

'Yes.'

'Come up.' She pressed the button to unlock the front door and stood, breathing deeply. Why was she so nervous?

A second buzz, at her own door. She opened it.

'Viv! Hello! Come in.'

The two had never been on kissing terms.

'Thanks, Belinda; I'm very grateful to you for this.'

'Quite like old times, isn't it?'

Belinda couldn't resist the remark. The two stood awkwardly appraising each other. Shit, Viv was still slim, still attractive, the legs still worthy of display. The hair was totally grey, but even that suited her.

'Bring your case through to your old bedroom. D'you want a drink? Tea? Coffee? Something stronger?'

'Nothing, thanks. Are you getting ready to go out?'

'What? Oh, well, yes, I was, but I've put him off. Thought you might need a bit of company. You sounded upset. What's happened?

'Belinda, I'm sorry, but what I need first of all is a shower. It's been so humid. Is that ok?'

'Sure. You know where it is. There's a clean towel on your bed.'

'Thanks. I'll be with you soon.'

At least that gives me a chance to look presentable, Belinda thought. She went to her bedroom, and began rifling through her clothes when the thought struck her – why not remain in the bath-robe? It was quite flattering, disguising a multitude of imperfections. Viv might well emerge from the shower wearing something similar. Better put on some knickers, though. These days Belinda wore knickers, not pants, and thongs were but a distant memory. She applied a fresh layer of make-up, brushed her hair and returned to the living room where she poured herself another glass of wine and sat waiting for Viv to join her.

She had to wait some time, and was about to turn on the TV (she always watched the ten o'clock news despite the feelings of bitterness engendered by the likes of Natasha Kaplinski and Fiona Bruce strutting their stuff) when Viv appeared at the door. She was wearing denim jeans and a low-cut black top. How could it possibly be that a woman of 61 still had an arse that looked good in jeans? Belinda felt a gripe of envy, and the screw was turned tighter as Viv sank onto the settee opposite and with coltish ease swung up her legs and tucked them beneath her.

'Feeling better?' she heard herself say.

'Much, thanks. This is very good of you, Belinda.'

'Sure you don't want a drink?'

'Not at the moment, thanks. Maybe a bit later.'

Silence.

'Well, are you going to tell me what's going on?'

'Oh, nothing really. I was the only woman there and the day began to turn into a boys' boozing session. I never was one for that.'

'You sounded upset when you first phoned.'

'Did I? Probably just annoyed. You know how juvenile men can get sometimes.'

A muffled ringing tone came from Viv's bedroom, and she jumped.

'Sounds like your mobile, Viv. Aren't you going to answer it?'

'No, it'll only be Eric wanting me to rejoin the party.'

'He knows where you are, I suppose?'

'Yes.'

She made no move to answer, and the phone stopped ringing.

'Things alright between you and Eric, I suppose?'

'Oh, yes, well enough.'

'And how did you find Nigel? Has he changed?'

'Not especially.'

Belinda's irritation deepened. She'd given the cow a bed for the night and she couldn't even be arsed to hold a civil conversation. Why was she bothering? In the awkward silence she poured herself another glass.

Viv's mobile rang again. This time she didn't jump.

'I'll let it ring,' she said calmly. 'He'll give up soon.'

God, you're a cold bitch, thought Belinda. For the first time she felt a twinge of sympathy for Eric.

'So, how's life treating you?' Viv asked when her phone eventually fell silent.

'Oh, pretty good. I'm retired now, of course.'

'You're enjoying it, then? You're not finding yourself at a loss? Eric did, when he retired. Not that he admitted it, of course.'

'No, no, plenty to do, time to do all the things –'

Belinda's assertion was interrupted by the ringing of her own phone. She hurried over to it, relieved.

'Hi.'

'Hello, is that Belinda?' An unidentifiable male voice.

'Speaking.'

'Is Viv there? Sorry, it's Nigel, I should have said. You remember me?'

'Nigel! Yes, of course. Yes, Viv's here.'

She looked across at Viv. There was a hint of unease.

'I need to speak to her. Tell her it's urgent, please.'

She held out the phone.

'He says it's urgent.'

Viv moved to the phone with a small sigh. Belinda returned to her wine. I'm buggered if I'm going to leave the room, she thought, this might be interesting; anyway, why should I leave, in my own house?

'Yes?' said Viv, then, after a few seconds, '*What?*', the question being accompanied by a widening of the eyes. In the silence that followed Belinda noticed the blood drain from her face.

'I'll go immediately. I'll get a taxi.' There was a tremor in her voice. She put down the phone, and stood, staring into space.

'Viv?'

'It's Eric. He's been hurt. He's in hospital. I've got to go. Is there a local taxi firm you use?'

'Which hospital?'

'UCL, Nigel said, near Euston.'

'Never mind a taxi, I'll take you. What happened? Is he badly hurt?'

'Yes, I think so.'

'Come on, then. My car's outside.'

Belinda moved over to Viv and squeezed her hand; the squeeze was not returned.

Chapter 15

THE GEORGE, BOROUGH HIGH STREET

'Where the hell have those buggers got to?'

Jim was getting restless, Alan thought, no doubt because he was desperate for yet another pint. Bloody hell, wasn't it enough that one of their number had already been revealed to be an alcoholic? Jim was well on the way to being completely pie-eyed, which was why Alan had exerted all his persuasive powers to get him to wait until Eric, Viv and Nigel arrived. He wasn't up to coping on his own with a drunken Jim, particularly as the booze seemed to aggravate his aggressive tendencies. The Market Porter was filling up, and Jim had already expressed loud exasperation at having been asked to 'Shove up a bit, mate, will you?' when a group of young men had swooped to occupy the remaining vacant chairs at their table. He'd told Jim to wait for his drink until they moved on to The George, which had quietened him for a while, but as the minutes ticked away with no sign of the other three Jim had got twitchy, fidgeting in his seat, glaring at anyone who made eye contact with him, his hand automatically reaching for his glass, further twitchings and mutterings ensuing each time he realised the glass was empty.

'Sod this,' he said, 'I'm getting another pint. D'you want one?'

'No,' said Al. 'Why don't you just make it a half? They'll be here any minute.'

'You said that fifteen minutes ago. And I'm not drinking bloody halves. Just because I'm queer it dunna mean I have to act like a fuckin' Nancy.'

He got up unsteadily and weaved his way across to the bar. It was hidden by a crush of waiting customers, and Alan hoped he'd be saved further embarrassment by the others arriving before Jim was served.

Alan watched him, daring not to look at the lads with whom he shared the table, whose conversation had come to an abrupt stop at hearing Jim's revelation, and who were now, no doubt, assessing the likelihood of his being Jim's partner. He didn't look the slightest bit gay, he told himself, then chided himself for again falling into the trap of stereotyping. What did gays look and sound like these days, anyway? Just like everyone else, he supposed, just as Jim did. When, after Eric's departure, Jim had admitted to his sexuality, Alan had expressed amazement and disbelief, to which Jim had responded with an explosive 'What did you fuckin' expect? Jules and Sandy?'

But Alan's surprise about Jim's sexual preferences had been transitory; it was, after all, no big deal. Less easy to accept was what he'd said about seeing Tony outside Vivienne's flat back in Leeds. It was, as Eric had said before departing, totally unbelievable. OK, perhaps Tony might have tried to chance his arm, but Viv, the fastidious Viv, would have given him short shrift, surely? All that flirting on the pub-crawl had just been a bit of fun, hadn't it? The sort of behaviour that attractive young people engage in after a few drinks?

If it had been Nigel that Jim had seen, then Alan would have been less surprised. Nigel, he knew, had always held a torch for Viv. His self-assurance had always evaporated in her presence, he'd hung on her every word, his eyes had followed her when he thought no-one was watching. But Alan had watched, for he was one of nature's observers. No-one else seemed to notice Nigel's infatuation, not Viv, Alan was sure. It was strange that Eric hadn't picked up on it – or had he? Was this the reason the Jacksons had not attended the Leeds reunion ten years previously? Was Eric even now concerned about his wife and Nigel being alone together, was that why he'd hurried off to meet them on the Millennium Bridge? Had jealousy stretched its long arm across four decades?

Do we really know our friends, he wondered? Probably not, for his friends certainly didn't know him. He knew he'd been the amiable make-weight of the group at Leeds, that he didn't have their good looks (Jim excepted of course), or their wit, or talent, but this didn't mean he was stupid. Just because he'd said little didn't mean he hadn't known what was going on, that he'd been unaware of the strains and tensions amongst them, unaware of the reservations that Vivienne had about Eric and the amused tolerance that Nigel had for him, unaware of the true nature of Jim's glum dourness and of the desperate insecurity behind Tony's brashness. But today his understanding of the past had been savagely undermined, and with it his own sense of self, for much of what we are in late middle age comprises the accumulation of our memories. One of Alan's former colleagues, admittedly a lonely old bachelor, had insisted that happiness is bound to past places and times, and to sights, sounds and people as they once were; that one is never happy in the here and now, only in the there and then. Never return to old places, for they will have changed –some for ever, not for better as Lennon had sung (what a mature observation for one in his twenties!) – better to remember them as they were. Was the same true of people, despite their superficial resemblance to their former selves? Was it a mistake to have seen them all again? Better perhaps to have taken to the grave his memories of them as they once were?

He never used to think like this, but then he never used to think much of his time in Leeds. Until recently it had seemed like a three year aberration, for it had been the only time he'd been separated from Sheila. They'd known each other since they were five, kids together at Primary School in Woolwich, where she was the only girl in his class who hadn't teased him for his tubby frame and ginger hair. For that he'd doted on her. Briefly separated when he passed the Eleven Plus and she'd been consigned to the local Sec Mod, they were reunited when he, succumbing to adolescent hormonal stirrings and his love of rock'n'roll, and tired of being a working-class fish in all-male middle-class waters at the Grammar School, had joined the local youth club. They'd soon begun 'going out together' as Alan's widowed mother had said, adding embarrassingly, because it was true, that it was love's young dream. He'd been surprised when he'd passed sufficient 'O' Levels to enter the 6th form, and amazed when his 'A' Level grades enabled him to scrape a place at University. Yes, he'd enjoyed his time there – who couldn't, in the 1960s? – but his enforced return to Woolwich, his marriage to Sheila and his years in Ealing were the true stuff of life. Some might say his life was a failure: his Maths degree was only a third, effectively barring him from promoted posts. But despite his academic limitations he'd been a good teacher, his easy-going affability serving to secure the co-operation of his pupils far more effectively than the more strident exhortations of his colleagues. He'd enjoyed his work without being obsessed by it, and without engaging in the sort of out-of-hours social networking with his colleagues that seemed to be increasingly de rigueur in the teaching profession. His life had revolved round his friends, his hobbies and his family. Mundane, he supposed some people would call it. It was good enough for him.

And yet, looking across at Jim, still waiting to be served, a scowl on the features that were so familiar to him from three years of shared experiences in life's springtime, he felt bitter regret that the last chance of his connecting with the past were evaporating in discord. This would be the last time he would see any of them, and, from the way they were behaving, none of them would wish to see each other either. What a sad end. The spirit of the 1960s, alive only when those who were young in that decade were together, would soon pass from collective memory. He'd had visions of them all, those that remained, meeting up together in the years to come, to toast his memory. It seemed unlikely now. They were the Peace and Love generation: why could they not be kinder to each other?

No! Why had he not thought of it before? There *would* be an occasion when they'd gather together again. They'd come to his funeral, surely? He'd not yet given much thought to his funeral. Perhaps it was time that he did. He must impress on Sheila the importance of their coming – to not just give notice of the event, but to issue a specific invitation to attend. Another idea came to him – he'd write them a letter. A letter from the grave, to be given to them at the wake. A last request that they forget their differences, that they continue to meet, perhaps every year on the anniversary of his death. And the letter should be read out aloud – a nice touch of ceremony. Who would be the best to read it? Nigel, of course. He was seized with a sense of urgency. The letter would need careful wording. He'd start planning it tonight, in the hotel.

'Ok, Al? Where's Jim?

Alan started: so deep had been immersion in his project that he'd not noticed Nigel enter. Eric was behind him.

'He's at the bar. Nip over and tell him you're here, can you mate, before he gets a drink in? I want to get on to the George.'

Nigel obliged.

'What took you so long?' Alan asked Eric. 'And where's Viv?'

There was no answer. Eric remained standing, despite the proximity of the chair vacated by Jim.

'Eric!' Alan shouted over the pub hubbub.

'Eh? Sorry?'

'I said, where's Viv?'

'Oh...... she's not feeling so good. She's gone to .... gone back to the hotel.'

'What, by herself?'

'Yes.'

Alan was alert to something having happened: Eric was usually reluctant to be parted from his wife, and was if anything over-solicitous when she was out of sorts, either physically or emotionally. To have allowed her to make the journey back to the hotel alone when she was ill – well! Alan tried to envisage him behaving thus towards Sheila: such an act was unthinkable. He examined Eric. It was difficult to read his expression: distracted, yes, but with occasional narrowing of the eyes and working of the mouth which spoke of some inner ferment.

'Are *you* all right, mate?'

'Me? Yes. Course I am. Never fucking better, me old *mate*, me old *cock-sparrer*, me old *china*.' Eric's words were spoken with an aggressive sneer, made the more threatening by his standing over the still seated Alan.

Bloody hell, Alan thought, something definitely *has* happened to rattle his cage like that. Eric rarely swore, and he'd never been one to take the piss over Alan's cockney origins. Viv's absence had something to do with it, he was sure. Another certainty was that, whatever had happened, there was little to be gained in tackling Nige about it. Nige was far too bloody discreet to reveal anything.

On cue, Nigel walked over to them, a scowling Jim in his wake.

'If you lot anna been so fuckin' long then I wunna wanted another pint, would I?' he was saying, then, as his eyes passed blearily over Alan and Eric, 'Where's Viv then?'

'She's not feeling so well,' said Nigel, 'She's decided to get an early night.'

'*Ha!*' Eric snorted dismissively.

'Wass wrong with her then? Can't be pissed, she wunna drinking.'

'She had a headache, didn't she, Eric?'

Eric ignored the appeal for confirmation. Alan noticed that he hadn't looked at Nigel since they entered: he had turned away slightly, evidently to avoid the possibility of accidental eye contact.

Jim persisted with his drunken interrogation.

'Bit sudden, wannit? She was all right at St Paul's. Won't she be around when we get back then?'

'I think she'll be in bed,' said Nigel, 'Don't you, Eric?'

'How the fuck should I know?' Eric exploded, 'You evidently know her better than I do.'

My God, Alan thought, something's happened between those two. But what, he wondered? Surely the admission of an undergraduate crush wouldn't provoke such vehemence? Bloody hell, he didn't think he could face any more surprises today.

Jim's booze-befuddled brain had evidently been assimilating Nigel's assertion that Vivienne would be in bed, and he suddenly gave a leering smile.

'In bed? Who with, I wonder, eh?' he hiccupped. 'Just like Leeds p'raps, only this time it's Tony who left the party first.'

Nigel pulled back his shoulders and gazed at Jim; he then said quietly 'You're drunk, Jim, so I'll make allowances for you. But do us all a favour and shut up, will you?'

Eric, Alan noticed, seemed not to have registered Jim's innuendo and was still staring into space. There was a prolonged, edgy silence made more pronounced by the chatter and laughter that surrounded them.

It was broken by Nigel.

'Right,' he said. 'Just one more pub, eh, Al? The George, is it? Shall we be on our way?'

A wave of tiredness settled over Alan. Not just tiredness – I'm weary, he thought, weary of everything. His mother had used the term frequently during her last illness. He'd come to know just how she felt: a great, lowering lethargy that seeped into every bone and into the mind, dulling every stimulus, inhibiting the capacity for any enjoyment, but a lethargy unrelieved by rest. 'There's no rest left in me,' she'd often said. He didn't want to go on to the George, he didn't want to go back to the hotel, he wanted to go home to Sheila, but he was without the energy to contemplate making the journey.

He pulled himself to his feet.

'OK, then,' he said. 'Last lap.'

He was scarcely upright before his chair had been seized by a hovering customer.

Outside, the light was fading, rendering the scene even more redolent of its Dickensian past, save for the garish hanging baskets on the pub walls. Knots of smokers stood, savouring the nicotine and the rare warmth of the summer night. Bare thighs, midriffs and shoulders abounded; laughter echoed up and down the street.

Nigel and Alan led the way back through the darkness of Borough Market. Eric was a few paces behind. Some yards behind him, and staggering slightly, followed Jim. He was suddenly feeling very drunk indeed. It wasn't a pleasant feeling. He'd forgotten what it was like, the waves of nausea, the lack of focus, the feelings of paranoia alternating with hatred and contempt for all about him, the inability to articulate his thoughts. Under the confused maelstrom of disconnected thoughts and conflicting emotions bubbled a cauldron of self-loathing that he had, after all these years, once more allowed himself to relapse into taking comfort in bingeing, something he thought was behind him, something he no longer needed now that he was reconciled to his nature and had the love and support of a partner.

In the darkness he blundered into a vegetable box left on the ground beside one of the market stalls and cursed when the pain seeped through the beery anaesthesia. He hopped about, clutching his knee. Fuckin' London bastards! Why cunna the Cockney twats clear up after 'emselves? He was seized with a hatred of all things southern. He should never have come. It was exposure to London and bloody Londoners with their whiney speech and their poncy pubs that had made him take refuge in ale. He should have stayed in Stoke. By this time on a Friday night he and Nicky would be having a quiet pint in the Greyhound, and there'd be no need to get pissed, surrounded as they'd be by the comforting accents of his own folk, the salt of the earth. Salt of the earth. That's what Potteries folk were. No one else to touch 'em.

'Are you with us, Jim?'

Nigel's clear voice, with its clarity and upper-class confidence, served to enrage him further. He glanced up: Nigel and Alan were silhouetted against the yellow glow of the street lights, now visible through market entrance. Eric had caught them up but was standing slightly apart.

'Quite easy to get lost, here,' said Nigel when Jim emerged into the street, 'and it looks as though you might need a bit of help crossing the roads.'

'Piss off, you patronising cunt,' Jim retorted.

'Suit yourself,' said Nigel evenly, and led Eric away towards a pedestrian crossing.

Blinking in the glare of the lights and disoriented by the roar of traffic, Jim was assailed by another wave of nausea. He leaned against a wall, vaguely aware that the busy road seemed to be devoid of pedestrians, and conscious of its rather reassuring run-down seediness. Just as dirty as parts of Stoke; fuckin' Alan and Nigel wunna want us to see this in daylight, he thought, forgetting that he'd been there earlier when the taxi had dropped them.

Need Viv here, he thought morosely, at least *she'd* talk to me, she always did, when I was down. Not like the other sods. They'd never understood. They don't understand now. They're fuckin' homophobes; they think they're so fuckin' liberal but when faced with a real-life gay it's like they've been contaminated. Should never have told 'em. Bloody

Alan's reaction in that last pub – patronising bastard, as bad as Nigel – have I told Nigel? No, I anna – but I bet Alan's telling him right now. And fuckin' Eric – showed himself in his true colours, didn't he? Should have thumped him before he left the pub. Only Viv had understood, and now she isn't here.

'You're right, Jim: he's a cunt.'

Jim jumped. He'd not been aware that Eric was standing close by.

'What? Who? What you talking about?'

'Nige. He's a devious bastard.'

'Thought he was a mate of yours. You shared a flat with him, didn't you. Two bloody southerners together.'

'Christ, he's a bloody Yorkshireman, had you forgotten? Look, let's cross over and find this pub. Come on.'

'Think I've had enough. Wouldn't mind getting back.'

'Well *I* need a drink, a stiff one. Anyway I don't want to let Nige out of my sight. Come on, Jim, strength in numbers.'

Jim allowed himself to be led towards the crossing, and found he was grateful for Eric's assistance, being saved by his companion's tug from being run down by a car which ignored the crossing and sped on, the bass thumping from its speakers all but drowning the jeers and catcalls of its occupants. He'd better stay with Eric. He couldn't find his way back to the hotel alone. Good old Eric – he hated Nigel too. A wave of inebriated affection for Eric swept over him, turning to maudlin remorse when he remembered what he'd said about Viv's departure. He braced himself to apologise. Saying sorry didn't come easy to Jim.

'Hang on a minute,' he said, as Eric led him towards the alley down which Nigel and Alan had disappeared.

'What now?'

'What I said about Viv. About her going back to the hotel to meet Tony. Didn't mean it. It was crap. Sorry.'

'Back to the hotel? What are you on about?'

'What I said earlier.'

Eric looked puzzled.

'You're pissed. What you said earlier was that Tony was outside Viv's flat in Leeds.'

Jim shook his head in an attempt to clear the fog of misunderstanding, then the mist dispersed.

'That too. I was wrong: no, he *was* there, but he probably hadn't been in her flat, I mean he probably –'

'Nothing would surprise me about my wife,' Eric interrupted.

Even through his drunkenness Jim was able register the loathing on Eric's face, but he was unsure where the hatred was directed. He blundered on.

'Didn't Viv ever tell you I was gay?'

'There's a lot Viv didn't tell me. And I'm sorry about what I said to you in the Market Porter.'

'We're quits, then?'

'Yes. Let's go. You can buy me a scotch.'

Despite his apprehension about the night still to come, Nigel's spirits lifted a little as they emerged from the alley into the courtyard of the George. He used to drink there occasionally when he was in The Service. He'd read up on its history, knew that it was the sole survivor of a number of galleried coaching inns that had once lined the London to Dover road, knew that it had been partially demolished at the end of the 19th century to make way for a goods office of the Great Northern Railway, and that the remainder had been saved and restored by the National Trust. A bit over-restored, he thought, looking at the white-painted balustrades that lined the gallery of the first and second floors –surely it would have been better to have left it as bare wood? And to do away with the ubiquitous hanging baskets that were suspended from it – though you couldn't blame the National Trust for the brewery's taste for 21st century floral arrangements, he supposed.

The courtyard outside was crowded with trestle tables, every one apparently occupied. Searching for a vacant place so that Alan could sit, he didn't notice immediately the modern building that had been erected on the opposite side. It was evidently a bar, its design attempting to complement the galleried frontage of the George, though executed in concrete, glass and steel. It was a brave attempt, but it didn't quite come off. The courtyard was evidently open to customers of both establishments, hence its overcrowding.

He noticed Eric and Jim emerging from the alley.

'Hang around here, Al,' he said, 'and see if you can grab a seat if one comes vacant. I'll go and get the drinks. What d'you want?'

'Orange juice, please mate. And d'you think they'd run to some crisps? Haven't eaten for ages.'

'I'll see what I can do.'

'Are you getting them in for Eric and Jim?'

'Let them get their own. We're all drinking at different rates. Silly to try and stick to rounds.'

He strode over to one of the entrances. Inside, it was reassuringly unchanged. A series of narrow connecting rooms ran the length of the pub; in many there was space only for a single table by the windows. There was a wealth of lattice on the windows and beams on the walls. Unlike the courtyard outside, most of the tables were unoccupied.

He was about to go and tell the others about the availability of seats when he thought again. Close confinement with Eric and Jim in a small empty bar would be unbearable – well, not unbearable, for Nigel was trained to cope with far more stressful situations. But such was the disharmony that had arisen between them that the company of strangers around them was needed to provide some measure of distraction, something else to look at when trying to avoid eye contact with one's erstwhile friends.

He ordered an orange juice, a small glass of house red and two packets of crisps. Nigel didn't like crisps, but there was no other food on offer except in the restaurant upstairs. He was hungry: the intention had been to go for a meal after completing the pub-crawl, but that was now unthinkable. Looming over him was the prospect of the conversation that he had to have with Eric. He'd promised to explain, but what was there *to* explain? It was a simple matter, a story as old as civilisation. Male and female meet after a space of years; there is immediate physical attraction, they fall in love, have an affair. What more could be said? What words could be used to alleviate the pain of the injured party? Was it worth even trying? In any case, Nigel had his own pain now. Melanie and Oscar came to mind. He was overcome by a sense of the hopelessness of his situation.

What had he been hoping for by seeing Viv again? Only an indication that she had regrets, perhaps a surreptitious squeeze of the hand under a table or a meaningful glance when they passed their old meeting places, something that he could take back to Stow and savour in those moments when the bleakness of his life with or without Melanie overwhelmed him. Then all his illusions had been shattered by Tony's revelations and by the agony of hearing

Vivienne's account of that night. During that embrace on the Millennium Bridge, that agony had been replaced by a welling of hope that all might not be lost, that there might be a future for them notwithstanding their advancing years and the cluttered baggage of their domestic situations. How long had that hope lasted? A minute, maybe? One minute in which he'd felt young again, eager to experience once more the long-forgotten adrenaline buzz of arranging secret assignations, those stolen moments when he could once more buy flowers, order theatre tickets, book restaurants. Perhaps it was as well that Eric had appeared when he had, before those dreams slowly evaporated in a growing awareness of the logistical impossibility of ever resuming the affair. But at what a cost! Viv had gone: he doubted he'd ever see her again, and whatever fellow-feeling he'd had for Eric was now mired in guilt. All that was left was to try to assuage that guilt by confessing to all that Eric wanted to know. He knew he'd have to answer all Eric's anguished questions, how it came about, how often they'd met, where they'd spent their times, what they'd discussed – but please God, not what they did in bed.. There was one thing he was thankful for – Viv had always resolutely refused to discuss her marriage: at least he'd be spared having to skewer Eric with that knowledge. He could be honest: he knew nothing of what passed between husband and wife.

He picked up the drinks and the packets of crisps and walked out into the courtyard. Alan was no longer standing where he'd left him. Another wave of guilt assailed him – he should be looking after Al. Had he collapsed? And where were the other two? The trestle tables immediately outside the George were all occupied by strangers, and his view across the courtyard was obscured by standing customers. Many of them were in the early stages of inebriation; it was a raucous, rowdy gathering that held the potential for trouble. He wondered why Al had chosen to finish the pub-crawl in an area of London that, at night, held a trace of menace. It would have been better to have started here and have worked their way back to the more salubrious Holborn and Fitzrovia.

He began a circumnavigation of the courtyard, drinks and crisps in hand, glancing surreptitiously at the occupants of each table, conscious that night-times in towns were becoming the exclusive preserve of the young. He felt out of place. He hoped he was not attracting attention by virtue of his clothes and his years, but no one seemed to notice him. Such is the invisibility of the old.

Eventually he spotted them, at the far side of the courtyard, just outside the modern bar. They were squashed together at one end of a table, Jim and Alan on one side, Eric opposite. Four young women occupied the other end. Jim and Eric seemed to be drinking shorts. How had they managed to be served before him? He hadn't seen either of them at the bar.

'Here you are, Al,' he said, 'Managed to get some crisps. Shove up, Eric, I'll sit on the end.'

Eric shoved up, not looking at him, and jogged the elbow of the young woman sharing his bench. Her drink slopped over the table. She rounded on Eric.

'Hey, watch it, you old drongo, I've lost half me drink.'

Her accent was Antipodean and her voice shrill. Eric mumbled what Nigel, still standing at the end of the table, assumed to be an apology. It was evidently not accepted.

'Cost me three pounds, that drink did,' she said, indignation adding to her shrillness. 'You'd better get me another one, hadn't you, mate?'

Three young men at an adjacent table had ceased their loud conversation and were peering across at the scene with expectant interest.

Eric made no response and no move, choosing to stare into his glass.

'Hey, did you hear what I said? You owe me a drink.'

Nigel, alert to the dangers of confrontation in such a crowded febrile environment, was about to rescue the situation by offering to go to the bar himself, when one of the watching young men detached himself from his party and approached.

'I'll get you another drink,' he said, 'Why don't you and your friends come and join us? Plenty of room if we all squash up.'

He was smartly if casually dressed, and his voice bore only a hint of Estuary English. The young woman flashed him a smile; she was attractive in a Baywatch sort of way and wore the obligatory next-to-nothing, as did her friends.

'All right mate, why not? Are we up for it, babes?'

The question was addressed to her friends who responded with the sort of enthusiasm that could only come from those who'd not been in the country long enough to assimilate the bored disdain so often affected by young Englishwomen in that situation. They moved to join the men: great play was made of making room for them on the benches. Nigel observed that Eric was the subject of stares which would have been intimidating had he not still been staring into his drink which, Nigel noticed, seemed to be a double Scotch.

'When did you get your drink?' he asked as he sat down.

Eric edged away from him.

'I got 'em in,' said Jim. 'Made sure I went to a different bar to you. Scotch is served quicker than poncy glasses of wine.'

Nigel registered Jim's hostility and thought about challenging him before deciding to save his energy for the looming confrontation with Eric. That, however, would have to wait. This was the last pub on Alan's carefully planned itinerary, and he deserved better than having to bear mute witness to the falling-out of his friends. Looking at Al, who was gazing round the courtyard with a wistful expression on his exhausted face, Nigel was seized by the certainty that this would be the last time they would share a drink.

'When was the last time you were here, then, Al?' he asked.

'Long time ago, mate. Before that monstrosity was built.' He nodded towards the modern bar.

'But it's better than the building it replaced.'

'Maybe, but at least it wasn't a bar. This courtyard was just for George regulars. Now it's swamped by all these youngsters.'

'I didn't think you were averse to young people, Al.'

'I'm not. It's just that they've taken over everywhere. There's nowhere left for old gits like us to go and drink without feeling out of place.'

'Well, we haven't done too badly today, thanks to you, Al. It was a wonderful pub-crawl. It was, wasn't it, chaps?'

Eric and Jim, to whom the question was addressed, were sitting opposite each other in silence. At first Nigel thought they'd either not heard, or had chosen to ignore him, but after a moment Jim, with barely-disguised ill-grace, conceded that it hadn't been a bad day, and Eric nodded what was evidently a reluctant assent.

Damn them, thought Nigel, they're not going to get away with that. He raised his glass of wine.

'To you, Al! Thanks for all your organisation, and for bringing us together again.'

Jim and Eric were embarrassed into compliance, and joined in the toast. Their muttered salutations were drowned by a loud echo of 'To you, Al!' from the young men at the adjacent table, delivered in an accent which mimicked Nigel's. Their female companions screeched in appreciation.

'Hey, you old buggers!' one of the young men shouted, 'Hoping to score tonight, are you?'

More screeches of merriment.

'Ignore them' Nigel muttered, but Jim was already staring at the source of the insult.

'Fancy a bit of Aussie arse then, do you granddad?' came a challenge, followed by a shriek of 'God, he's disgusting!' from one of the females.

Jim made to stand up, but seats fixed to trestle tables do not lend themselves to speedy ascent even when sober: his thighs banged against the underside of the table, forcing him back into an ungainly sitting position. More hilarity ensued from the Anglo-Australian party. Customers at adjacent tables turned to watch.

Nigel hurriedly began to attempt to engage his companions in a discussion about which of the pubs they'd visited had been their particular favourites. At first only Alan participated, but eventually Jim joined in, provoked by Alan's assertion that only London could offer such a variety of drinking establishments. Even Eric contributed the odd remark. Nigel continued to provide conversational openings, all the while keeping an ear cocked towards the adjacent table where the young men had evidently decided to abandon the entertainment of mocking their seniors in favour of none-too subtle attempts to persuade the women to join them for the rest of the night. He began to relax, insofar as relaxation was possible given what lay ahead.

The courtyard was becoming yet more congested as more revellers piled in through the alley. A glass, or a bottle perhaps, smashed to the ground over by the pub entrance, followed by ironic cheers. A loud argument broke out between two cropped-haired lads standing a few yards away; their disagreement became physical when the larger of the two began shoving the shoulder of the other, then their female partners intervened, none too politely, and the hostility was extinguished as quickly as it had ignited. At the table beside them, Anglo-Australian relations had evidently taken a turn for the worse: a short altercation, culminating in a 'Fuck you, mate' from one of the women was followed by her rapid departure, followed immediately by her three friends. The young men began an ill-tempered dispute as to which of them was responsible for ruining their chances, then sank into a morose, twitchy silence which boded ill for anyone who had the misfortune to cross them.

'I think it's time we made a move,' said Nigel, 'It's London Bridge tube station we want, I suppose Al?'

'That's right. It's just round the corner.'

They extricated themselves from the benches and headed across the courtyard; their table was immediately swooped upon by the cropped-haired lads and their partners. As they negotiated their way through the crowds towards the alley leading to the street, none of them looked back: they were therefore unaware that the three young men had also risen and were heading in the same direction.

Eric fell behind the other three as they made their way up Borough High Street. The last hour had been torture. To have to endure the company of a person who was now anathema to him; to have to pretend that all was well, to have to engage in meaningless pleasantries, to have to agree that they'd had an enjoyable time, and all this because Nigel, fucking Nigel, had blackmailed him into rejoining the party by his insistence that Alan's day should not be spoiled. And it *was* blackmail, no doubt about it, for there had been the implication that explanations, excuses, apologies, whichever it was the bastard might provide, would not be forthcoming unless he first went through this charade. He, Eric, should have set off in pursuit of Viv as soon as she'd left, have insisted that they return to the hotel to talk, or maybe have given her a chance to calm down and then have turned up at Belinda's place – no, that wasn't on, for he didn't know Belinda's address. Did Nigel know it? Had Belinda been party to the affair, if that was what it was? Did assignations take place in Belinda's flat, on all those occasions when Viv had claimed she'd gone to London to stay with her friend? Was he the victim not just of duplicity but of a conspiracy?

He followed the others as they turned towards the tube station, but was blind to his surroundings. His mind searched the past: if it had been an affair, when did it begin? Surely not at Leeds, oh God, not when he and Nigel were sharing a flat? No, no, impossible, there were no opportunities, when he and Viv weren't together than he was with Nigel, and Nigel showed no interest in women anyway. There was no evidence of mutual attraction on the few occasions Nigel had visited the cottage. They must have met up much later, by accident perhaps? When was it Viv started visiting Belinda? Perhaps it wasn't an affair?

Viv had never shown much enthusiasm for sex. Perhaps it was platonic? Perhaps Nigel had problems, and Viv had counselled him, just like she used to with Jim? No, he was too self-assured, too confident, too bloody debonair and good looking to have problems.

What had prompted Viv's infidelity? It hadn't been a bad marriage, had it? They'd always jogged along well enough – ok, Viv could be a bit impatient sometimes, a bit dismissive of his enthusiasms back in the days when he'd had enthusiasms. He'd been a good provider, hadn't he? Worked his balls off to secure promotion so she could have the house, the clothes, the holidays, the lifestyle to which she'd aspired? Ok, maybe his immersion in work had militated against a fulfilling social life, but after the kids had left she'd found her own friends, friends with similar interests, and all of them women as far as he was aware. Was it raising the kids that had soured her? She'd not been the most doting of mothers, was happy to leave him in charge when they were old enough. She'd never voiced any specific discontent, in fact they spoke of little except domestic trivia and occasionally current affairs. They never discussed their own relationship, even in the early days of their marriage when they still had sex, after which, he'd read in *Guardian,* most couples spoke of what was in their hearts. With a jolt, he realised that he'd never heard her say that she loved him – or if she had, it was so long ago that he'd forgotten.

His eyes were assailed by garish fluorescent lighting and he found himself to be in the underground station. He was being shouted at – it was the others, standing by the ticket machine. And it was Nigel doing the shouting, telling him to get a move on, that they didn't want to be separated, they'd have to change trains at Bank.

Suddenly, he was filled with a stomach-churning, head-spinning whirlpool of rage, jealousy and humiliation, underlain by a pent-up desire to shout, swear, bash, thump, *hurt* someone. Instead, he groped in his pocket for change for his ticket.

Chapter 16

THE NORTHERN LINE

It was christened The Misery Line back in the 1970s, and the term stuck throughout the following decade as the delays became more frequent, the overcrowding more acute, the carriages more dilapidated, dirty and graffiti covered. It was loathed by the squashed and sweating commuters whether from Edgware and High Barnet in the north or Morden in the south. Despite improvements that occurred with the introduction of new rolling stock in the 1990s, delays and overcrowding continued and the carriages were still, like all in the London Underground, devoid of air conditioning.

Between eight and ten in the evening however the trains are relatively empty; no one is forced to stand; the yellow grab-rails that replaced the old dangling straps are unutilised and revealed in all their garish modernity; there are no exhortations to stand clear of the doors, for then is that hiatus which occurs between the departure of the daily commuters and the later influx of homeward–bound concert- and theatre-goers and, after them, the late-night revellers making their boisterous way back to the suburbs from the clubs and bars of Soho and the West End.

That night, the passengers in the third carriage from the front on the northbound train from Morden were typical of the hour, a largely silent assortment of night-workers reconciled to their forthcoming un-social toil and a few tourists who'd been defeated by the complexities of the Underground system and had found themselves in parts of London never featured in brochures. Three such, oriental in appearance, were the only ones conversing; they were in what sounded like agitated debate, pointing at the stylised map of the line displayed above the windows opposite them.

Maria Bimenya, sitting under the object of their discussion, guessed the cause of their agitation. She, when first making this journey, had been similarly confused by the way the Northern Line divided after Elephant and Castle, and had panicked before realising that the two branches came together again at Euston, her destination. That was when she'd just arrived from Uganda and had been forced to take accommodation out at Morden. She'd found the journey from there to University College Hospital, where she was a nurse, too stressful, and had moved to share digs with a compatriot in Borough, where the squalor of the environment was a price worth paying for the shorter length of exposure to the Underground. After two years in England she still hated the tube, especially at this time of night when there clung to the carriages a moist, warm dankness, pungent with the odour of the departed daytime hordes. At such times she longed to smell again the wood smoke of her native village and to walk amongst the matoke plantations on the terraced hillsides of Kigezi.

'The next station is – London Bridge,' intoned a disembodied female in an accent that Maria recognised from the BBC World Service but which she'd not heard anyone speak in London, 'Change here for – the Jubilee Line.'

The announcement provoked more furious discussion amongst the Orientals, one of them jabbing angrily at a map in his guide-book and gesticulating back at the map above Maria's head. She knew better than to offer advice: tourists from the Far East, she knew from experience, tended to assume that anyone with a black skin would be as ignorant as they about Britain's capital city. In fact her advice was evidently not required, for as the train drew to a halt the Orientals, still jabbering animatedly, stood up and made for the doors which opened, permitting their egress and the entry of four men who stood hesitantly before taking their seats, three opposite, one next to her. The doors remained open and then there began that disconcerting whirring, whining sound that often occurred when underground trains, for some inexplicable reason, remained stationary. The first time Maria had been exposed to this she was alarmed, wondering whether it signalled the approach of some subterranean horror, but she was now blasé about the arcane workings of Transport for London and sat patiently waiting for onward transmission.

'What's the fuckin' hold up?' came from the man who'd chosen to sit next to her. Maria was by now accustomed to the obscenity which seemed to accompany most utterances made by the English, though admittedly the frequency of its use usually bore an inverse relationship to the age of the speaker, and the one who had voiced the question seemed advanced in years. Or was he? Maria still had difficulty in gauging the ages of the natives. The English seemed either to cling to youthful clothes and hairstyles until reaching their three-score-years-and- ten, suddenly to melt into a mess of wrinkles, bent backs and shuffling feet; or, and this was particularly the case in those parts of the city in which she moved, to disintegrate into a premature old age by the time they were thirty-five, grey-faced, lank-haired, obese and malodorous. She had still to become accustomed to how the natives stank.

The question posed by the man next to her remained unanswered by his companions, and Maria heard him mutter to himself that he was dying for a slash. She risked a sideways glance at him: he was lined and gaunt, his sparse hair closely cropped, but wore the obligatory tee-shirt and jeans. He belched loudly, and Maria blanched at the waft of beery breath that assailed her.

'For God's sake, Jim.' The remonstration came from one of the men sitting opposite. He was tall, slim, well built, with a healthy head of fair hair and was smartly dressed in white trousers and a linen jacket: he reminded Maria of the sort of Englishmen she remembered from her childhood, those few who haunted the hotels of Kabale, rather sad remnants of her country's colonial past. She found him rather comforting. He caught her eye and smiled apologetically: she returned the smile. He seemed an unlikely companion for the man next to her.

The other two men had less definable characteristics. One had curly grey hair framing kindly if undistinguished features: he wore a shapeless jacket and baggy fawn trousers. Looking at him with her practiced nurse's eye, Maria thought he looked ill.

She began to appraise the fourth, but her attention was diverted by a commotion at the doors. They had begun to close, but juddered open again as a man forced his way between them and entered: he was followed by two others. The doors closed again, but the train remained stationary. The three men stood and peered round the carriage. One caught sight of her.

'Well, well,' he said, loudly, 'I see we have the company of one of our valued immigrant workers.'

Immediately, the fair-haired man who had smiled at her rose, crossed the carriage and sat next to her: she was sandwiched between him and the one he'd called Jim. She was reassured, but only slightly: safety was not necessarily to be found in numbers, as she knew only too well from her experiences in the crowded A & E department on Friday and Saturday nights.

'Shut up, Dave,' said one of the other new entrants, 'Our coloured brethren aren't the target tonight.'

The train started. 'This is a Northern Line train bound for – Edgware. The next station is – Bank. Change here for – the Central, and Waterloo and City Lines.'

The three men remained standing by the doors. Maria knew better than to make eye-contact with them. She had gained a fleeting impression when they'd entered; they were youngish, she thought, and quite smartly dressed, all with neat slicked-back hairstyles, not the sort that she normally associated with overt racial abuse, though she knew that anti-immigrant sentiment extended across a broad spectrum of English society. They began to make loud comments, first disparaging, then increasingly abusive, directed at the elderly men. Maria maintained her gaze at the floor but sensed that the gaunt man, Jim, was it, was the object of the most offensive vituperation. 'Looks like he needs a good wash', 'Thought he could make it with our women, the seedy old bastard', 'Disgusting old paedophile', 'Reckon he needs a lesson teaching him', were a selection of the insults hurled at him. The few other passengers remaining in the central part of the carriage got up one by one and moved down to the far end. Maria was left, a lone woman sitting amongst a group of old men who seemed destined to be on the receiving end of continued verbal abuse, if not worse. She was rooted to her seat, fearful that to move would attract attention back to her.

'Where are you getting off?' the fair-haired man whispered to her.

'Not till Euston.'

'We're getting off at the next stop. When we get up, I'd make a move down the carriage if I were you, just in case, but I think it's likely that this lot will want to follow us. And I apologise for the ignorance of my fellow-countrymen.'

Maria nodded and gave him a fleeting smile

The train slowed. The disembodied female announced they were approaching Bank, and repeated her litany of the other lines served by the station. The fair-haired man stood, and led his companions towards the door. The three young men immediately moved to block their exit. Maria made good her escape to the far end of the carriage.

When the three men entered, Nigel had recognised immediately that they were the ones who'd taunted Jim back at the *George*. He cursed himself: he should have been more alert, should have looked behind him when leaving the pub, but his mind had been occupied by other things. It could be coincidence of course, they might just be bound for another pub seeking more compliant female company than that provided by the Australian girls who'd deserted them, but there was something in their demeanour that was threatening. He avoided looking at their faces, keeping his eyes on their feet, any movement of which would give the first indication of the direction of any attack. Some things from his training were never forgotten.

He heard the offensive remark directed at the black woman sitting opposite, and was surprised by its articulacy; it was not the usual oafish grunting of the working-class racist. Nigel, notwithstanding his progressive political opinions, did not idealise the lower orders. His duties in various European cities had convinced him that there was no socio-economic group quite so viciously ignorant and chauvinistic as the English proletariat. But these men were the more sinister for their relative sophistication, as evidenced by the remark about tonight's target, delivered by one who spoke with the assurance of a leader to whom the others deferred.

At all costs he must stop Jim being provoked, and he must also try to give assurance to the black woman, who was obviously terrified. He moved across the carriage to sit next to her, taking the opportunity to whisper words of reassurance and advice. He hoped she would not think he was being patronising, and was rewarded by her smile. The men began their tirade of insults: Nigel glanced across the girl at Jim, expecting to see signs of agitation, but he just looked very drunk. Across the gangway, Eric and Alan were as statues, apart from the nervous working of the former's mouth and the beads of sweat on the latter's brow.

When the train slowed he rose, saying quietly 'Our stop, chaps,' and led them towards the door. The three young men moved to form a phalanx in front of it, and stood, arms folded, looking not at him but above his head. They were smiling, sneeringly. Nigel stood still, held out his arms to stop the further advance of his companions, and did rapid mental calculations. Their tormentors were not especially well-built, and there were only three of them, but they had the advantage of youth, and Nigel was in essence alone, for Jim was drunk, Alan ill and Eric obviously petrified. It would be suicide to tackle them. Best to make a tactical withdrawal, sit down again, stay on the train until the young men got bored – they'd be unlikely to initiate an attack with the carriage half full, though all the other passengers were now huddled at the ends. But more travellers would be bound to get on as the train entered central London. Yes, stay on board: the young men wouldn't want to be carried out to Edgware, surely? As soon as they got off it would be a simple matter to catch a return train to Euston.

He turned round.

'Sit down again,' he hissed to his companions, 'and keep quiet. We'll get off later.'

They resumed their seats. The young men made no comment, made no move, but remained standing by the doors, still smiling. The silence was frightful. The train eased into Bank station: behind the men the doors slid open.

'Excuse, please.'

A slightly built, heavily bearded swarthy young man – Arab probably – insinuated his way between two of the three guarding the entrance. Suspended from one shoulder was a bulky back-pack, and as he turned to make his way down the carriage it swung and struck the smallest of the young men a glancing blow on his chest.

'Hey! Watch it!' came an aggrieved shout.

The Arab must have heard the protest, must have been aware that his back-pack had made contact with something resilient, but made no apology, didn't even look round. He heaved the pack off his shoulder and sat between Nigel and Jim in the seat vacated by the black woman, and began rummaging in the bag, his face close to its opening.

'Hey, you! Ain't you got any manners?'

Nigel saw the Arab look up to face his interrogator, and knew that by doing so his race would immediately be revealed to those whom he'd offended. It proved to be the case: he was immediately subject to a torrent of abuse.

'Fucking Paki! Islamist bastard! What's in your rucksack, you Jihadist scum? All set for a bit of matryrdom, are you, Mohammed? Getting ready for your 40 virgins? Pig. Muslim pig.'

The relief that Nigel had briefly experienced when the attention of the young men was diverted from Jim evaporated on realising that the potential for more serious trouble had arisen. These fellows were dangerous. They obviously knew something of current political issues; they were parroting the sort of phrases to be found on extreme right-wing websites. He examined them: they were smart, all wearing white shirts, black trousers and shiny leather shoes – they could almost be in uniform. Fascists undoubtedly. Members of the BNP perhaps? That organisation's lieutenants had recently smartened up considerably at the behest of the odious Nick Griffin.

The stream of invective continued. The bearded man looked appealingly at Nigel, then across at Alan and Eric, then sideways at Jim. The thugs began to move towards him, slowly, menacingly.

'Please help me,' he whimpered.

Nigel knew he was obliged to act. He was honour bound to do so, but he would have to take them on alone. The Arab looked no more capable of resistance than Alan, Eric and Jim. It would be a rout, of course, and damage would be done. Fellows such as these were usually tooled-up.

They were standing in front of him and the Arab, still spewing invective. Nigel's vision had narrowed to a bubble encompassing just the three men; the rest of the carriage was a meaningless blur. Should he wait for the first blow to be delivered, or launch a pre-emptive strike? A kick to the groin of the shortest perhaps? From a seated position it would have little force. Horrified, he realised he was frozen in indecision. Minutes seemed to pass. Then, with studied deliberation, the stockiest of the men reached down and seized the Arab's beard, pulled him to his feet. 'Please, please,' he entreated in a voice close to tears.

'Leave him alone, you bastards!' came a shout from behind the men, who turned, releasing the Arab. Nigel was confronted with the sight of Eric, his face contorted with fury, ineffectually lashing out with over-arm, womanish blows. After only a second an evidently well-rehearsed plan of assault swung into action: Eric was grabbed from behind, had his arms twisted up behind his back, while two of the men began an almost leisurely volley of punches to his face, stomach, groin. After each blow Eric grunted, no more than that; no screams, no yelps, just a series of exhalations.

Nigel was experiencing a secondary horror: a realisation that his courage or his training, perhaps both, had deserted him. The reactions that had once been so automatic no longer kicked in. He was frightened of being hurt. The scene in front of him was being played in slow motion: the assault was lasting hours. With a massive effort of will he stood, sizing up which of the assailants he should target, when Eric was suddenly released. He slid to the floor and was immediately subjected to a vicious kicking, directed at his groin, his kidneys, his head. Nigel, adrenaline surging at last, aimed a karate chop at the throat of the nearest thug, but he mistimed it, and his intended victim swung round and kicked at his legs, causing him to stagger back to his seat. He became aware of screams from the far end of the carriage and an announcement that the next stop was Moorgate. The men clustered round the doors, and calmly stepped off when they opened.

Nigel dropped to his knees beside the prone Eric: he was horribly bloodied, his features swollen and unrecognisable. Two passengers had entered, a middle-aged couple: they stood, aghast, then turned and hurried through the doors which had just begun to close. The train set off.

'Pull the alarm handle, for Christ's sake!' Nigel yelled at Jim, the nearest to that device. Jim's response was to vomit, copiously, on the floor, splashes of the day's beer and fragments of his lunchtime sandwiches covering the trickle of blood that had begun to seep from Eric's ear. Alan remained comatose in his seat.

Nigel staggered to his feet and reached for the handle.

'No! Don't pull! Don't stop the train!'

It was the black woman. She grasped Nigel's arm.

'But we must get help, he's badly –'

'What use stopping the train in a tunnel? Listen. Only four stops to Euston. Hospital near there. Train get us there quicker. You get off at next stop, phone for ambulance, tell it to go to Euston. I stay with your friend.' Even in his distress, Nigel registered that her accent was African, not Carribbean.

She turned and knelt beside Eric, put her ear to his face, then felt his wrist.

'He's alive, but not good. Help me turn him, in case he vomits – no, not you!' as Nigel bent to assist, 'You get off the train very soon. Stand by the doors.'

She looked up at Alan and Jim. 'You two! Help me with your friend, please.'

Before they could comply, she was joined by another passenger.

'I help you,' he said. It was the Arab.

Nigel leapt through the opening doors, and pulled his mobile phone from his pocket. He waited for the noise of the departing train to subside, then keyed in 999. No signal. Oh Jesus, got to get to ground level. He took the escalator steps two at a time, reached the top: ticket barriers. Oh God. Leap the barrier? No, the staff would be on to him, might be arrested before he could make the call. Fumbled for ticket, found it, inserted it – charged through into entry hall, keyed in 999 again.

The usual questions. *Which service do you require?* Ambulance. *Where are you calling from?* Angel underground station, but I need an ambulance to go to Euston. My friend's badly hurt. *Euston Station?* Yes, but the underground station. *Where is the injured party?* On a train, an underground train, bound for Euston. *Which line?* Oh, does it matter? *Yes.* Northern Line. *Which branch, Bank or Charing Cross?* Oh for God's sake. Look, send the ambulance to the Main Line entrance. Tell the paramedics to go to the top of the escalator. *Your name?* Templeton.

He turned off the phone to forestall any further inane questioning. That African woman seemed to know what she was doing; she'd get help to get Eric off the train, tell the station staff to meet the paramedics. She was cool in a crisis, just like he used to be.

He found himself trembling, felt an overpowering urge to sit down, get his breath, take stock. No time. He'd got to hurry to Euston. As his adrenaline subsided, he was overtaken by weariness at the thought of what lay ahead.

The hospital. The medics. The police. Witness statements. And, oh God, Viv. He had to tell Viv.

Sick with foreboding and guilt, he turned on his phone and keyed in Vivienne's number.

Chapter 17

WC 1

Giacomo was listlessly polishing the glasses. His duty tonight was to serve in the bar. The hotel manager was very proud of the bar – Art Deco, it was, he said. Giacomo thought it was old fashioned. In any case, bar work was not to his taste. He was not a happy young man: he wasn't really enjoying England. The weather was just as dispiriting as his friends in Roma had led him to believe it would be, though he was constantly assured by his Inglesi acquaintances that this summer was unusually cool and wet, that he should have been here last year, it had been, what did they say? A real scorcher.

As usual at this hour, the bar was almost empty. Those who'd been in earlier had repaired to the Jacques bistro to eat. In fact, there was only one customer, sitting over in the corner, a rather disreputable looking character. He was wearing what was by English standards a well-cut suit, but like the owner it was rumpled, and, Giacomo had noticed on the three occasions when the man had approached the bar to ask for a double Scotch, was dirty and stained down the lapels. He'd shuffled into the bar about an hour ago, bleary eyed and shaking slightly. Giacomo had assumed he was drunk, but apparently not, for the double Scotches had had no discernable effect apart from serving to reduce his unsteadiness. When he ordered his first drink he'd tried to engage Giacomo in conversation, some of it in an absurd pidgin-Italian which was impossible to understand. At one point the manager had entered the bar, and, noticing the dishevelled man, had whispered to Giacomo to keep his eye on that one and not stand any nonsense: he'd been offensive towards Su on reception earlier that afternoon. Giacomo was hoping that he'd soon leave.

It was not to be: he rose and approached the bar.

'Another double Scotch, *senor*,' he said.

'*Senore*,' corrected Giacomo, reaching for the bottle of Red Grouse.

'And one for yourself, Luigi.'

'Thank you, sir,' said Giacomo unsmilingly, 'but it is not allowed to drink on duty.'

'Suit yourself,' was said amiably enough, and the man shuffled back towards his seat, sipping at his drink as he went.

Tony eased himself into the chair and took another sip at his Scotch. He was feeling better for his sleep and the snort he'd had before leaving his room. He'd been totally disoriented when he woke – where was he for God's sake? Television on a wall mount; tray containing cups, sachets, plastic cartons of milk; a trouser press: must be a hotel – ah yes, he was in London. He was on a pub crawl, wasn't he? Yes, with Jim and Alan and Viv and that bloke with the beard, and Nige. He'd go down to the bar, have a few quick ones and then rejoin them.

But now he wasn't sure he wanted to. It would be too much effort. He was nicely settled in the bar. He quite liked drinking by himself. In any case, he didn't know where the others were. How long ago had he left them?

He glanced at his watch – eleven o'clock. How long had he been here, and why was he here alone? Hadn't Nige come back with him? Yes, he had, and he'd been angry, for some reason. Why? What had he done?

He shook his head from side to side. The fog cleared slightly. He remembered being attacked by Jim in one of the pubs, and Nige had intervened. Yes, that was it; Nigel had brought him back here in a taxi. But Nige had been unfriendly, not nice to him at all. He must have done something to annoy him. Perhaps he'd misunderstood something he'd said. That often happened – people often misunderstood him. It had been the same with his wives, and with that bitch Tracey and with Bevin, his business partner. It had started long before that, though. It had started with his father.

A vision of his choleric, red faced father swam before him, swishing his cane, taunting him with how much it would hurt before he was bent over his desk in the study, and six, or more, swipes cut into his backside. He'd never meant to be naughty; he never was really naughty, he was beaten for just saying the wrong thing, or having the wrong expression on his face. He'd never dared seek solace from his mother: she feared his father as well. He'd sometimes heard her sobs coming from the parental bedroom despite covering his head with his pillow to muffle the awful sound.

He sipped his whisky and groped in his pocket for his panatellas. He lit one, inhaled deeply, then noticed there was no ashtray on the table. His rage, inwardly focussed on the memory of his father found outward expression in the direction of the barman.

'Hey, Luigi!' he shouted, 'There isn't an ashtray here! Get me one, can you?'

The barman glanced up.

'There is no smoking sir, please put out your cigar. And my name is not, Luigi sir, it's Giacomo.'

'What sort of name's that, then?

His question was ignored. Gazing round, Tony noticed that none of the tables was equipped with smokers' requisites. He suddenly remembered the smoking ban and stubbed out his panatella on the sole of his shoe. Bloody Nanny State, bloody Blair, or was it Brown now? Sometimes it seemed to Tony that the entire weight of the apparatus of the state was being brought to bear down on everything that made his life enjoyable. It was just like his adolescence when everyone had conspired against him to make his existence intolerable. That bloody public school he'd been sent to: he'd thought it would at least provide a means of escape from his father's attentions, but at the hands of some of the masters and many of the prefects he'd suffered a sadism almost as bad as that at home. And for no reason. Why was it that no-one appreciated his sense of humour?

All his life he'd been unappreciated, apart from his time at University. He'd hated his father for insisting that he study in his home town – his one thought had been to escape his clutches – but, being the son of wealthy parents he was ineligible for a student grant, and his father would only give him an allowance if he stayed in Leeds and lived at home, and studied bloody Textiles, so he could be of some use in the family business. But once he started he'd found there were advantages to be had in being wealthier than the average undergraduate – his Mini was great for pulling chicks – and he'd got in with a crowd who seemed to like him; well, much more than he'd ever been liked before. That was why he was here, wasn't it? To see old Al and Nige and Jim and Viv again, particularly Viv. Ah, Viv. She'd been gagging for it, when she was a student, anyone could see that. He should have got her away from that prat – what's his name – Eric – long before that last pub-crawl. He'd left it too late; she'd never had a chance to get to know him, to find out what a good time he could give her.

He downed the remainder of his Scotch. It was good. Pity whisky didn't lend itself to taking quick nips when out and about – the advantage of vodka was that it didn't smell. Women didn't like the smell of whisky on the breath, and there was always the chance, even at this hour, that he might find himself in a situation where he could pull. Must be a few solitary women in the hotel, surely? He was still a good-looking fellow after all; had all his hair, not like Eric; definitely thin on top was Eric. Nige had a good head of hair on him though, the bastard. Probably because he had no pressure in his life; none of those bloody public servants knew what stress was.

No-one had understood the pressure he'd been under, being a captain of industry. The old man had had his uses, dying when he did; it had saved him from entering the family business, had allowed him to use his inheritance to set up in property, just at the time when textiles was on its last legs in the West Riding, and Leeds was at the threshold of being a financial services boom town. Good job he had the acumen to understand this and take advantage of it. But by God it had been hard work. He had to carry most of the load himself; most of his managers didn't have the first idea about entrepreneurialism, and that went for his partner as well. No wonder he'd had to spend so much time shouting at them and chivvying them. And they'd all let him down in the end.

Just like his women. His wives had all been willing enough to spend his money, but didn't understand that he had to spend long hours away from home in order to generate it. Wife number three had been the worst – going on all the time about how he drank too much, that he was getting to be dependent on it. Absolute bollocks. Alcohol helped oil the wheels of business, helped dull the loneliness of those long evenings in the office. But he wasn't dependent on it – wasn't then, wasn't now. He could cut out drinking just like that, if he wanted to. Once he got on his feet again he'd give it up. He didn't need bloody Bevin as a business partner. There were still plenty of opportunities to make money in Leeds – all those new flats down by the canal, ripe for buy-to-let; he'd get a loan and start up again. Tracey would soon see which side her bread was buttered; she'd come back to him like a shot.

He was summoning up the energy to make a return trip to the bar when two men entered. They seemed familiar.

'Come on, Al,' one of them said, 'A brandy will settle our nerves. Help you sleep as well'

Tony experienced the joy of recognition – it was Jim and Alan! People to talk to. He felt up to talking now; they'd be impressed by his plans for making money. He stood up and approached them.

'Now then, you two fuckers!' he greeted them boisterously, 'Where the bloody hell have you been? Where are the others? Where's Viv?'

'Oh. Tony.'

'I'll join you in that brandy,' he said. 'My shout.'

'On second thoughts I don't want a drink,' Alan said, 'Think I'll get to bed. Got to phone Sheila anyway. And write a letter. 'Night, Jim.'

'What's wrong with *him*? The night's young. C'mon, Jim, let's have a session. Lots to talk about. When are the others coming?'

'It'll only be Nige who comes,' Jim said, 'and the last thing I bloody want now is a long session. Just one brandy for me, and I'll get my own.'

Tony felt the familiar lurch of aggrieved disappointment that always came when his offers of company were declined. He peered at Jim – what was wrong with the miserable bastard?

'Where are Viv and Eric, then?' he persisted.

Nigel hurried along the Euston Road towards the hospital. He had to get there and support Viv, to explain what had happened. That was all that had been in his mind on the tube: how much time had he lost at Angel station phoning for the ambulance? Then the delay at Euston – he'd been met at the top of the escalator by Jim and Alan surrounded by a posse of police, shirt-sleeved, slow moving, impassive, the paraphernalia of law enforcement dangling from their belts, their radios crackling with staccato gibberish – more time wasted while he'd explained to the plods his role in the incident. At last, names and addresses duly noted, requests to report to the police station the following day to make full statements solemnly delivered, they were released, Jim and Alan then leaving for the hotel, while he, Nigel, set off on his mission to comfort, explain, apologise.

His haste did not prevent his constant re-living of the scene on the tube, nor the agonies of self doubt that had assailed him ever since. What had happened to him – was he losing his grip? Why hadn't he intervened sooner? All the trained responses to such situations were still there in his head – why hadn't he employed them? Was it really fear of being hurt, or fear that he would prove to be unequal to the task, too old, too unfit? Or – and the first glimmerings of the dreadful possibility had only just begun to dawn – was it that his subconscious had registered that an injured Eric would be unlikely to insist on the explanation that had been promised him? Nigel knew the depths to which humans could descend in pursuing self-interest. But he'd always believed that he, a liberal humanist lacking the passionate intensity of those who are convinced they hold the monopoly of truth, was, if not immune from self-centredness, then possessed of a code of honour which required one to be honest with one's friends. But dishonesty had begun twenty years before: it was atonement that he was seeking.

He hurried past the entrance to Euston Square tube station, then came to an abrupt halt. The hospital, a gleaming glass and steel edifice, was on the other side of the road, and there was no obvious crossing point – the central part of the carriageway was about to start its plunge into an underpass and the central reservation had a barrier along it. The A & E Department sign beckoned to him from across the torrent of traffic: he had to get straight there; there could be no retracing his steps. There came a break in the constant stream of headlights coming from his right: he charged into it, made the narrow central reservation to the accompaniment of a blaring of horns, looked left, leapt over barrier, then took another leap into hazard just as the advance guard of motorised mayhem was released from the starting block of traffic lights back at the junction with Gordon Street.

He entered the building. He was vaguely conscious of a brightly lit concourse filled with people slumped on serried ranks of seats, of others standing, of scurrying uniforms, of walls festooned with garish posters, but he was instantly assailed by the noise – shouting, singing, swearing. He cast round for reception; spotted it, approached one of the females seated behind the high counter, waited with ill-concealed impatience while she finished a telephone conversation, and told her that he was there to enquire about the welfare of a Mr Middleton who he believed to have been admitted very recently with serious injuries.

The woman consulted a computer screen on the desk top behind the counter, then peered at him with an expression that managed to combine boredom and suspicion.

'Are you a relative?'

'No, but I'm a close friend.'

'Sorry. You'll have to speak to a nurse.'

She turned towards a colleague seated beside her and began a conversation which seemed to relate to the possibility of their exchanging shifts next week. Nigel, mindful of the notice fixed to the counter which stated that the Trust would not tolerate abuse towards its people, fought back his anger and adopted a calm, measured tone.

'Perhaps you tell can tell me how he is?'

The woman turned back to him with a sigh. She was middle aged and conspicuously plain.

'He's with the doctors now.'

'Is that all you can tell me? How can I get to know his condition?'

'When he's stabilised his wife'll probably come out while he's taken to a ward. Course, she might be taken to a private room; depends how he is. You can wait here, if you like.'

She turned back to her colleague, her duties evidently completed to her satisfaction. Nigel swallowed his irritation and turned to seek a vacant seat. As he did, there was a commotion at the entrance and a trolley bearing a prone man was pushed through. It was accompanied by a green-overalled paramedic bearing aloft a transparent plastic bag attached to the man by a tube, and by a young female wearing the obligatory Friday-night minimum. She was staggering, wailing and sobbing, and as the procession passed Nigel she launched into a stream of invective directed at the paramedic when he raised his arm to prevent her embracing the prostrate man. Two policemen who had followed the trolley moved to restrain her, resulting in another volley of obscenities which continued as they led her, none too gently, towards a door at the side of the waiting area. They were accompanied by a chorus of jeers and curses from many of those seated. The trolley continued its passage and was met at the entrance to the corridor by a white tee-shirted youth with a day's growth of stubble and lines of exhaustion on his face. It took Nigel a few moments, accustomed as he was to the collars-and-ties, white coats, dangling stethoscopes and distinguished grey hair of private medical practitioners, to realise that the lad was a doctor.

He resumed his perusal of the room. He couldn't see a vacant chair. All were occupied, it seemed, by the dross of the capital: rowdy, uncouth, ill-proportioned, hulking, slouching, scabrous, simian *untermenschen* of both sexes, faces disfigured by ironmongery which studded ears, eyebrows, lips; bodies decorated by garish tattoos covering all those places unreceptive to metallic adornment. The faint smell of disinfectant failed to disguise the reek of cheap perfume, beer and vomit. His lip curled in disgust: was it for these people that his father's generation had fought for a health service free on the point of demand? He'd read of the mayhem to be found every weekend in A & E Departments, but had assumed a degree of journalistic exaggeration. Now he felt a shaft of understanding for the unhelpfulness of the woman at the reception desk, confronted nightly as she probably was by the drunken aggression of those who knew their fuckin' rights, and who wanted a fuckin' doctor to come and see to their mates now, right?

What was the point of staying? Viv might not return here: the reference to her being shown to a private room pointed to Eric's condition being serious, life-threatening, perhaps. And would she want to see him? In situations like this uxorious loyalty came to the fore: he imagined his reactions were Melanie ever to be in danger, and was then consumed with guilt about the ambiguity of his feelings for her.

He became aware of quiet sobbing from a seat immediately in front of him. It was a middle-aged woman: next to her a man of similar age was clutching her hand in a silent gesture of support. Drunken shouts suddenly burst from some of the seats behind them: the couple cowered visibly. Poor bastards, thought Nigel, parents perhaps? Here on the assumption that an injured son or daughter was being attended to in a place that would provide succour and safety for them as well as their child?

He peered round the room again, this time noticing that in the midst of the Hogarthian sea were dotted small islands of respectability and sobriety, soberly dressed, mild features pinched by worry and fear, referred here no doubt by the answering messages on the phone of their General Practioners' emergency service which had informed them that such a service was not available after 5pm. What was happening to this bloody country? When had it all started to go wrong? Who could be trusted to put it right?

'Nigel?'

He started, unaware that he'd been approached. The voice came from an overweight, blondish woman, whose over-made-up face spoke of a desperation to cling to the remnants of youth. She was vaguely familiar.

'Nigel, it's me, Belinda.'

It took a few moments for recognition to dawn, such had been the deterioration in ten years.

'Of course. Belinda. Did you come here with Viv?'

'I brought her here. Nigel, you haven't changed a bit.'

'How's Eric, d'you know?'

'I don't know, Nigel; he was admitted before we got here. Viv was allowed straight in to see him. I'm assuming she'll remember I'm here.'

'How was she?'

'Tense. Not saying a lot. Look, let's get a coffee. There's a machine over there. I haven't dared get one by myself, with all the riff-raff hanging around. It'll probably be undrinkable.'

Polystyrene cups of brown liquid in hand, they stood together at the edge of the room.

'It's been a long time, Nigel.'

'Which way did Viv go? We need to keep an eye out for her.'

'Through those double doors over there. How are you, Nigel?'

'How do you think I am? Worried sick.'

'What happened?'

'Eric was beaten up by some thugs. Look, I've already had to explain what happened to the police and I'll have to do it again tomorrow. I don't want to go over it again now, if you don't mind.'

And I don't want to have to converse with you at all, he thought. He didn't want her here. He'd never liked her, had always thought she was a most unlikely person for Vivienne to have as a friend, hated having to use her as a go-between. He stood, coffee untouched, staring at the double doors while she made various attempts to engage him in conversation, eventually falling silent when she elicited no response. The digital timepiece on the wall opposite clicked away the minutes, the electronic read-out next to it informed new arrivals that the waiting time for non-emergencies was three hours.

When Vivienne finally appeared, accompanied by a nurse, he charged over to her.

'Viv, Viv, how is he?'

She stared at him. Her face was expressionless.

'Where's Belinda?'

'Over there,' he gestured towards the coffee machine, but she was making her way towards them.

'I'm staying here with Eric,' she said as Belinda reached them. 'No need for you to hang on. Thanks for the lift.'

'How is he, Viv?'

'I don't really know.' Her voice was icily calm.

'He's being taken to intensive care,' the nurse informed them, her gentle Caribbean lilt almost drowned by the hubbub around her, 'Mrs Middleton will wait in a private room until he's all fixed up.'

'Fixed up?' Nigel rounded on her, 'What do you mean, fixed up?'

The nurse ignored him.

'If you're ready, darlin',' she said to Vivienne, 'Let's get you to that room.'

Nigel, for the second time that day, had the chastening sensation of events being removed from his control. If Viv left now, when would he ever be able to explain? By tomorrow each of them would be ensnared in procedures that might dictate that their paths wouldn't cross again for days, weeks, maybe ever.

'Viv, wait,' he said sharply.

She was already turning to follow the nurse, but stopped and looked at him, for the first time with recognition in her eyes.

'What?'

'I'll wait here as well, out here. You might need some support.'

'It's Eric that needs support, not me. Where were you when this happened?' The question seemed simply to request information, there was no trace of accusation.

'I was with him, we all were; it was on the tube, a gang of thugs.'

Her eyes narrowed: Nigel noticed for the first time how haggard she was; she looked her age. She appeared deep in thought, then –

'You're not hurt, are you.' A statement, not a question.

'No.'

'And Alan and Jim? Are they?'

'No. Viv –'

'Not much use to Eric, then, any of you. You always told me you could handle yourself.'

'No excuses, Viv. I lost my nerve.'

The nurse returned. 'Please, darlin', I've got other things to do.'

Vivienne turned and allowed herself to be led away.

Nigel felt a tug at his elbow. He found himself walking with Belinda towards the exit.

'Let her go, Nigel,' she said, then, 'What *did* happen?'

'Just as I said. A bunch of thugs.'

'But what had happened to make Viv leave you all?'

Nigel stopped.

'For Christ's sake, is it important?'

'Sorry. Look, Viv's things are at my place. D'you think she'll remember that? She might need her stuff.'

'I doubt that the location of her overnight case is at the forefront of her mind right now.'

He began walking again. Belinda waddled alongside him; they reached the exit. She stopped, grabbed him by the hand.

'What about you? You must be in a state of shock. Look, my car's nearby. Why don't you come back with me and collect Viv's stuff? You look as though you could do with a drink.'

'I've had more than enough for one day.'

'OK, well, you could certainly do with some company. I could as well. You can stay over if you like, bring Viv's things back here tomorrow.'

He turned to look at her for the first time since she'd greeted him.

'Thank you very much for the offer,' he said with measured politeness, 'but at a time like this one needs to be with one's friends, don't you think?'

Jim awoke from his doze with a start. He checked his watch: 12.30. He was alone in the lobby. He noticed he was being observed discreetly by the receptionist, a new one, a male: there must have been a change of shift while he was asleep. He hoped his presence had been explained to the man when the shift-change took place. The young lass who'd preceded him on duty had accepted with equanimity Jim's need to be near the entry to intercept a friend the time of whose arrival was uncertain, though he had embarrassed himself by explaining that the awaited friend was a man, an explanation made lest she thought, given the lateness of the hour and the proximity of the hotel to main-line rail stations, that he was waiting for a whore.

His behaviour must have seemed bizarre, if not suspicious, even before that. Faced with Tony's evident determination to stay with him until Nigel arrived, he'd had to resort to subterfuge to escape him. This had involved him telling Tony he was going to bed, asking the receptionist to phone him in his room once his erstwhile companion had left the bar and entered the lift, then returning to the lobby once the all-clear had been received. By the time he'd got to provide a reason for his vigil by the entrance, the lass was already regarding him with bemusement and was obviously enjoying herself, giving him the occasional conspiratorial wink. No doubt all this information had also been passed on to her replacement. Just so long as *that* bugger didn't start winking at him. Jim, now totally sober, had resurgent feelings of provincial naivety faced with the knowing sophistication of late-night Londoners.

He had been more shaken by the brief account of the assault on Eric he'd tried to give to the police than he had by the event itself. That was because his recollection of the fracas had been fogged by inebriation. Sobriety had rapidly ensued once he'd vomited, but then it was too late, too late to help Eric, too late to assist Nigel. The reproachful looks bestowed on him by the black woman as she took charge during the interminable journey to Euston still haunted him. He was dreading Nigel's arrival, fearful not just of what news he might bring of Eric's condition, but of Nigel's scorn for his utter uselessness. He remembered the feelings of resentment of Nigel which he'd harboured for most of the day, and shame was added to his guilt.

When the doors opened and Nigel walked in. His youthful appearance, so well maintained over the years, had evaporated. The upright stance, the purposeful gait, had gone – he was stooped, shuffling almost, diminished. His long fair hair was no longer pushed back in a jaunty quiff but straggled over his forehead.

'Nige, what's happened? Is Eric…. has Eric…' he tailed off, unable to frame the question.

Nigel slumped in the seat beside him.

'He's in intensive care. That's all I know. Viv's with him.'

'Did you see Viv? Didn't she tell you –'

'She didn't have time. Got taken off by a nurse.'

'So, when do we get to know? Do we go to the hospital tomorrow?'

Nigel shook his head resignedly. 'I don't know, Jim. Don't know what we do.'

'Fuckin' hell, what a mess.'

'It's that all right. Where are Alan and Tony?'

'Both in bed. Al was knackered. Took me a while to get shot of Tony, though.'

'Thank God you did. If he'd been here I wouldn't have been responsible for my actions.'

Jim wondered briefly what Tony had done to earn Nigel's opprobrium, apart from being Tony of course, but the moment passed. He had an apology to make: he found apologies embarrassing.

'Sorry I was so useless,' he grunted.

'What?'

'On the tube. I was pissed. Should have helped.'

Nigel touched him on the shoulder.

'I was pretty useless myself, Jim, and I didn't have the excuse of being drunk.'

'And …. and I think I may have been a bit of a shit towards you, earlier on. Sorry about that an' all.'

'Not important, Jim. Nothing's important now, except our own survival.'

'What d'yer mean by that?'

'Think I was trying to avoid the cliché about life being too short. I'm going to bed now. Sort things out in the morning.' He hauled himself to his feet.

Jim shared the lift with him to the second floor, dragged himself along the corridor and on reaching his room collapsed on the bed. He'd promised to phone Nicky when he'd returned to the hotel. Too late now; he'd be asleep, tucked up in bed in Stoke. Jim wished with all his heart that he were with him.

Chapter 18

'Can you manage?' said Vivienne as Eric hauled himself from the taxi, 'Don't forget your stick.'

'I've got it.'

'You go ahead, then. I'll catch you up by the barrier.'

She watched him as he walked under the canopy, thinking that he really was much steadier now and that the stick was more an affectation than a necessity. She paid the cab driver, swung the small suitcase down onto the pavement, extended its handle and began wheeling it in pursuit of her husband.

The train was already in. Eric presented the tickets and the couple walked together down the platform to the front carriage which they boarded, managing to secure seats side-by side facing the direction of travel, something on which Eric always insisted. It occurred to Vivienne that this was the return journey to Leamington that they were supposed to have made together last July: instead she had travelled alone, leaving Eric in the London hospital where he'd spent a month before being transferred to the Walsgrave in Coventry. On that journey she'd been wracked by the prospect of a lifetime spent nursing an invalid, but things had not turned out so badly as she'd feared. Her prayers had been answered, in that respect at least.

The train pulled out. Eric settled back in his seat and exhaled in relief.

'Well, that wasn't a bad send off,' he said, 'And it was good to see the others again. Except for Tony, of course. I wonder why he didn't come?'

'Didn't you hear what Sheila said? They tried phoning; the line was dead. They wrote as well, but didn't get a reply.'

'She's a homely character, Sheila, isn't she? A real East-Ender. Old Al never said very much about her. D'you think he was ashamed of her?'

'Heavens, no, Alan was never like that, was he? It was obviously a good marriage. And what a family. Four children and God knows how many grandchildren. They'll all be a great comfort to her in the coming months.'

'He had a lot of friends, Alan, didn't he?'

'That's what comes of staying in one place all your life.'

As she said it, Vivienne had an uncomfortable vision of the dearth of friends there would be at Eric's funeral, or at hers for that matter. For the first time, realisation came that she hoped she would be the first to go.

'I liked the ceremony, didn't you?' Eric was off on another tack. 'D'you think Al planned it – the music I mean? Good job the sound system wasn't too bad. They're often terrible in crematoria. Hey, fancy him choosing *Mr Tambourine Man*! Al never admitted to being a Dylan fan. He was always a rock'n'roll man, before he discovered the blues of course. Perhaps it was Sheila's choice. Mind you, I bet it was Al who chose *Whiter Shade of Pale*. He always liked that.'

In fact the funeral had not been to Vivienne's taste. Not that such events were meant to be enjoyed, of course, but she was unhappy with the way in which such ceremonies were now conducted with no reference to the afterlife in which she believed, and she'd vowed long ago never again to listen to Procol Harum's 1967 anthem. She missed the Christian ceremonial, which she thought must surely provide the comfort of familiarity even to those who professed themselves unbelievers. Even the modern form of Christian service was, for her, unsatisfactory: the rolling cadence of 'I am the Resurrection and the Life, saith the Lord', heard as it had been by generations of her antecedents as coffins entered church or chapel, and which provided a continuity with the past so disparaged by today's throw-away culture, had been replaced by a bland statement to the effect that Jesus said he represented the resurrection. Vivienne had begun regular attendance at chapel again, for the first time since her school days, and was rediscovering her faith. It was such a pity that the old familiar hymns were no longer sung, that many of the old rituals had been discarded in the interests, her minister had explained, of enfranchising the younger worshipper.

But at least Alan's ceremony had been led, no, *facilitated*, by a Humanist officiant who'd given a sense or order and dignity to the occasion, unlike the do-it-yourself funeral of a non-believing Library colleague Vivienne had attended where the proceedings had been so shambolic as to be embarrassing. The eulogy by one of Alan's former colleagues had been painless, though his voice had the loud but slightly beseeching resonance that spoke of years of verbal exposition to those reluctant to listen. It was a pity that he had been followed by one of

Alan's old school friends whose embarrassed panegyric was rendered meaningless by his inarticulate delivery in an Albert Square accent.

'Jim looked well, didn't he?' Eric was persisting in his post-mortem of recent events. 'Must be living with that fella that's doing him good.'

'Oh, you've remembered that Jim's gay, have you?'

'Course I have. I remember him telling me in, what was it ….. oh God, what was the pub? Don't tell me …… I know! The Old Bank of England.

If there was one aspect of Eric's slow recovery about which Vivienne was ambivalent it was the gradual improvement in his memory. To her shame, her first reaction on learning of Alan's death was less one of sorrow, more one of dread that the funeral, which Eric of course had insisted on attending, would serve to upset the equilibrium of the past six months. She had no concerns about its effect on the steady improvement in Eric's physical health, for he was making great strides. His mental state, however, was hard to assess. Much of the time he was almost serene. Restricted to a wheelchair in the early days of his recuperation, he'd begun to read assiduously and his old interest in local history was re-awakened: recently he'd begun to visit the County Record Office and he spoke of taking up research. At other times, when events served to highlight his memory lapses, he became agitated, but such occurrences were becoming fewer. The medics said that he might eventually achieve total recall. She hoped and prayed, however, that the events of that day last July would be for ever consigned to oblivion.

The prospect of the funeral had been fraught with many doom-laden scenarios. Least amongst them was her seeing

Nigel again: they'd not been in contact since that evening at the hospital. She guessed he was fearful of phoning lest Eric pick up the receiver. At first she'd been hurt that he hadn't written to enquire after Eric, until she remembered her dismissal of him in the A & E Department: he no doubt thought she'd drawn a line under the past, which of course she had.

More dreadful had been the prospect of Tony wreaking renewed havoc. There was no guarantee that funereal solemnities would inhibit the ramblings of an alcoholic. She'd resolved to leave the ceremony immediately if there was so much as a hint of misconduct, notwithstanding the disappointment this result in for Eric and the hurt that it might cause Alan's widow.

Worst of all had been the possibility that a visit to London and contact with his old friends would serve to jog Eric's memory about the events on Millenium Bridge. For that eventuality she'd had no game-plan, and for its probable consequences she felt only impotent despair.

'Hey, Viv, I thought old Nige seemed a bit different, somehow,' said Eric, as the train pulled in at Gerrards Cross.

'Really?'

'Yes. Didn't you think so? He seemed edgy, at first. But he also looked older, and a bit sad.'

'Well, that's hardly surprising. He and Melanie have spilt up.'

'What? Really? How do you know that?'

'He told me when you and Jim went in the house to get some more drinks.'

'But why? What about the kid?'

'I think it was Oscar that precipitated it. Melanie wanted to move nearer to his Special School. Nigel decided to stay in Stow.'

'Weren't they getting on, then?'

'Oh, Eric, who knows what stresses and strains are put on a marriage when trying to cope with a handicapped child?'

Eric considered this for a moment.

'Yeah, I suppose so,' he said eventually, 'but Nigel – '

'Eric, would you mind very much if I read my book for a bit? I always find funerals emotionally draining: I'd like to escape into someone else's reality for a while. And we'll be passing through the Chilterns soon, won't we? You know you always like to look at that scenery.'

'Yes. Right. OK then.'

Vivienne pulled her novel from the zipped outer pocket of the suitcase, opened it and stared at the pages. She was in no mood to read, but wanted to escape from Eric's persistent re-running of events of the day. The funeral *had* been emotionally draining, but not in the way that Eric presumably thought she'd meant, though Tony's non-attendance had been a great relief, and the hurdle of the first meeting with Nigel, outside the crematorium after the ceremony, had been overcome without incident.

She'd registered the look of surprise on Nigel's face when Eric had greeted him with a bear-hug, and the quizzical glance he'd shot her after bending to kiss her cheek. There had been no awkward stumbling for opening remarks, for Eric had immediately treated Nigel to a protracted bulletin on the nature of his injuries, the treatment he'd received and the progress he was making, followed by an enthusiastic account of his historical researches and the book he was hoping to write in due course. Then Jim had joined them and the conversation turned to Alan, during which Vivienne had registered the evident regard which Jim and Nigel seemed now to have for each other. The shifting sands of personal allegiances she found unsettling.

Back at Sheila's house for the wake, she'd begun to relax. For the late middle-aged, once hushed condolences have been offered, such gatherings are life affirming events, for they are still there, only just past their prime, and life goes on. The younger people at the gathering had already sought each other out and had begun to chat animatedly and even laugh – well, for them it was just another party, really, wasn't it? Death would never happen to them, for they were indestructible. Vivienne had just begun to chat to Jim, who seemed in the past ten months to have become a light-hearted conversationalist, when their group was approached by one of Alan's daughters bearing an envelope, which she gave to Nigel.

'Dad asked me to give this to you,' she'd said.

Nigel peered at the envelope: Vivienne noticed he blanched, then recovered, and said that perhaps the four of them ought to go into the garden as this would appear to be a private matter.

Outside, he passed round the envelope. The legend on it read –

To the Second Division – Nigel, Jim, Tony, Eric and Viv. The enclosed to be read out by Nige, who has the voice for it.

Jim had asked what the bloody hell Alan could mean by the Second Division, Eric said he didn't know, Nigel feigned ignorance and Vivienne had found herself unable to reply, such was the foreboding that gripped her.

She couldn't remember the precise wording of the enclosure. Alan had written that he was sorry to have been a drag on the party last July, that he hoped Eric had made a full recovery, that he hoped they'd all meet up every year to drink to his memory, and that they should be kind to each other and keep the spirit of the 1960s alive because the decade would one day have gone from collective memory. She could, however, remember the tremor in Nigel's voice as he read it out.

After the reading, Eric and Jim had returned to the house to refill their glasses and Vivienne had been left alone with Nigel.

'D'you think old Al knew?' Nigel had asked.

'I doubt it.'

'Viv, Eric's so .... relaxed, friendly. Can't he remember what happened?'

'Not much. For a long time he had no recall of anything that happened that day. But recently things have been coming back. Last week he suddenly remembered the fracas in the pub when you had to take Tony away. Today he remembered Alan being taken ill at St Pauls.'

'So you think there might come a day when he – '

'Yes, he might. I'll cross that bridge when I come to it.'

'Viv, I never had the chance to apologise properly for – '

'Don't. Water under the bridge. Another bloody bridge.'

'Well, it looks as though we're honour bound to see each other again once a year.'

'Nigel, don't you see I can't take that risk? If Eric's memory were to be jogged further...'

Nigel had looked crestfallen, then carefully replaced Alan's letter in the envelope.

'So much for the Second Division, then. You never told Eric about that, did you?'

'No. He'd have been most upset.'

'Ah, yes, you mustn't upset Eric, must you?'

The bitterness in Nigel's voice still haunted her. Glancing across at her husband, peering at the passing landscape with a slight smile on his face, she had to fight down the resentment she felt for the way things had turned out for him given the tragedy of Nigel's situation, which he'd recounted briefly in the few moments before they'd been rejoined by Eric and Jim. On hearing it she had, for a while, wondered whether to relent, to agree to honour Alan's last request, but the risk was too great. She'd survived today; she couldn't bear another angst-ridden meeting. Her duty lay in keeping Eric on an even keel, encouraging his academic pursuits, helping him to develop some sort of social life amongst those who shared his interests, and at all costs to keep him from further contact with Nigel. The more time that passed before any eventual recollection came to him, then the more likely it would be that his advancing years would dull the emotional response. And she could always deny it, say he was getting confused. That's what happened in old age, after all.

Eric was enjoying the journey. Now the train had left High Wycombe the worst excesses of commuterland were hidden by the beechwoods. At this time of year and in the evening light the Chilterns were at their best, the fresh green of the beech leaves not yet so dense as to disguise the mist of bluebells on the forest floor. He must get Viv to join him for a weekend in a pub or hotel somewhere and explore the area, perhaps stay in Henley and revisit his youthful haunts. He was sure she'd agree: Viv was much more amenable to his suggestions these days.

It had been good to see Nige and Jim again, notwithstanding the circumstances, and old Al had been given a good send off. It was a shame about Tony, but hadn't he been ill for some time? He seemed to remember there'd been something wrong with him at the reunion: no doubt it would come back to him soon. His memories of the events of that day were coming back to him with increasing frequency. No use asking Viv: she seemed never to want to talk about it.

He glanced at his wife, sitting beside him, nose in a book as usual. Some things never changed. But she was much more attentive to him, since his accident. He still thought of it as an accident, though he'd been told many times that it was an assault. Once he'd left hospital Viv had been assiduous in her caring role, at times even showing an affection for him, casually expressed of course, but welcome none the less. She seemed far less prickly now she saw less of her literary friends, but perhaps this was more to do with her taking up regular attendance at chapel. Eric remained a vague agnostic, but if Viv's renewed faith brought dividends for him he wasn't going to challenge her.

The train pulled in at Princes Risborough. Eric took in the scene, familiar to him from his childhood cycling excursions. Strangely, since his accident, he no longer looked back with nostalgic yearnings. The past was interesting, of course, but no longer the land of lost content. It was the same with the 60s – a fascinating decade, worthy of a sociological treatise, but not one that he had any wish to re-live. Even the music sounded a bit silly: now, he listened to Radio 4 on Saturday mornings, not Sounds of the Sixties. His long convalescence had reconciled him to growing older, for each day had brought gradual improvements in his condition, improvements which masked that long, gentle decline of the previous years which he used so bitterly to resent. Once he'd cast the wheelchair aside he felt like a new man, and the walking stick soon became merely a reassurance rather than an essential prop. In fact, he could dispense with it, but he rather enjoyed the jaunty air with which he could now carry it. Perhaps he'd replace it with something less solid, more elegant, with a straight hand grip – a cane rather than a stick. Yes, and given that it might turn out to be a warm summer, a Panama hat would be a suitable accessory, and maybe a cravat? He pictured himself, a spry elderly gentleman, sauntering down the Parade on a Saturday morning, tipping his hat to the ladies, calling in at the café in Jephson Gardens. Almost as debonair as Nigel.

Poor old Nige. Thinking about it, of all of them it was Nigel who faced the bleakest future. Jim had got his partner – what was her name? It would come to him eventually. And Sheila – well, yes, tragic to be widowed, but she had her children and grandchildren. But Nige: he felt a wave of pity for his old flatmate. He regretted not having had the chance to talk more to him today. And there was something, lurking in the recesses of his memory, that he was sure he had to ask him, or was it something that Nigel had to tell him? He felt a vague sensation of there being unfinished business.

'I've been thinking,' he said.

'Yes?' Vivienne put down her book. 'What about?'

'How it's all turned out for us. Al was right; we ought all to get together now and again. Maybe invite Sheila, and Jim's woman.'

'He's a man, Eric.'

'What?'

'Jim's partner. He's a man, remember?'

Eric thought for a moment.

'Oh, yes, so it is. When you remind me, things come back to me.'

'Look, Eric; I'm not sure that a get-together would be a good idea. Not much fun for Sheila, and of no interest to Jim's partner. And do we really want to spend more time with them? Don't you think we've said all we've got to say to each other?'

'Oh.'

'I'm just thinking you ought to start thinking more about the future, now you're recovering. Concentrate on your research.'

'Maybe you're right.'

He was silent for a while. The train resumed its progress. An idea came to him.

'Look, I've been thinking about Nige.'

'Yes?' Vivienne's eyes remained on her book.

'He must be lonely, poor bugger. Why don't we invite him to stay with us for a weekend? We're not that far from Stow. Viv?'

'Yes, I heard you. He won't want to come; he's a proud man, you know.'

'He'll come. He's our oldest friend. Old friends are the best to be with when you're down. Though it must be hard on him, seeing how things have turned out for the rest of us, those of us still here I mean.'

Vivienne put down her book again.

'What d'you mean?'

'Well, Jim's happy enough, isn't he? And us: *we're* all right, aren't we?'

She seemed to be giving this question careful consideration.

'Yes. I suppose we are,' she said eventually.

'So, I'll phone him and invite him. We're not doing anything the weekend after next. It'll be good, just the three of us.'

The End

Printed in the United Kingdom by
Lightning Source UK Ltd., Milton Keynes
141023UK00001B/3/P